Dark Water

Dark Ship

Dark Horse

Dark Shadows

Dark Paradise

Dark Fury

Dark Hunt

Dark Path

Dark Prey

Dark Path

© 2020 Evan Graver

www.evangraver.com

All rights reserved. No part of this publication may be reproduced, distributed, or transmitted in any forms or by any means, including photocopying, recording, or other electronic, or mechanical methods, without the prior written permission of the publisher, except in the case of brief quotations embodied in critical reviews and certain noncommercial uses permitted by copyright law.

ISBN-10: 1-7338866-9-9

ISBN-13: 978-1-7338866-9-7

Cover: Wicked Good Book Covers

Editing: Novel Approach Manuscript Services

This is a work of fiction. Any resemblance to any person, living or dead, business, companies, institutions, events, or locales is entirely coincidental.

Printed and bound in the United States of America

First Printed July 2020

Published by Third Reef Publishing, LLC

Hollywood, Florida

www.thirdreefpublishing.com

DARK PATH

A Ryan Weller Thriller

EVAN GRAVER

CHAPTER ONE

East of St. John U.S. Virgin Islands

The speedboat came out of nowhere, its sleek, colorful hull slicing easily through the two-foot waves. The roar of its powerful engines drowned out everything else as it swept past the sailboat.

Paul Langston stood as the speedboat's wake violently rocked the sailboat. He grasped the steering wheel, trying to keep himself upright and maintain the boat on its original heading. His gaze shot to the compass mounted on the bulkhead beside the cockpit door, then back to the flashy orange, red, and blue Cigarette boat.

Diane Langston looked at her husband as the speedboat slowed to turn, sensing this had something to do with their sudden departure from St. Thomas. She ran a hand through her shoulder-length brown hair. She was a few inches shorter than her husband at five-foot-six, and her sixty-six-year-old body was still trim from hours of yoga and jogging along the mountainous roads near their home. Diane took pride in her youthful figure, and unlike her girlfriends back in New Jersey, she'd never had plastic surgery. She had changed into a black one-piece swimsuit once they were aboard and had been lounging in the cockpit ever since, enjoying the sunshine and wondering why they had made such a hasty exit from their home.

Paul watched from his place at the wheel, his eyes squinting against the afternoon sun even behind his designer Ray-Bans. She'd always thought he was a handsome man, even though his once thick brown hair had dissipated into a thinly disguised comb over. He was well-tanned from lying by their pool or on one of the secluded beaches on the island, but his lack of physical activity over the years had left him with what he liked to say was "Dunlap's disease," his joking explanation as to why his gut done lapped over his belt.

"Who are they?" she asked.

"I don't know."

There was something in Paul's tone of voice that made Diane believe he might not know the men in the boat, but he knew *why* they were there. Paul was an accountant who had passed the bar and become a lawyer. In the late seventies and early eighties, he had worked at a firm in New Jersey before he'd quit and opened his own practice. She remembered visiting him at the little storefront in a strip mall in Perth Amboy, not far from the Harborside Marina, where he'd kept a thirty-foot motor launch for entertaining clients. Paul's office had been spartan, with just two rooms: Paul's inner office, where he spent long hours, and an outer reception area where a heavy-set blonde woman named Karen had worked. Diane was never quite sure if she and Paul were sleeping together, and if they were, she certainly didn't understand the attraction, especially when he had a fit, willing wife at home.

She had never seen or met any of his clients, but she knew

he had worked for the Mob. Almost everyone had a connection to them during those chaotic years in New Jersey, and Diane was happy that Paul had somehow kept them away from her family.

When their three children had left home to begin their own journeys in the world, Paul had taken Diane on a vacation to St. Thomas. After a week in the tropics, he had announced they were moving there. They'd settled on a modest house set on a hill off Frenchman Bay Road, which offered stunning views of Long Bay and the Caribbean Sea. Diane had fallen in love with the place at first sight, and it met Paul's primary requirement that it have a pool. He continued to work remotely and had a small office on the second floor of a building across from the cruise port. The kids came periodically throughout the year, but they would all gather to celebrate Christmas together in the warm weather.

Now, standing in the sailboat's cockpit and watching the speedboat full of men armed with large black guns, Diane Langston knew their life had come to an inglorious end, thanks to Paul's nefarious dealings. She wanted to scream at him, but she knew she was just as complicit as him because she had taken the money the Mob so handsomely paid her husband with and created an enjoyable life for them and their children. Still, she couldn't help herself. "Dammit, Paul. What did you do?"

"Get below," Paul ordered, ignoring her tirade. He reengaged the autopilot and stepped around the wheel. Pushing his wife into the cabin, he jumped down beside her and went to the V-berth. Outside, the Cigarette slowed alongside the sailboat, matching its speed.

"What do they want?" Diane asked, watching her husband lift the mattress.

Before he could reach for the shotgun he kept there, bullets punched through the sailboat's delicate fiberglass hull.

The men in the speedboat continued to pour round upon round through their target.

Diane flattened herself to the cabin sole, watching her husband squat beside the bed and rack the shotgun. He poked the barrel through a hole in the hull and fired. The boom was deafening inside the confined cabin. Diane covered her ears, trying to make everything go away. She had known they were in trouble from the moment they'd set sail. Paul had been acting jumpy the last few days, and their flight from the island was so sudden that she'd barely had time to grab her purse. Paul had told her to leave everything, and yet he'd carried a yellow waterproof box under his arm as he'd grabbed her by the elbow and steered her toward their car.

What had Paul done to cause these men to destroy their precious sailboat?

Paul racked the shotgun again, thrusting a fresh shell into the chamber. As he stood to move, it looked to Diane as if an invisible hammer struck a blow to his body. He spun and fell to the floor; the shotgun flying from his grasp. She could see blood gushing from the wound to his hand. It dripped into the water, pooling on the cabin floor and turning an ugly black color.

Diane crawled to her husband through the rising water. The sailboat listed heavier to starboard. The waves caused little geysers to erupt through the bullet holes as the water gushed in. She glanced up through the clear hatch cover at the jib, luffing in the breeze. Despite the damage to the canvas, the boat was still moving forward.

"Paul! Paul!" she cried, her tears mingling with the seawater.

Her husband rolled onto his side and looked at her with fear and sorrow in his eyes. He gripped her hand in his. When he spoke, his voice was hoarse and full of pain. "I'm sorry, Di."

She glanced around the bullet-riddled berth. The shooters were higher in the speedboat, firing down at an angle with their shots, creating holes above the waterline on the port side upon impact and perforating the hull beneath the waterline on the starboard side on exit. If she and Paul stayed close to the port side and low to the sole, they might survive the intended massacre.

An explosion rocked the stern of the boat and a wall of water flowed through the cabin, smashing the couple against the V-berth bed. Diane fought to keep ahold of her husband, but the raging water forced them apart. It was in her mouth, her nose, and her eyes. She gagged and fought her way to the surface, reaching underwater to pull her husband up with her. She couldn't let him drown.

As Diane struggled to stay afloat, the boat began to sink by its stern, gently pulling the Langstons into a watery grave.

CHAPTER TWO

The sun-dappled water of the Caribbean Sea rolled endlessly to the western horizon, where there was nothing but water meeting the sky. To the east were the green hills of Peter and Norman Islands. A light wind billowed the white sails of the thirty-five-foot Lafitte 44 sailboat, *Windseeker*, heeling her over in a gentle four-degree list to port as she made her way north from the British Virgin Islands toward St. John in the USVI.

Ryan Weller stood in the cockpit, checking the speed on the GPS screen mounted to the pulpit in front of the sailboat's wheel. Not for the first time this trip, he thought, *There's something wrong with sailing north*.

It felt weird to be heading for Florida. His journey as a commercial diver working on the *Peggy Lynn* with his old crew had ended, and a new adventure was beginning with his girlfriend, Emily Hunt. Ryan had no idea what lay ahead, and part of him dreaded it. It wasn't his new relationship that bothered him, but the prospect of having to find another job. Had his life aboard his boat, bouncing from island to island

and risking life and limb as a troubleshooter for Dark Water Research, really come to a screeching halt?

He had promised Emily that he'd give up that life and step away from doing dangerous things in the service of his friend's company, but part of him didn't know if he could keep that promise. It gnawed at his stomach, twisting his gut into knots.

He looked at Emily, resting on the starboard cockpit bench, her long legs propped on the port side. Her thick blonde mane, the color of harvest wheat, waved in the wind, blowing strands across her face. She must have felt his gaze on her because she turned and looked at him with those cornflower-blue eyes that he found so intoxicating. Emily brushed a strand of hair from her cheek and smiled. She was just two inches shorter than his six-foot height, and she wore a blue bikini over her lithe body. The sun had kissed her, making her skin glow.

Yeah, he thought with a grin. *Everything is gonna be all right.*

But was he trying to convince himself that it would be?

And what the heck were they doing sailing north during hurricane season?

Before leaving Trinidad over three months ago, he and Emily had prepared *Windseeker* for cruising. Ramesh, the hulking owner of Five Islands Yacht Club, had done as Ryan had asked while Ryan was working off the coast of Nicaragua and *Windseeker* had been sitting on the hard at Five Islands. Ramesh had replaced the aging Perkins diesel with a brand-new Volvo Penta, scraped the hull, and re-coated it with antifoul paint. He'd changed the bearing on the propeller shaft and repacked the stuffing box where the shaft ran through the hull, then he'd added a folding propeller that collapsed when not in use.

Ryan and Emily had done even more work to *Windseeker*

when they arrived at Five Islands. They'd inspected the rigging, replaced lines and halyards, scrubbed the sails to remove the mold that had accumulated from being folded up in the lockers, or rolled up on the mainmast boom and the jib roller furler. Then they'd put the old girl in the water and taken her for a test run. The Lafitte 44 was a true bluewater boat. She'd seen her previous owner around the world and had now taken Ryan around the Caribbean.

After saying goodbye to Ramesh, Emily and Ryan sailed north, stopping at every island in the necklace of green gems that made up the Lesser Antilles. Some islands had sheer volcanic walls that rose straight out of the water and were topped with dense jungle, while others had lush tropical beaches uninhabited by man. Ryan enjoyed both, and this trip was a dream come true for him. He had finally found a woman who wanted to sail with him to exotic ports and run wild on the beaches.

He should have been happy, but there was a part of him that wouldn't fully let go. When they reached Florida, they would have less time together. Emily would want to go back to work, and he would be left at loose ends. Ryan didn't need to work. There was more money than he could spend in a lifetime deposited in his Cayman Islands bank account. The bankers had invested well and increased his holdings, firmly banishing any financial worries he might have had.

What was he going to do? He wanted this relationship to work, but he also knew he couldn't give it his all while he felt that a piece of him was missing. He wanted to continue chasing criminals.

Even though Emily had told him that their work wasn't all that different, he thought it was. Investigating insurance fraud was a far cry from disarming bombs, fast-roping onto ships, and dealing with the scum of the earth.

He ran a hand through his thick brown hair. Like his girlfriend, his lean muscular body was deeply tanned. Today, he wore orange swim trunks that Emily had picked out for him, saying they flattered his shapely behind, and a white T-shirt bearing the logo of his old employer, Dark Water Research, the global commercial dive and salvage firm.

Emily interrupted his thoughts by suddenly pointing at the horizon. "Do you see that smoke?"

Ryan grabbed a pair of binoculars and held them to his green eyes. He fidgeted with the focus dial, but whatever was burning was over the horizon. He glanced at the GPS screen and radar, verifying there was nothing but empty sea between themselves and the smoke. Standing in the cockpit, he could only see for three miles, but the radar dome mounted on the mast fifty foot above him gave a sweeping view of nine miles, and it showed the burning boat to be near the edge of their screen.

He punched the starter button on the diesel engine. It rumbled to life and idled smoothly before he engaged the drive and shoved the throttle forward.

"Get the mainsail down," he ordered while grasping the jib's furling line, jerking it hard and causing the jib to furl around the forestay.

"What is it?" Emily asked.

"I don't know, but smoke like that can't be good. Somebody is in trouble." He caught her worried glance, but they both knew they had to find the source of the smoke.

Windseeker's original Perkins engine had made just fifty horsepower while the Volvo that Ryan was now throttling up was nearly twice that. The extra ponies pushed the sailboat to ten knots at max throttle, and that was where the GPS speed number hovered as the bow bucked through the waves.

Emily had the main sail collapsed into the lazy jacks and

was strapping it to the boom. Ryan put the binos back to his eyes, centering on the smoke, but they were still too far away to see anything.

Windseeker surged through the waves, making impressive progress courtesy of the vessel's upgrades. As Ryan continued to watch through the binos, a mast head appeared above a sinking sailboat. Its tattered main sail hung over the cockpit, and black smoldering smoke rose into the air. More than half of the hull was underwater. Suddenly, a woman pushed aside part of the main sail and fell over the side of the boat.

"Get the life ring, Em," Ryan ordered.

She moved with urgency, grabbing it from the rail and loosening the coil of rope attached to it, so she was ready to throw the ring when commanded.

Ryan drove *Windseeker* straight toward the distressed boat. Five minutes later, he was abreast of the sinking vessel and bringing his sailboat to a stop. Emily threw the life ring to the bedraggled woman, who was struggling to stay afloat in the water. She snagged the life ring with both arms. Ryan reflexively hit a button on the GPS, marking their location, before helping Emily drag the woman through the water and pull her aboard the sailboat.

Shivering as she sat on the cockpit bench, the older woman looked up at Ryan and said, "You have to help my husband. He's in the V-berth."

As the last words came out of her mouth, Ryan saw the nose of the sinking boat tip up into the air as the stern slipped beneath the waves. Within seconds, the boat was fully submerged. Ryan ripped off the bench seat cushions and retrieved the box that contained his dive gear.

In the middle of mounting his wing and backplate buoyancy compensating device, or BCD, to a tank, Emily said, "What are you doing?"

"I'm going after him." Ryan pulled on his mask, dive boots, and fins, then shrugged into the BCD.

"Help him!" the woman shrieked.

Emily jumped into action, grabbing the tank and aiding Ryan to stand. She steadied him as he stepped over the lifelines.

Ryan turned to Emily. "The current will take us north as we come up. Watch for my surface marker buoy and then drop a weighted line for us to ascend along. I'll give three jerks on the line to let you know I have it, then pull up the SMB."

"Okay."

He shoved the regulator into his mouth and took a giant stride off the side of *Windseeker*.

Ryan splashed through the surface in a burst of bubbles. He had dumped the air from his BCD so he would drop like a stone. He took a moment to reach between his legs and fasten the BCD's crotch strap, then he kicked furiously downward, chasing the sailboat in a head-down position.

Beneath him, the sailboat arrowed stern-first into the dirt, throwing up a cloud of sediment. With a quick glance at his Shearwater dive computer, Ryan saw he was approaching one hundred feet in depth. *Twenty minutes of dive time*, his mind automatically told him. The sunken boat was still another fifty feet away and rested on its starboard side with its bow over the edge of a precipice that dropped thousands of feet down into darkness.

At the recreational dive limit of one hundred and thirty feet, he had ten minutes of bottom time; at one fifty, he had less than five. The computer beeped as he approached the sailboat, letting him know he was surpassing the recreational limits and was now accumulating decompression time. He ignored it. If he could save a man, then the decompression obligation would be worth it.

He noted the name *Balance Sheet* lettered across the stern in gold leaf, then pulled aside the nylon sailcloth and pushed through the cockpit door. Snapping on his dive light, he shined it around the cabin.

Cushions and clothes floated in the confined space. Dishes, books, and other gear had fallen from the port side and lay strewn across the starboard settee, cabinets, and hull, making the place a snag hazard that threatened to trap Ryan. Nevertheless, he continued forward, ensuring he was neutrally buoyant. He couldn't afford to bump the boat and send it sliding over the edge into the deep, where the weight of the water would crush to death both himself and the man he was trying to save.

At the door to the V-berth, he poked his light inside and moved it around, seeing a tangle of sheets and clothes. The next thing he saw was the blood streaming from the man's wounds, then a pair of thin legs, poking out of surf shorts. Moving the light upward, he saw the man was clutching a yellow waterproof box as a flotation device. His head was above the water in the space created by the trapped air.

Ryan inhaled and his body moved up. His head broke the surface to see the man staring at him in wide-eyed disbelief.

"We need to get out of here," Ryan said. "Do you have any dive experience?"

"Yeah. I'm Open Water certified," the man said in a thick New Jersey accent.

"Cool." Ryan handed the man his primary regulator and then reached for his secondary reg, which hung from a necklace below his chin.

"I can't leave the box."

"What's your name?" Ryan asked.

"Paul."

"Okay, Paul, we don't have enough air to worry about that. We need to go. *Now*."

"I have a scuba tank in the starboard bench of the cockpit."

"Great; we have some extra air for deco stops. Let's go."

Hugging the box a little tighter, Paul said adamantly, "Not without this."

"Have it your way. See ya." Ryan jerked the regulator from the man's hand and turned to swim away. The man screamed for him to stop, letting go of the box and thrashing after the diver. Ryan rose back to the surface and handed the reg to him. With the seven-foot hose attached to the reg he'd given Paul, they didn't need to swim side by side, and Ryan could lead the way with Paul following behind him.

Once clear of the hull, Ryan opened the starboard bench seat and found the scuba tank, a jacket-style BCD, and a set of regulators. He dumped everything into the dirt beside *Balance Sheet*, fastened the tank to the BCD, and hooked the reg to the tank valve. Paul grabbed a mask and put it on while Ryan worked. When he had the kit together, Ryan helped Paul into the BCD, then gave him an okay sign. Paul returned the gesture, and Ryan indicated they were to head for the surface with a thumbs-up.

They continued to use Ryan's tank and regs as they ascended. Ryan knew his air consumption rate, and, for him, the tank would have lasted through most of his decompression stops, but he would need another tank to finish. With Paul breathing heavily on the octopus, the air in the tank was rapidly being depleted. Even with both tanks, they wouldn't have enough air to complete their deco obligations.

The normal ascent rate was no more than thirty feet in a minute, meaning that if a diver was ascending a line, he would place one hand just above the other to maintain that rate. Ryan understood that Paul would be nervous about spending so much time in the water and would want to get to the surface as soon as possible. He tapped his dive computer and held it so Paul could see. Paul nodded. Ryan pointed to the deco time, then at Paul, and flashed five fingers on his right hand, meaning Paul needed to do an additional five minutes.

Paul's eyes widened, and he shook his head vigorously. Ryan held up his fists side by side and acted like he was bending an invisible bar. Paul nodded. He would get bent if he shot to the surface.

At seventy-five feet, Ryan forced them to stop. He tapped the computer and flashed five fingers. They would stay at the current depth for five minutes. Normally, it would be half the time at half the depth, but Ryan added a few minutes to compensate for Paul's longer bottom time.

Paul did not have thousands of dives under his belt like Ryan, and his neutral buoyancy was shit. He kept bobbing up and down, adding and removing air from his BCD. Ryan gave him a few silent pointers but eventually slapped his hand away from the inflator button. While they waited for the minutes to tick by, Ryan pulled the SMB from his BCD and attached a finger spool to it. With a small breath, he inflated the SMB, and they watched as it shot upward, unspooling line behind it. When the SMB reached the surface, Ryan tied the line to a bolt snap, clipped it to his BCD, and wrapped his free hand around the shoulder strap of Paul's BCD.

When they had depleted the air in Ryan's tank, they changed to Paul's, putting the new regulators in their mouths. The line to the SMB went taut and jerked hard several times. Ryan swiveled his body to look at the surface. There was a shadow above them, and he hoped it was *Windseeker*. He motioned for Paul to hold and let out some air from his BCD, compensating for Paul's overinflation.

As they watched, a weighted line dropped through the water column five feet in front of them. Ryan grabbed it and gave three jerks on the line. It stopped falling, and he figured Emily had tied it to a boat cleat.

Ryan pulled his companion over to the ascent line. He unclipped the SMB and jerked it hard several times. Emily grabbed it and began pulling it up to the boat.

With the ascent line, they didn't have to worry about their buoyancy, allowing the boat above to do the work. Ryan guided Paul through the decompression stops. Emily dropped a fresh tank to them, knowing they would need more air, and at the last stop at ten feet, they took turns breathing one hundred percent oxygen to help clear the last of the built-up nitrogen from their body tissue. Ryan liked to keep a pony bottle of oxygen aboard his boat in case of emergencies and to help off-gas after long dives.

As the two men made the final ascent and broke the surface, they saw the women leaning over the railing, staring at them.

Ryan and Paul shed their BCDs and passed them to Emily before climbing up the boarding ladder. Paul sat wearily on the bench beside his wife. Ryan had looked at the older man's wound while they were decompressing and had wrapped a piece of Paul's shirt around it to stop the bleeding.

"Emily," Ryan said, "grab the first aid kit, please."

He used his dive knife to slice the makeshift bandage away from Paul's hand.

"You're lucky it didn't hit any bones, or you'd be a lot worse off," Ryan said as he applied a bandage to the deep cut on Paul's palm.

Paul leaned back against the rail, cradling his right arm against his chest. Ryan handed him four acetaminophen tablets and a bottle of water. While Paul washed down the pills, Ryan hauled in their ascent rope and stored their gear. He'd seen the bullet holes in the sunken boat and the shattered shotgun on the deck. Fortunately, the current had carried them a long way from the wreck site and hopefully even farther from the men who'd sunk her.

When *Windseeker* was back on course with her sails trimmed, Ryan sat beside the rescued couple. He extended his hand to Paul. "I know we met earlier, but my name's Ryan. That's Emily, and we're on our way to St. John."

"Thanks for coming to my rescue." Paul shook his hand and then Emily's. "This is my wife, Diane. We just left St. Thomas."

"What happened?" Emily asked. "Were you attacked by pirates?"

Paul nodded. "I think so. It was one of those high-speed racing boats."

Diane's shoulders shook as she spoke. "They just started shooting at us."

"You're out of danger now," Ryan said, "but you need to get that wound looked at."

"Yeah," Paul agreed. "Can you take us to St. Thomas? I know a doctor there."

"Is it wise to go home?" Diane asked him.

"Fuhgeddaboudit." Paul waved his hand. "Those yutzes aren't coming near us again. Me and Ryan will go up to the house and get some stuff. You girls'll stay at the marina."

Ryan saw the look that Paul shot his wife. He took it to mean she should shut up and not talk in front of the strangers. That was fine with Ryan. The sooner he dropped them off, the sooner he and Emily could get to St. John, and whatever danger the stranded couple was in would be behind them.

Paul turned to him with a smile. "Please, let us take you to dinner as a 'thank you' for saving us."

"Yeah, I think we can do that," Ryan agreed.

Paul smiled gregariously. Despite his problems and having to drag him out of a sunken sailboat, Ryan liked the man. Even his wife had a staunchness about her.

Ryan moved behind the wheel. "What's the closest marina to your house?"

Paul got up and came over to look at the GPS plotter. "We can put you in at my old slip at American Yacht Harbor."

Ryan tapped it into the touch screen and hit the *Go* button. A white line populated over the blue ocean.

"Might as well settle in," Ryan said, checking the arrival time. "We have two and a half hours to get there."

"Once we're abreast of Cabrita Point, it's best to go in on the motor," Paul advised. "It can get pretty crowded in there between the ferries and the fishing boats."

"Roger that," Ryan replied.

As they sailed, the rescued couple seemed to relax, but Ryan saw how Paul vigilantly scanned the horizon. Emily found a cover-up for Diane and fixed tea for the two women. They stayed in the cabin, chatting.

"What do you do for work, Paul?" Ryan asked.

"I'm an accountant. Me and Diane moved here about ten years ago."

"Are you retired?"

"I still work a few days a week. What about you?"

"Emily is an insurance investigator and I'm a commercial diver. We both took a sabbatical from our jobs. We're on our way back to Florida."

"Is that where you live?"

Ryan smiled. "I live wherever my boat is. Em has a place in Tampa."

"You make a nice couple," Paul said.

An hour from St. Thomas, Ryan used the Customs and Border Patrol's ROAM app to notify them of *Windseeker*'s arrival. After putting his information into the app, he called the CBP office at the Port of St. Thomas, and the agent said to go straight to the docks at American Yacht Harbor.

The low green hills of St. John slipped past as they

entered Pillsbury Sound. Not much later, the green and red dirt hills of St. Thomas appeared. Ryan started the engine, and Paul helped Emily lower the mainsail and put the sail cover in place. Paul called American Yacht Harbor on the radio and explained that an accident had befallen his boat and that *Windseeker* would take her place in his slip. The harbormaster asked that Ryan and Emily have their paperwork ready.

Paul guided Ryan into the slip and leaped onto the dock to secure the mooring lines to the dock cleats. The man might not have been a great scuba diver, but he was a more than capable sailor, and his fastidiousness showed when he coiled the ends of the spare dock line beside the cleat. The harbormaster greeted Paul with a handshake and looked over Ryan and Emily's paperwork, scanning the pre-approved ROAM application number into his smart phone.

"Ryan, do you have a shirt I can borrow?" Paul asked. "I want to go to our house and get us a change of clothes."

"Are you sure that's wise, dear?" Diane asked.

"It's okay, Di. There's nothin' to worry about."

Ryan went below and pulled on a pair of khaki cargo shorts over clean underwear, slipped into a clean T-shirt, pocketed his wallet and CRKT tactical folding knife, then grabbed a light green guayabera shirt for Paul.

Back on the dock, Paul shrugged on the shirt. He couldn't button it over his stomach and left it open. The two men headed for the marina office to call a taxi.

They rode across the island to the Langstons' residence. Fifteen minutes later, both men got out of the cab after asking the driver to wait and they walked to the front door. Ryan grabbed Paul's arm and pointed at the door frame where someone had forced the lock open and left the door ajar.

Paul shoved the door open, standing right in front of it while Ryan stepped off to the side, invisible and protected behind the solid wall. When Paul stepped through the door and no one took a shot at him, Ryan followed.

The place was a wreck. Someone had tipped over, ripped open, smashed, or otherwise destroyed everything in the place. Ignoring the disaster that was his home, Paul headed across the living room to a bedroom. Ryan followed cautiously. What were the odds that a man and his wife had their boat shot out from under them on the same day that someone had robbed them?

"Is anything missing?" Ryan asked.

"Not that I can tell," Paul replied from the bedroom. "Give me two more minutes."

Ryan stepped over the piles of debris and walked to the sliding glass doors that overlooked the pool. They, too, were open.

The hairs on the back of his neck stood up. Someone was watching them. He was sure of it.

An icy coldness clutched at his chest at the thought of a sniper's crosshairs centered there. He ventured no farther outside and instead returned to the safety of the house's concrete block walls.

"What the hell's going on, Paul? Why are people shooting up your boat and ransacking your house?"

"The wife and I had a little argument. That's why the place is a mess," Paul answered. He came out of the bedroom, carrying two bulging suitcases.

Ryan looked past him and saw the open wall safe. "Uh-huh." It was hard to tell how a person would act just by meeting them, but Ryan suspected Mrs. Langston would never destroy her own home in such a manner.

"Let's go. I'm starving," Paul said, his New Jersey accent dropping the R and G in starving.

Ryan stopped the older man before he could get to the

front door. "Paul, I've made a good living out of helping people in trouble. Maybe I can help you."

"Fuhgeddaboudit, Ryan. This ain't no big deal. Let's go get the girls." He patted his belly. "All this excitement's worked up an appetite."

When all the signs pointed to trouble, there was no way Ryan could forget about it.

CHAPTER THREE

Ryan and Paul exited the trashed house and walked to the waiting taxi. Ryan carefully scanned his surroundings, looking for any signs of trouble. He wished he had his Walther in his back pocket, but, despite the USVI being a part of the United States, his gun rights didn't extend beyond the mainland. He hadn't declared them to Customs either, and it was a hefty fine and jail time for not doing so.

As he climbed into the cab, he said to Paul, "Do you need to see a doctor about your hand?"

"No. You did a good job patchin' me up. Take us back to American Yacht, driver."

Ryan watched the scenery slip past, moving his head to get a glimpse out the rearview mirrors to determine if anyone was following them. Trees crowded both sides of the narrow, twisting road, making it impossible to tell if someone was tailing them. If whoever was after the Langstons was smart, they'd use multiple vehicles to follow them, swapping out at varying intervals. It was like playing defense in football, the cornerbacks, safeties, and linebackers trading off on the receivers before converging for a tackle.

He glanced at Paul, who was staring out the side window. Maybe this man was used to people destroying his life. He seemed cool under pressure, and eating was usually the furthest thing from most people's minds if they'd just been through a traumatic experience like being trapped in a sunken boat and then discovering that someone had robbed their house. Ryan knew something wasn't right here, but if the guy wouldn't accept his offer of help, Ryan wasn't going to pry. He decided that, after dinner, he and Emily would put as much distance between themselves and the Langstons as possible, maybe even striking out for St. John this evening.

Back at the docks, both couples showered in the marina's private restrooms, changed into clean clothes, and walked to a steakhouse in the same building as the yacht club. Ryan ordered a New York strip steak with a baked potato and steamed vegetables. Emily gave him a strange look for ordering such an expensive meal, but Paul said it was all good because Ryan had saved his life and a hero deserved a steak dinner.

When they finished eating, Paul asked Ryan, "What did you do before commercial diving? Something tells me you're ex-military."

"I was in the Navy," Ryan replied.

"What'd you do—SEAL teams?"

"No, I was a diver." It wasn't a complete lie. Ryan had been an Explosive Ordnance Disposal technician, and as part of that training, he had gone through the Navy's rigorous dive school where they'd taught everything from the use of basic scuba gear to surface-supplied diving operations. Once he'd passed the EOD school at Eglin Air Force Base in the Florida Panhandle, he'd gone on to learn how to dispose of underwater mines while using closed circuit rebreathers.

Ryan had left home the day after high school graduation to sail around the world. When he'd returned, he joined the

U.S. Navy to fight for his country after the devastating attacks of September 11, 2001. He'd spent ten years as an EOD tech, completing multiple tours in Iraq and Afghanistan before calling it quits and moving back to his hometown of Wilmington, North Carolina. There he had worked for his father's construction company, renovating houses. While he enjoyed spending time with his family and getting to know his nieces and nephews, he'd missed the sea and craved adventure. Pounding nails didn't give him the same thrill as chasing bad guys or diving wrecks.

When Greg Olsen, his former EOD team leader and owner of the commercial dive and salvage company Dark Water Research, had asked him to be DWR's liaison with the Department of Homeland Security, Ryan had jumped at the chance to get back into action, and for the last two years, he'd bounced around the Caribbean, doing commercial diving jobs and combating terrorism.

Then Emily had come back into his life and everything changed. The two of them had met while he was investigating pirates in the Gulf of Mexico and they'd had a short but intense relationship before she'd dumped him for putting her life in danger. Several years later, when she needed help to find a stolen freighter, Emily had turned to Greg Olsen, who paired her with Ryan, forcing them into an uneasy truce as they worked together. The passion they had shared in those early days had returned, and they'd been inseparable since. He looked at her now and grinned. She returned the smile and reached for his hand. He winked at her and waggled his eyebrows suggestively, and she giggled and shook her head.

"I can see you lovebirds are ready to be alone," Paul said. "Youse guys go on. I'll get the bill."

"You sure?" Ryan asked. "Can I get the tip?"

"Fuhgeddaboudit. You saved my life."

Emily and Ryan stood, and Diane gave them each a hug. "Thank you so much for your help."

"You're welcome," Emily told her. "Call me anytime."

Diane smiled. "I will, dear."

Ryan took Emily's hand and he led her out of the restaurant.

"What's the hurry?" she asked as they stepped onto the wooden dock that ran along the waterfront.

"In a minute," he said, continuing toward *Windseeker*. When they were in the cockpit, Ryan unlocked the cabin door and went below, returning with a beer for him and a glass of wine for Emily.

Ryan took a sip of beer and said, "Someone ransacked their house, Em, and it was probably the same people who sank their sailboat. I think Paul screwed up and now his enemies want him dead."

"What do you think he did?"

"I'm not sure, but the whole time I was at their house, I felt like a sniper was watching me through his scope. It was the same feeling I used to get when I was disarming IEDs in Afghanistan. Those AQ and Taliban bastards liked to take potshots at us while we worked."

Emily raised her eyebrows. Ryan rarely talked about his time overseas. If he did, it was not about the tragic secrets he kept locked inside, but about the good things that had happened. He had come to terms with most of his demons. Sailing, diving, and working helped to keep them at bay, but they still surfaced occasionally. They came out in nightmares, paranoia, or bursts of anger that led many to believe Ryan was a rogue actor, a loner with trust issues. Emily knew better. She'd seen him at his best and at his worst. She accepted it for what it was—post-traumatic stress—and she loved him anyway.

They sat in silence on the cockpit bench, watching the

sun set behind the homes perched on the hill across the bay and listening to the sounds of their environment. Birds sang in the nearby trees, ropes creaked, and water lapped against the boat hulls. A flock of pelicans swooped over the water and settled onto dock posts.

Then they heard a woman scream Emily's name.

Emily sat bolt upright as Ryan stood.

"What the hell was that?" he said.

The next shout was louder and longer. "*Emily!*"

She pointed across the docks. "It came from over there."

Ryan grabbed the binoculars from the pulpit and scanned the adjacent boats. He saw two black men horsing Diane Langston aboard a large gray yacht. One clamped his hand over her mouth so she couldn't scream again, while a third man guided Paul up the boarding ladder with the muzzle of his pistol.

"Do you see anything?" Emily asked.

He handed her the binoculars and pointed at the yacht. "Diane is on that Viking."

Emily put the glasses to her eyes as Ryan dashed into *Windseeker*'s cabin. He went straight to the navigation table, lifted the lid, and removed his Walther PPQ nine-millimeter pistol from its hiding spot. He kept it in a Kydex holster that he clipped inside his waistband.

When he came back topside, Emily said, "They're casting off."

Ryan closed and locked the companionway door before they raced down the dock to shore as the Viking began pulling away.

"There." Ryan pointed at a Renaissance Prowler 36 fishing catamaran with twin Suzuki four-hundred horsepower outboards docked at the fuel pumps. The rocket launchers mounted on the Prowler's T-top were full of heavy-duty offshore fishing tackle.

They ran to the boat where the captain, a middle-aged white man with silver-flecked hair, had just finished fueling his boat and was casting off his dock lines.

Ryan stopped at the edge of the dock. "Are you for hire?"

"Yeah," the captain said, "but I'm taking her to her berth and going home for the night."

"I need you to follow that Viking." Ryan nodded toward the yacht leaving the harbor.

"What?"

"A friend of ours is on that boat," Ryan said. "We think they kidnapped her."

"Call the cops," the captain said.

"I'll pay you cash. Double the rate," Emily said.

Both Ryan and the captain turned to look at her. She stepped over the Prowler's gunwale. "Let's go."

"Where's the money?" the captain asked.

Emily pulled off a gold necklace and laid it on the console. "That's worth five hundred dollars. I'll give you the money when we get back."

The captain held up the necklace and examined it in the low light, then pocketed it and started the engines. He eased them away from the dock and clicked on the running lights as they glided through the black water.

"I'm Captain Stuart. Normally, I'd tell you about the fishing spots we're going to, but I don't think you're interested."

"Just follow the boat," Emily said, sitting on the seat beside Stuart.

Ryan leaned against the seat and held onto the aluminum tubing of the T-top. Stuart glanced over at him. The breeze lifted the T-shirt around Ryan's side and Stuart saw the butt of the Walther.

"You got a permit for that gun?" Stuart asked.

"You let me worry about that, Captain."

Stuart turned back to the wheel and adjusted the brightness of his GPS screen. They trailed the Viking at a safe distance, appearing to be just another vessel going night fishing. Ryan kept one eye on the GPS, the yacht making a nice fat blip on the screen, and the other on the vessel as it pushed out into Pillsbury Sound and turned south.

"What do you want me to do?" Stuart asked.

"Stay with them, and when I tell you, run up fast on their stern. I'll hop across, and you back off. You stay on the starboard quarter, and when I'm ready for you to pick me up, I'll flash a light three times in quick succession."

"Okay," Stuart agreed.

"What did you do before you became a fishing guide?" Ryan asked, trying to occupy the guy's mind while they waited for the vessels to get clear of the traffic in the channel.

"I'm a recovering attorney. I worked for a major firm in D.C. until I got burned out. Then I moved down here and bought a boat."

"Recovering attorney. That's an interesting way to put it," Ryan said.

"After twenty-five years, two divorces, and one heart attack, I figured it was time to do something else."

They rode in silence for a few more minutes, the yacht gaining ground on them until Ryan said, "Okay, Captain—let's see what you've got."

Stuart threw the throttle to its stop, and the catamaran shot forward like it had been kicked in the stern. The nose came level, and they rocketed through the water.

When they were within ten feet of the Viking, Ryan moved to the casting platform on the bow of the Prowler and waited as Stuart maneuvered his vessel into place. When the gap closed to two feet, Ryan sprang across to the Viking. He crouched at the base of the steps leading to the main deck as the Prowler veered away into the darkness.

CHAPTER FOUR

The steps up from the Viking's swim platform led to a small seating area. Beyond it was an open sliding door. Ryan saw a man at the helm and another guy who held an M4 rifle to his shoulder, coming toward where he was kneeling.

The Viking had only one set of steps from the swim platform up to the cockpit, so Ryan pressed himself close to the hull, hoping the guard wouldn't see him. The Prowler came darting by, and Emily screamed in delight as the two boats almost collided. This drew the attention of the man with the M4, and Ryan ran up the steps. The guard with the long gun spun on his heel, detecting nearby motion in his peripheral vision, and Ryan struck him with an open palm strike on his chin. As he staggered backward, Ryan hit him with a judo kick to the chest, sending him tumbling over the rail.

Moving across the deck, Ryan jammed his pistol against the helmsman's head. "Put it on autopilot."

The man complied, then raised his hands from the controls.

"Jump overboard," Ryan ordered. They were only a mile

from the nearest island, a little chunk of awash stone called Dog Rocks.

"No, man. Are you crazy?" the captain asked.

Not wanting to spend any more time dealing with him, Ryan crashed the butt of his gun against the man's temple, and he fell to the deck. Ryan saw nothing handy to tie him up with and hoped that he'd be out long enough for him to get to Diane and Paul and get them off the boat. He quickly patted the man down and chucked the pistol he found overboard.

The door to the main cabin was beside the driver's controls. Ryan pushed it open and saw steps leading to the lower level. He aimed his pistol at a thin black man in his late twenties who stood in the center of the salon. His hair was styled in cornrows and he wore black dress pants, black square-toed shoes, and a gold dress shirt. A small soul patch jutted out from under his lower lip and a close-cropped goatee graced his chin, with a thin strip of hair connecting the two. Soul Patch grabbed Diane and forced her to her knees, pressing his pistol against her head.

"Drop it or I'll kill her!" Soul Patch warned.

Ryan kept his gun trained on Diane's would-be executioner. "Go ahead, but if you pull that trigger, you're dead." He stepped off the companionway stairs and stood five feet away from Diane. She was sobbing. The tears streaked her face and dripped from her chin.

Paul Langston sat on the sofa, his hands bound in front of him. He looked at Ryan and shook his head, his eyes silently pleading for him not to do anything rash.

Ryan felt cold steel against his back and guessed that the captain was now awake.

"Looks like we got ourselves a Mexican stand-off, eh, playa?" Soul Patch said.

"You get to keep Paul because he screwed you over. But

his wife has nothing to do with this. Let her go and we can all walk away from this happy."

"I thought you didn't care about the woman," Soul Patch jeered.

"She's innocent," Ryan said.

"And who are you?"

"I'm the hostage negotiator," Ryan replied, his gunsight never wavering from Soul Patch's head.

Soul Patch thumbed the hammer back on his semi-automatic.

"He can dive for the box," Paul blurted out. "He's a Navy diver."

"Oh, he is, is he?" Soul Patch said. "Then let's make a deal, playa. You get the box from Paul's sailboat and you can have Mrs. Langston back."

Ryan assumed the box in question was the same one he had convinced Paul to leave behind in *Balance Sheet* not more than six hours ago. "I'm not leaving without her."

Soul Patch wrapped his hand in Diane's hair and wrenched her head back. She screamed in pain and flailed against Soul Patch's hand.

"Shut up!" Soul Patch screamed, and he smacked her in the face with the barrel of his gun. Blood gushed from a cut on her cheek.

Ryan's voice rose in anger. "She's an old lady, asshole. Why don't you pick on someone your own size?"

Soul Patch slung Diane out of the way, her head hitting the floor hard, and she was still. He raised his gun gangsta style and stepped closer to Ryan. "You wanna go hostage negotiator?"

Paul scrambled off the couch and knelt over his wife, putting his finger to her neck.

"Is she okay?" Ryan asked, looking around the gangster at the older couple.

"I think so," Paul said shakily. "Her pulse is strong, and she's breathing."

"Good. See if you can wake her up."

"Leave her alone," Soul Patch ordered through gritted teeth.

Paul stroked his wife's cheek before bending and kissing her on the lips.

Soul Patch jabbed his gun at Ryan. "You still wanna go, playa?"

"Yeah, and I'm taking the woman with me."

"Bullshit! You're gonna take that worthless piece of shit Paul, who thinks he can steal from me, and you're gonna bring me that box with my documents in it. Diane is gonna keep me company. If you're not back in twenty-four hours, I'll feed her to the fish."

"I need forty-eight hours to get my gear in order and make the dive," Ryan said.

"No," Soul Patch spat. "Twenty-four hours. Starting right now." He raised his left wrist to look at his gold Rolex. "Ten-thirty."

Ryan rolled his wrist and looked at his Citizen dive watch. "Okay." He holstered his pistol and held up his hands.

Paul helped Diane sit up against the couch and held her hand. "I'm sorry, Di. I promise we'll be back soon."

Diane raised a hand to probe the bleeding gash on her cheek and looked past her husband at Ryan. Despite the dazed look on her face, her eyes bored into him, and he knew he had no choice but to comply with Soul Patch's demands and figure out a way to rescue her. Ryan knew that as soon as Soul Patch had his box, he would kill everyone involved.

"Let's go, Paul," Ryan said.

The older man heaved himself to his feet, a defeated expression on his normally gregarious face. Ryan slowly turned and faced the helmsman, who had found a pistol from somewhere and kept it trained on Ryan as he backed up the accommodation ladder.

At the steps to the swim platform, Ryan asked Soul Patch, "Can I borrow a flashlight to signal my boat to pick us up?"

"What's the signal?" Soul Patch asked.

"Three quick flashes to the boat on your starboard rear quarter."

Soul Patch flashed the light just as Ryan had said, then he aimed his pistol at Ryan's head. "Get the hell off my boat, playa."

Ryan saw the running lights of the Prowler turn toward them, and he stepped onto the rail. Paul jumped first, and with a sigh and a shake of his head, Ryan reluctantly followed him into the water.

———

EMILY AND STUART must have seen them jump because the Prowler slowed and they snapped on a spotlight, instead of pursuing the Viking.

The light centered on the two swimming men as the Prowler approached. Stuart and Emily helped Paul climb aboard, and Ryan pulled himself up between the Prowler's twin outboards.

"You guys okay?" Stuart asked.

"We'll live," Ryan said, wiping the water from his face.

"Where's Diane?" Emily demanded.

"She's being held hostage while Paul and I do a little recovery dive." Ryan stood and stepped to the center console. "What are you doing tomorrow, Captain? I need your help."

"I'm supposed to take a charter out in the morning, but I can get a buddy of mine to do it if you make the pay right."

"Emily said she would pay you double your normal rate. Does that work for you?"

"Sounds good," Stuart said. "The pickin's have been slim lately."

"I need to borrow a vehicle to run some errands in the morning," Ryan added.

"Yeah, no problem. I'll be at the dock at seven."

Ryan slapped Stuart on the shoulder and asked Emily for his cell phone. He pulled up his favorite contacts and hit the call button beside Rick Hayes's name. Like he'd done for Ryan, Greg had plucked Hayes from a mundane life and brought him into the fold at Dark Water Research. He and Ryan had worked several ops together since, and Rick was both Ryan and Greg's go-to man when they needed extra muscle.

A moment later, Rick came on the line. "Hey, buddy, what's going on? Long time, no hear."

"Where are you at?" Ryan asked.

"In Nicaragua with Greg. We're still working on the port contracts for Bluefields."

"That sucks."

"Tell me about it; I'm over Central America. Why are you calling me, anyway? Is it playtime?"

"Yeah, I need some backup on St. Thomas."

"Wish I could make it, brother, but I'm tied up here. You need to call Jinks."

Ryan hung up, his mind racing through scenarios and trying to figure all the angles.

When they returned to the dock, Ryan steered Paul toward *Windseeker*. After retrieving the money from the sailboat, Emily paid Stuart, and he handed her necklace back to her. Ryan took a quick shower and called Roland "Jinks" Jenkins. Ryan had met Jinks when Jinks had still been on active duty as a Navy SEAL. After his retirement, he'd agreed to head up Greg's private military contracting company, Trident.

The short Samoan answered with, "You're like a bad penny, Weller; you keep turning up."

"Yeah, but you like shiny objects."

Jinks laughed.

"What are the chances of you getting a strike team to St. Thomas by nine tomorrow night?" Ryan asked. "I'm in the middle of a hostage exchange."

"Now you're speaking my language, but bad news, buddy—we're tapped out."

"How about two guys? I can manage with just a sniper team."

"That, I can do, but your timing sucks."

"Doesn't it always? If it makes you feel any better, this is interrupting my vacation."

Jinks snorted. "I'll get two guys and a gear package to you by tomorrow night."

"Thanks, Jinks."

Ryan returned to the sailboat and found Emily and Paul sitting in the salon, drinking beer. "Okay, Paul, spill it," he said. "Who's the guy holding your wife hostage and what's in the box?"

"Can I get another beer?" Paul asked.

Ryan retrieved three beers, handed them out, and collected his gun cleaning kit from the V-berth. He sat at the table and disassembled his Walther. "Now, what's in the box that Soul Patch wants so badly?"

Paul looked momentarily confused. "Oh, you mean, Terrence Joseph."

"Yes." Ryan nodded.

"Papers that can incriminate me and Terrence Joseph in criminal activity."

"What kind of criminal activity?" Ryan asked dubiously. He'd helped a lot of people over the years, but he always felt that if a person was a criminal, they would get what they deserved. Maybe that was why Ryan himself had spent six months in a Venezuelan prison. The universe had dished out punishment for all the hell he'd rained down on various factions during his lifetime.

Paul toyed with the beer bottle for a moment, then said, "I'm a smurf."

"You don't look blue," Emily said with a giggle.

"I'm not a cartoon smurf. My job is smurfing. I launder money through shell companies and offshore banks. Every day, I move a small amount of money through the accounts, nothing over the ten-thousand-dollar threshold set by the U.S. government so the deposits won't attract attention. It's all set up automatically, so all I have to do is babysit the payments. Once the money moves through one set of accounts, it goes into another and another, until the person who owns the money uses it to purchase hard assets."

"Let me guess," Ryan said, running a bore brush through the barrel of his pistol, "you smurfed some money into your own account."

"To be fair, I've been doing it for years," Paul said. "The amount of money that flows through the books is so large that I skimmed a little extra for myself. I created several dummy accounts, just like I normally would, siphoned off tiny amounts, and then I cooked the books to make it all look legit."

"Don't you get paid a percentage?" Emily asked.

"I do, but when the money is in the tens of millions, I figured I could skim a little extra off the top. It's easy to do by stealing a few dollars here and a few dollars there. Nothing big."

"But it all adds up over time," Ryan said.

"Yes."

"How much?" Ryan asked.

"Almost seventy million dollars," Paul said.

Ryan rolled his eyes. "And you stole it from Soul Patch?"

"No, Terrence is just the middleman."

"So where did the money come from?"

Paul Langston glanced around the cabin as if someone might overhear their conversation, then leaned toward Ryan and lowered his voice. "Venezuela."

Ryan ran a hand through his hair and sighed. He'd had enough of Venezuela for one lifetime. "Okay, Paul, tell us how Terrence fits into your scheme."

"Terrence is like a middle manager. He runs a local gang that does everything from snatching purses to running drugs."

"I think now might be a good time to turn a copy of your paperwork over to the police," Emily said.

Paul shook his head. "No. I have to save Diane."

"What was your plan for this incriminating evidence?" Ryan asked.

The older man shrugged. "I thought it might buy me immunity if the police investigated, or maybe it would keep Terrence from doing something stupid."

"Like trying to kill you or kidnapping Diane?" Emily noted.

"Yeah."

"How do you know him?" Ryan asked.

"When Diane and I lived in New Jersey, I used to work for some Italians."

"The Mob?" Emily asked.

Paul nodded. "After we moved here, I was looking for some clients to help offset some expenses, so my old contacts hooked me up with Joseph. He needed some money laundered and I helped him do it."

Ryan shook his head in disbelief as he disassembled the trigger assembly and pulled the Walther as far apart as he could. He needed to clean the saltwater from the weapon to keep it from corroding.

"So, you kept a record of your activities?" Emily asked.

"Yeah." Paul nodded. "I kept a record of all the money I'd laundered for Joseph, figuring that if there was a RICO investigation, I could disclose the records and get immunity. Kinda like an insurance policy. You know?"

"Did you keep a history of your withdrawals?" Ryan asked.

"Yeah, I did," Paul said. "I thought I'd kept everything clean and neat. I still don't know how Terrence figured out what I was doing. I never told anyone about that account, not even Diane."

"Where did you keep the records?" Ryan asked.

"In my office, but when we took off, I put the most important ones in the box."

"He might have been monitoring your place with a bug or a keystroke logger," Emily offered.

"How are we gonna get Diane back?" Paul asked.

"I'm working on that," Ryan said. "By this time tomorrow, I should have help. Speaking of that, we need accommodations for the team."

"Youse can use my place," Paul said.

"No," Ryan said. "If Joseph has people watching your place, I don't want to tip them off that we have help."

Paul thought for a minute, then said, "I know a lady who runs a small bed and breakfast not far from here. Her house is on a cliff that overlooks Vessup Bay. You can see this marina from the back patio."

"That'll work," Ryan said. He sprayed the components before him with gun oil and then reassembled his pistol. When he put the slide on, he racked it back and forth a dozen times and dry-fired the gun. Satisfied the Walther was clean and ready for use, he washed the magazines, holster, and bullets in fresh water. He set the bullets aside and loaded brand-new hollow points into the mags. "Paul, after you call your friend about the house, you can take the V-berth. Try to get some sleep, and we'll get a fresh start in the morning."

Paul made his phone call and told Ryan everything was set, then headed for the bunk.

Emily took Ryan topside. "Do you think they're watching our boat?"

"Without a doubt," Ryan replied.

"I assume you have a plan."

"I need to collect some things that will make the dive easier and get my rebreather bottles filled, then I'll get the box."

"You make it sound simple," Emily said.

"It should be, as long as Mr. Murphy doesn't show up."

CHAPTER FIVE

In the morning, Ryan was up early. Normally, if they were in a marina, he and Emily would go for a run, but today, he sipped coffee and waited for the scuba shop in the yacht club building to open. When it did, he asked about getting his rebreather bottles filled with trimix and oxygen. The owner told Ryan that he could accommodate the oxygen, but not the trimix. The best place to get trimix was at the University of the Virgin Islands.

He called the university's dive center and found they weren't filling tanks because their shipment of helium had been delayed. They recommended a dive shop on St. Croix because it was one of the few technical diving centers in the area.

Ryan purchased the other supplies he needed from the ship's chandler at the marina, including a two-hundred-foot coil of line, a Danforth anchor, and a round rubber fender. When he had his gear together, he carried it to Capt. Stuart's dock. Emily and Paul helped carry the dive gear and four spare aluminum tanks. If something went wrong with the rebreather, he would bail out to the other bottles.

When everything was aboard the Prowler, Ryan stepped aboard and said, "First stop, Christiansted."

Stuart whistled and raised his eyebrows.

"I need to refill my trimix tank at St. Croix Scuba. On the map, there's a dock at the end of King Cross Street."

"More like pilings," Stuart said. "The hurricane wiped out the docks, but I haven't been there in a while."

"Just get us close and I'll wade ashore if need be."

"Yes, sir." Stuart started the whisper-quiet Suzukis and put the boat into drive. When they rounded Cabrita Point, he turned and followed the ferry route between St. Thomas and Great St. James Island. Stuart pointed out the Straggler Islands, keeping clear of the dive boats shepherding their divers around the coral reefs, and aimed south for St. Croix.

The Prowler sliced through the water with ease, and they made the forty-mile crossing in just over an hour. Only a portion of the King Cross Street dock had been rebuilt, and old dock pilings jutted from the water like discarded toothpicks. Ryan tied off the Prowler, and he and Emily walked up the street to the dive shop. While they waited for the shop worker to fill the tank, Ryan spotted a wall-mounted display of lift bags and purchased two of the largest ones the shop had in stock.

With the bottle full and his wallet lighter, Ryan and Emily headed back to the boat. He gave Stuart a slip of paper with the coordinates for *Balance Sheet* written on it. Stuart punched them into the Prowler's GPS plotter and drove to the fuel dock at St. Croix Marine Center to top off the fuel tanks. Once complete, they raced across the water toward the resting place of the Langstons' sunken sailboat.

As Stuart held station above the wreck, Ryan tied one end of his line to his new Danforth anchor and the other end to the big rubber fender. He checked the fish sonar and saw the wreck was almost directly beneath them. Ryan had Stuart back off the wreck, and he dropped the anchor overboard. At the one-hundred-foot mark on the line, he tied on two aluminum tanks with short whips and tossed the rubber fender overboard when the anchor hit the seafloor.

Stuart spun the boat around to face into the current and dropped his own anchor rode. He backed down on the hook as Ryan donned his dive gear and his rEvo III rebreather.

Sitting on the bench, ready to go into the water, Ryan looked up at Paul. The older man dropped his eyes to the deck and looked away. They were only here because he had gotten greedy, and he'd put a lot of lives in danger as a result, especially that of his wife.

Ryan stood and stepped to the swim platform. Emily patted his shoulder after he'd washed the defogger from his mask and fitted it to his face. He turned to look at her. She kissed him and said, "Be safe down there."

He smiled. "Yes, ma'am."

After fixing his mouthpiece between his teeth and opening the breathing loop, he took a breath. With one last glance at Emily, he stepped off the back of the boat and swam to the fender.

The slack rope hung in loops. Ryan pulled it taut against the anchor, then hauled himself down the line. Several minutes later, he was on the bottom. He checked his computers; one for his oxygen tank, one for the trimix tank, and a third to monitor depth and time. Everything looked good.

Next, Ryan pulled the line through the anchor until it was tight against the fender overhead. After tying off the line, he surveyed the sunken sailboat. The visibility was decent, but he couldn't see the bow nearly seventy-five feet away. He pictured how things had looked the last time he'd been here, and as he swam forward, he noticed the boat was teetering on the edge of the precipice. According to the nautical chart he had looked at last night, the cliff sloped to a ledge at a depth of six-hundred-and-fifty-feet, before dropping vertically for another two thousand feet.

The box was in the V-berth, which meant Ryan had to traverse the full length of the cabin and be conscious of knocking anything askew that might cause the boat to slip over the edge. He had also prepared for this by factoring how the currents might have moved the boat since his visit yesterday.

Swimming out over the abyss, he stared down for a moment. A memory of his very first dive popped into his mind. He'd been doing his open water checkout dives and had jumped off a boat into the Atlantic. As he'd floated on the surface, he'd gotten his first glimpse of the abyss, and his breath had caught in his throat in a moment of panic. Staring into the abyss now made him feel the same way.

He looked at his computers again before pulling out the two lift bags he'd purchased at the dive store. After tying both to the port side bow cleat, he opened the valve on his bailout bottle and used the regulator to gush air into the lift bags. He flooded them until the relief valves popped open and the two bags lifted and stabilized the bow.

Back at the stern, Ryan dropped his bailout bottle in the dirt. He glanced at the length of line laying slack on the ocean floor beside his buoy anchor and had an epiphany. Swimming over to the anchor, he dug the anchor flukes as deep into the mud as he could before he ran the rest of the line to the stern of *Balance Sheet* and tied it off to the prop shaft.

Satisfied that the lift bags and the anchor line would hold the sailboat in place, Ryan swam around to face the open cockpit. The sail no longer blocked the entrance, and he swam freely through the cabin door. Once inside, he snapped on his light. Not much had changed. The contents of the boat's cabinets and shelves were still scattered across the deck and bulkheads. He paused for a moment to sense what the sailboat was doing as a vibration ran through the hull. After a moment, he pushed forward.

The yellow waterproof box floated against the ceiling where they'd left it. The pocket of air Paul had been breathing from had disappeared.

Ryan grabbed the box and pulled it after him as he backed out of the V-berth. The rebreather hit the bulkhead and he squeezed himself down, but the buoyant box kept him from getting back through the door. He let go of the box, and it slammed up against the hull, sending a shiver through the boat. Despite the anchor and the lift bags, the hull seemed to tilt toward the depths. Slowly, it stabilized itself, and Ryan took a deep breath, thankful his rebreather didn't dispense bubbles of spent oxygen that might cause the boat to move any further.

He pulled himself into the V-berth and pushed the box down and out the door, then maneuvered himself back into the main salon. The fact that the box wanted to float was frustrating to Ryan, and it was a challenge to get it to the cabin door. He knew that once he got the Pelican case into the cockpit, he would have to let it shoot to the surface.

Leaving the box just inside the companionway door, he rummaged through the cockpit bench storage areas and found a length of line. He swam over the stern and tied a loop around the line running between the prop and his buoy anchor, planning to send it up the anchor line. Back at the door, he tied the box to the line and pulled it into the cockpit. As he predicted, the box shot straight up when he let it go. When it reached the end of the line, there was an audible *pop* as the handle ripped off.

Around his mouthpiece, Ryan muttered, "*Shit*."

The box continued toward the surface at rocket-like speed while the handle and line gently floated down to drape across the hull and lifelines.

He sliced the line tied to the prop shaft with his dive knife and after loosening the anchor flukes; he ascended the line. His total bottom time had been a little over fifteen minutes. Above, he heard a pair of engines start and a boat race away. He figured it was Stuart going to retrieve the box.

Ryan shook his head. *He should have made Paul swim for it.*

He concentrated on his computers and his ascent. The visibility had decreased around him as the current had picked up. What had been slack water was now tugging at his body as it rushed past.

Above him, the boat returned to his ascent line. He looked up and saw the hull, dark in the fading light of the approaching storm. Ryan remembered seeing something about a tropical storm but had paid little attention as he focused on preparing for the retrieval of the case, mainly on account of the weather service saying it was at least a day out. As usual, they were wrong.

The rebreather's computers monitored his breathing and oxygen intake, automatically calculating the stops he would need to ensure he didn't get decompression sickness. As he moved up the line, the computers pumped in more oxygen, continually adjusting the mixture of gas he breathed, and greatly reduced his decompression time.

When he finally surfaced, Ryan saw the Prowler bobbing nearby. He held on to the fender buoy as the boat backed toward him; the waves washing over its swim platform. Emily helped Ryan over the gunwale and out of his rebreather while Stuart swung the boat bow around to face the waves.

They pulled the ascent line in and recovered the stage bottles before they headed for the marina. Clouds darkened the southeastern horizon and lightning streaked the sky, followed by the low *boom* of thunder.

Halfway across the bay, heavy sheets of rain began to fall,

obscuring the landscape ahead. By the time Stuart pulled up to the dock, they were all wet and shivering. Stuart left his boat in the slip and headed for his truck. Emily and Paul carried their gear to *Windseeker* and changed into dry clothes after showering while Ryan made a quick dive near the gas dock.

As the rain continued to pour outside, Ryan grabbed a beer from the boat's fridge and checked his messages. Jinks had sent a text, letting him know that Scott Gregory, a member of Trident and a former Navy SEAL, was inbound aboard Dark Water Research's Beechcraft King Air, accompanied by two others. He looked up from his phone. "Hey, Em, Mango and Jennifer are coming."

"What?" She snuggled in close beside him on the chart table seat and read the text. "I thought they went back to the South Pacific?"

"You and me both. But Jinks says they're on the plane. I guess Mango wanted to get in on the action."

Emily rolled her eyes, and Ryan knew she was thinking about the danger that lurked ahead.

Ryan turned to Paul. "How well do you know Terrence? How many men does he have at his disposal and where would he hole up in a storm like this?"

"I don't know him that well. We used to meet at my office. Until yesterday, I didn't know he had a yacht."

Emily got up and started boiling a kettle of water. "Is there anything at your office that could help us? More paperwork or evidence we could turn over to the police?"

"It's all in the box," Paul replied.

"It wouldn't hurt to look, you never know what we might find," Emily said.

Ryan liked the way she thought. There might be something at Paul's office that could help them locate Joseph and get a jump on the meeting. He glanced at his phone to see if his friends had messaged him, but there were no notifications on the screen.

Emily poured herself a cup of tea, and Paul asked for one as well. They sat sipping from mugs while Ryan drank coffee, which was much needed after the exertion of the dive. When they finished, she suggested they borrow the yacht club's car to go to Paul's office.

The trio pulled on rain slickers, walked to the marina office, and got the car keys. Paul drove because he was used to driving on the left side of the road. They parked in a narrow lot between two buildings, and Paul led them through the rain to a set of stairs to the second floor of the office building. The upper balcony had a view of the harbor across the street. Ryan looked out on the luxury yachts that lined the docks. Not long ago, he and his crew had run a sting there to take down a sex cruise operation.

Paul didn't have to use his key to open the door. The doorknob was in pieces. Someone had ransacked the interior, much like his house. The small outer office contained a desk and a few chairs for waiting clients, while Paul's office was larger and better furnished, although none of it was usable anymore. The intruders had slit open the sofa cushions and pulled the stuffing from them, and they'd cut open the backs and bottoms of the chairs. Desk drawers lay on the floor, empty of their contents, and the filing cabinet drawers stood open.

"My computer is gone," Paul said, stepping over the piles of stuffing to reach the desk.

"Anything else?" Ryan asked.

"No clue." The accountant shrugged. "Look at this mess." Paul righted his desk chair and dropped wearily into it. He placed his elbows on the desktop and cupped his face with his hands. "I really screwed up."

"What if you gave the money back?" Emily asked. "I've

dealt with insurance fraud cases where the clients returned the funds in exchange for reduced charges."

"He can give the money back, Em, but whoever he stole from will still kill him and Diane," Ryan said. "They'll use them as an object lesson for the other members of the network."

Paul started sobbing.

Emily raised her eyebrows and crossed her arms. "Really?"

Fortunately for Ryan, his phone started ringing. "It's Mango," he said.

Before he could answer, Ryan heard a man order him to put the phone down. Then the ominous click of a pistol's hammer being cocked reached his ears.

Ryan glanced at Emily, who was staring at the person behind him. She slowly raised her hands and nodded her head toward the desk.

Ryan pressed the button to answer the call, tossed the phone onto the desk, and said loudly, "Don't shoot."

CHAPTER SIX

The green hills of the U.S. Virgin Islands reminded Oscar López of his home in Venezuela.

He was sitting at a fast-food restaurant across from the St. Thomas Skyride, but the skyride wasn't his target. While he ate his burger, he kept an eye on a building across the street with a natural food store on the ground floor and a series of offices and apartments above it. There was no one on the sidewalk because of the rain, but cars still entered and exited the parking lots and sped along the road. He'd been casing the place since yesterday, after trailing a money launderer there. He popped a French fry into his mouth and watched the office window.

Oscar had grown up in the seaside town of Güiria, and St. Thomas prompted memories of his childhood. His father had been a fisherman, plying his trade in the Gulf of Paria. Oscar remembered going out with his father and hauling in giant Spanish mackerel and kingfish. Those were carefree days. They didn't have to fight off pirates or smugglers or pay for protection just to do their job. Oil money flowed through the country like water, and even his poor father had a brand-new Ford F150.

In 1998, Hugo Chávez took his presidential oath of office after making widespread promises of social and economic reforms, gaining him the trust and favor of the poor and the working class. The economy slowly tapered off as Chávez implemented his "reforms." Desperate to help his struggling family, Oscar had joined the Venezuelan Marine Corps, where he became a member of the 8th Marine Special Operations Command.

His reminiscing stopped when he saw two men—one of them the smurf—and a gorgeous blonde get out of a car and head up the stairs toward the smurf's office. Then he saw a black man step out of the shadows of another building and put a phone to his ear. Oscar wiped his hands on a napkin as he watched the caller put away the phone and follow the trio, pulling a pistol from his waistband as he went.

Oscar knew instinctively that the gunman was after the smurf. He jumped up, dashed out of the restaurant, and ran across the parking lot, ducking his head to shield his eyes from the rain. He didn't slow as he entered the four-lane road.

A horn blared, but Oscar kept running. The man with the pistol disappeared through the door at the top of the stairs. Oscar took the steps two or three at a time, using the railing to help himself leap upward. At the landing, he stopped and pushed the door open just enough to see through the crack. The hallway was empty.

He slipped inside and held the door as it closed to keep it from banging against the frame. Oscar stayed on the balls of his feet as he crept toward the office. He heard a man say, "Put it down," and another male replied, "Don't shoot."

Glancing around for a weapon, Oscar spotted a fire extinguisher. He lifted it gingerly from its hook on the wall, hefted it with both hands, and tiptoed through the smurf's outer office. The gunman had his back to the door.

Oscar thought the man should have moved to his right where he would have been out of the line of sight of the outer office door, but he was grateful for the man's tactical blunder. He drew the extinguisher back and slammed it into the back of the gunman's head.

The man spun to face Oscar, but he only made it halfway around before the younger man in the trio being held hostage struck the gunman with an open palm strike to his jaw. Completely dazed, the gunman fell to the floor. The man's pistol slid across the tile and stopped at the feet of the statuesque blonde.

Before Oscar could react, she snatched the Beretta up and ordered him inside the office. Oscar set the fire extinguisher on the floor, raised his hands, and stepped inside. The younger man patted him down. Between the thoroughness of the pat-down and the quickness of the palm strike, Oscar believed the man had some Special Forces training.

"Who are you?" the man asked him.

"I'm here for the smurf," Oscar replied.

"Are you working for Terrence Joseph?"

"No." Oscar shook his head, not knowing who Joseph was.

"What do you want with Paul?" the blonde asked.

Oscar's eyes went to the phone on the desk when a tinny voice called, "Ryan? Ryan, can you hear me?"

The man Oscar now knew as Ryan snatched up the phone and said to the woman, "Keep him covered. Paul, tie both these guys up."

Oscar watched as Ryan stepped out of the room with the phone and Paul grabbed a roll of Scotch Tape. He bent to wrap the black man's hands. Oscar kept his face impassive, but inside, he was smiling. The tape would be easy to free himself from. It would have been better to secure him, the greater threat, before the unconscious man, but the Marine kept that tidbit to himself.

Paul glanced up at the blonde when she said, "Use the printer cord."

As the smurf ripped the cord from the printer, the woman motioned toward Oscar with the gun and said, "Tie his hands first."

At least she has some common sense, Oscar thought.

Paul tied Oscar's hands in front of him, and the blonde told him to sit in the chair behind the desk.

Ryan stepped back into the room. He helped Paul truss up the black man, working in silence.

When they finished, Ryan stood and turned to Oscar. "Who do you work for?"

Oscar looked away.

"Are you here to kill Paul?"

Again, Oscar refused to answer the question. He'd been through torture training, and this guy wouldn't break him. The cord around his wrist was loose and he could escape if given the chance. He slowly moved his wrists, testing the bonds.

Paul's phone rang. He held it up and said, "It's Terrence," before he and Ryan stepped into the outer office.

Despite the distance, Oscar could hear the conversation.

Paul said, "I have the documents. Where do you want to meet?"

Oscar knew immediately that he needed those documents.

"I want to talk to Diane," Paul said. A moment later, he said, "Are you okay, Di?" Silence as he listened, then, "We have the box, and I'm coming to get you." After another silent moment, he said, "Okay, he'll be at American Yacht at midnight."

Ryan said, "Tell him to make it three a.m. There's less chance someone will see the exchange."

Whoever was on the other end of the line agreed after he and Paul went back and forth several times, then Paul ended the call.

The whole time they'd been talking, Oscar had been working on his bonds. His hands were below the desk where the woman couldn't see them. Despite aiming the gun at Oscar, she had paid more attention to the phone conversation. He loosened his right hand, then pulled the cord from his left wrist. At the same time, he planted his feet by the chair's wheels and readied himself to strike. It would be a shame to hit such a beautiful woman, but Oscar had to escape. Then he could tail these people to the documents and steal them.

When the woman looked away, Oscar sprang onto the desk. The sudden movement startled her, and she took a step backward, the gun swinging toward the floor. Jumping from the desk, he snatched the pistol from her hand and shoved her through the open door. He jerked the door shut as she crashed into Ryan.

With a twist of his fingers, Oscar locked the doorknob and turned to the window. He used the butt of the pistol to smash the glass and looked down at the parking lot. The jump from the second-floor window to the pavement was about twelve feet, but below him was a compact sedan. Oscar mounted the window frame as the office door splintered and flew open. He jumped onto the roof of the car, bending his knees to absorb the shock, and rolled down the rear hatch to the ground. As he sprinted toward the bushes at the rear of the building, he tucked the gun into his waistband.

He knew where they were going and when they'd be there. Now all he had to do was lie in wait.

CHAPTER SEVEN

Ryan Weller leaned out the broken window of Paul Langston's office and watched as the man they'd just been holding captive escaped into the brush at the far end of the parking lot. He thought about going after him, but he didn't want to jump on the car and bring any more attention to them than they already had. Despite the rain, people were still grocery shopping, and some had stopped to watch the action, so he pulled back from the window.

"Is there a back way out of here?" he barked at Paul.

Paul paused in the frame of the splintered door, looking around his once immaculate office. He nodded and pointed through the outer office. "There's another set of stairs."

"Good. Let's go."

Paul led them out the back entrance, and they got in the car. As they pulled out of the lot, Ryan told Paul to call the building supervisor and have him fix the window. He figured by the time the super got around to repairing it, the unconscious assailant would have disappeared. Now they had time to kill until their late-night meeting.

"What did Mango say?" Emily asked as Paul drove them

on an extended, rain-soaked tour of the island while the wipers sluiced back and forth on high.

"They had to divert to Puerto Rico until the rain lets up," Ryan replied.

"Will they get here before we meet with Joseph?" she asked.

"I don't know." Ryan checked the weather forecast on his phone. The bands of rain around the storm made it appear larger than it was. He sent a quick text to Mango, letting him know the time and location of the meet, along with a description of Joseph's yacht. He put the phone in his lap and stared out the window.

He hoped Mango and Scott arrived before the meeting time. If they didn't, he wasn't sure how things would go down. And now there was a third element in the mix.

Turning to Paul, he asked, "Do you know that guy who jumped out the window?"

Paul shook his head. "I've never seen him before in my life. This whole situation has brought out the crazies, if ya know what I mean?"

"Maybe you shouldn't have been skimming money," Emily suggested.

They remained silent as Paul circumnavigated the island. It took just over an hour for them to get back to American Yacht Harbor, where *Windseeker* waited patiently at the dock. Ryan wanted to get on her and sail away, but, once again, he'd been swept up in a life-or-death situation, and he couldn't let Diane die at the hands of some deadbeat street thug.

He and Emily had talked about his lifestyle several times during their sail north. She had come to terms with the fact that Dark Water Research might call him back to work, even though Ryan had told Greg he was done being his troubleshooter. He wanted to stop putting himself in harm's way so he could build a life with Emily, but trouble seemed to be drawn to him like a magnet to steel.

When they arrived at the yacht club, they returned the car keys and ran to the boat. The cabin door lock lay broken in the cockpit and the door was wide open, allowing the rain to pour in. They stepped inside and looked around. The interior of *Windseeker* was in complete disarray.

"You and your stupid box," Ryan muttered to Paul. He closed the door while Emily grabbed towels to mop up the rainwater.

"I'm sorry to get you into such a mess," Paul said, sinking into the settee and holding his head in his hands.

"Just shut up," Ryan retorted. He started shoving things back into cupboards and cubbies. It was one thing to tear up Paul's office and home, but now these bastards had done the same to his.

"Sit down," Emily ordered her boyfriend.

Ryan stopped slamming pots and pans around and glared at her.

"You're pissed," she said, holding up her hands. "I get it, but don't make it worse. Sit down and take a breath. I'll make some coffee."

"Thanks." He dropped into the seat at the navigation station and rubbed his face with both hands. This was the kind of shit he wanted to avoid for Emily's sake, but she seemed to be handling it better than he was, or at least she hid her frustration better. After a few deep breaths to help force the anger from his body, he checked the weather. He wanted to have his friends backing him up with a long gun, but he would have to make do if Mango and Scott didn't arrive soon. He would have to be the shooter and send Emily into the fray with Paul. While she was more than capable of taking care of herself, he *did not* want her to be involved any more than she was.

Emily handed him a steaming cup of coffee, and he sipped it while he scrolled around on a map application, looking at the marina and Vessup Bay. Across from American Yacht Harbor were mooring balls for boat owners who didn't want to pay for dock space, and farther on were houses scattered among the trees on the low hills. The houses were too far away for Ryan's needs, and the shooter would be blind to the action taking place on the dock side of Terrence's yacht.

Unsatisfied with the results of his search, Ryan pocketed his laser rangefinder from its place on the navigation table, pulled on a rain slicker, and told Emily he was going for a walk. Not only did he want to scout the area, but it would help him cool off, because he was still intensely angry.

His quickness to anger had increased since spending time in prison. Emily wanted him to talk to someone about it, but he wasn't ready yet. He didn't know if he would ever be, but he needed to do something. It wasn't healthy to always be angry about something. He drew in a deep breath and tried to push the fury from his belly by imagining it was roaring out like a dragon breathing fire upon its enemies.

The rain was now just a steady drizzle, and Ryan hoped the break in the weather would give the DWR crew a flight window. Ryan walked along the waterfront dock beside the rear of the long, low building that housed the yacht club and various shops. The area was more commercial than residential, with shopping centers on both sides of the street.

The walkway ended in a thick clump of mangroves and palms, so he turned around and started back. He took a left and walked to the street where he turned right and headed east again. As he walked, he peered into the thickets and up at the buildings, looking for the perfect place to position a sniper hide, disappointed there wasn't any cover for his operation.

Ryan kept walking until he spied a parking garage, and a

grin spread across his face. He pulled his hands from his pockets and ran across the access road into the structure. Even though he was now out of the rain, he left his hood up to hide his face in case there were cameras around. The structure was only two floors high and serviced the many ferries that operated from the terminal building on the waterfront.

Ryan took the stairs to the second floor and walked to the edge closest to the water. The garage offered a perfect view of the gas docks at American Yacht Harbor. He pulled the laser rangefinder from his pocket, held it to his right eye, and focused on the gas pump at the end of the dock. The distance was just shy of five hundred feet, an easy shot for an expert like Mango. Ryan wondered how rusty the man's skills were after spending a year as a charter boat captain in the South Pacific. He guessed they'd find out soon enough.

Mango would also have to contend with the wind, the humidity, and the sailboats parked along the private dock between the garage and the gas pumps. Ryan lowered the monocle from his eye and slipped his hands back in his pockets. A gust of wind buffeted him as he looked across the bay.

His phone rang as the rain began again. He ran down the steps and stood under cover as he answered with, "Hey, Mango."

"We just landed, bro. Let me tell you, Chuck is *the* man. He had the plane practically sideways on approach and snapped it straight right before touching down. I about shit my pants."

"Sounds like a good story for beer thirty."

"I need a stiff shot of something right now."

"How soon can you get across the island?" asked Ryan.

"It will be another hour. We have to clear Customs and get a rental."

"Okay. Get a van, one of those big cargo ones. Here's what I want you to do." Ryan sketched out his plan.

"Sounds good, bro. I'll text you when we're in place."

"Roger that." Ryan hung up and stood with his hands in his pockets for a few more minutes, giving the rain time to abate. When it didn't do so right away, he tucked the slicker around him and headed for the boat.

When he reached *Windseeker*, he had to change out of his wet clothes. Emily had the mess inside almost squared away, giving him time to clean his Walther and Emily's Smith and Wesson M&P9 Shield. He didn't expect her to see any action, but it never hurt to be prepared, especially when a rogue actor was on the loose.

An hour later, the three of them were having a late dinner when there was a knock on the boat hull. Ryan stepped out to find a short woman with a runner's physique, dirty blonde hair, and watery green eyes standing on the dockside. She wore tan shorts, white canvas shoes, and a pink blouse under a bright red raincoat. She came aboard without asking permission, and Ryan moved out of the way to let Jennifer Hulsey go down the steps into the cabin. Emily rose from the table and embraced her friend.

Jennifer pulled away and handed Ryan a small box from her pocket. "Scott sent this."

Ryan opened it to find a Bluetooth earpiece. He glanced at the instructions, downloaded the app to his smartphone, and paired the earpiece to his phone so he could communicate hands free over the network, then he turned on the earpiece and slipped it into his left ear. "Hey, Scott, you copy?"

"I gotcha, loud and clear. We're set up on the parking garage."

Ryan checked his watch. "We have six hours until showtime."

"I'll let you know when I see your boy pull up in his yacht."

"Hey, bro," Mango said, wearing his own earpiece.

"Glad you guys could make it to the party," Ryan said, relieved that he wasn't running the operation on his own.

"You know me, bro—I'm just here to save your ass again."

"I appreciate it," Ryan said. Mango had done just that on multiple occasions, including their first op together in Mexico hunting a drug kingpin. Since then, it had become a running joke between the two men and had spilled over to their friends, including Jennifer. She and Emily had remained friends despite Emily and Ryan having split up a few years back, and she was one of their biggest supporters for their rekindled romance. If Mango hadn't lost his right leg in a ship-boarding accident, he would probably still be saving lives as a sniper on the Maritime Security Response Team, the Coast Guard's version of Special Forces, but the Coast Guard had retired him, and their loss had become DWR's gain. He'd been Ryan's partner for several operations before he and Jennifer had gone off to explore the world aboard their sailboat, *Margarita*.

The men fell silent as they completed final equipment checks. Ryan didn't expect Joseph to arrive until right at the appointed hour, so he told his team he was turning off the earpiece to save the battery and to call him on his phone when the Viking arrived.

Now it was a hurry-up-and-wait game. Ryan had gotten good at it while serving in the Navy, but he was conscious of the nervous energy inside the cabin. He had to tell Paul to sit down numerous times in response to him spontaneously jumping up and pacing the length of the cabin. Even Emily, who was used to stakeouts to nab insurance defrauders, was getting antsy. She and Jennifer conversed in hushed tones, catching up on what had happened in their lives since last seeing each other at a mutual friend's wedding.

Ryan lay on the bunk in the aft stateroom, his eyes closed

but his senses on high alert. It was nice to have an overwatch, and he knew Scott and Mango would be just as bored and ready for action as he was. It was always like this: brief moments of action preceded by long, dull hours of planning and waiting. He wondered how Diane Langston was fairing, and if Joseph and his goons had treated her well.

He awoke to the ringing of his cell phone. Adrenaline surged through him as he grabbed it and answered.

"I've got eyes on the Viking," Mango said.

"Good. We're coming out." Ryan ended the call and looked at Paul. "You ready to do this?"

The older man squeezed his eyes shut for a moment, then opened them and nodded. His skin looked pale under the cabin lights.

"It's going to be all right," Ryan assured him. "We'll get Diane back, and you guys can go into hiding." He turned on the earpiece and reinserted it into his ear before doing a radio check. Everything was five-by-five.

Paul stood on shaky legs as Ryan led him outside. The rain continued to fall in fat droplets as they started for the fuel dock where the Viking had berthed for its brief visit. All the bars and restaurants were dark, and few cars passed on the street. This was when the world slept, and when watch standers were the most vulnerable. Ryan hoped the late hour would also keep bystanders out of the line of fire and that Terrence's goons would be less alert. If they were professionals, they would know how to compensate for his tactics, but he suspected these guys were more used to shepherding their boss from nightclub to nightclub rather than conducting a military-style operation.

"We've got you," Scott whispered in Ryan's ear as they emerged from *Windseeker*.

As Ryan and Paul moved through the dim light along the walkway and turned onto the fuel dock, Ryan scanned the bushes, buildings, and boats for anything out of the ordinary. The two men stopped twenty feet short of the Viking. Joseph and two of his goons stepped onto the yacht's aft deck.

"Where's Diane?" Paul shouted, a quiver to his voice.

"Not until I see the documents, playa," Joseph responded.

Ryan knelt and reached under the dock. A moment later, his hand found the line attached to the back of a post. He heaved the yellow box out of the water. It was heavy with all the dive weights he'd used to keep it underwater. He'd planted it there after Stuart had brought them back to the dock. At the time, he'd been afraid that if he kept it on *Windseeker*, someone would search his boat as they had Paul's house, and he'd been right.

Once Ryan placed the box on the dock and removed the rope and weights, he opened it and tilted it so Joseph could see the contents. The gangster motioned with his hand, and a third goon pushed Diane out of the salon onto the aft deck where she stood, trembling, beside her captors. Her face was red from crying and her left eye was black-and-blue, but other than that, she looked unharmed.

Ryan relocked the box. "Send Diane and one of your men. We'll make the exchange here."

Joseph motioned for the man holding Diane to do as Ryan said, and they stepped down to the dock. Ryan placed a hand on Paul's arm to keep him from rushing toward his wife. He needed her separated from Joseph. He would take the single goon making the exchange while Mango dispatched the other two. They would take Joseph alive.

"Ready?" Ryan whispered to his overwatch.

"Roger," Scott said.

When Diane and her minder were five feet from Ryan, Joseph ordered them to stop. Ryan pushed the box with his foot along the rough and weathered boards of the dock as he stepped forward. When he reached Diane, he grabbed her by the arm and jerked her toward Paul.

"*Now!*" Ryan commanded.

The sniper crew went to work while Ryan hit the goon who'd held Diane with a palm strike to the jaw, then pummeled him with two more, followed by a punch to the side of the face just under the ear.

The man dropped like a rock.

While Ryan was dispatching his man, Paul had grabbed Diane and rushed her off the dock. Mango shot the two goons beside Joseph with suppressed rounds. The gangster rushed to cast off the lines and escape from the carnage that had exploded all around him.

Ryan leaped onto the Viking and tackled the black man, riding him to the ground. Joseph hit hard, but he immediately began flailing his arms and rolling as Ryan struggled to get him under control.

"Who's the clown stealing the box of papers?" Scott asked in Ryan's ear.

Ryan was too busy battling with Joseph to respond. He had to end this fight quickly, so he drew his pistol and smacked Joseph on the temple with the gun butt. Ryan popped him again for good measure and jumped up to run after the mystery man. He had a feeling he already knew who it was.

The same guy who'd escaped from Paul's office.

CHAPTER EIGHT

Emily Hunt and Jennifer Hulsey had followed Ryan and Paul off *Windseeker* at a safe distance. Emily didn't want Ryan to know that she was backing him up, because he had told her to stay on the sailboat out of harm's way, but that wasn't who she was. She had to protect her man.

The two women skirted through the building's shadows, keeping a low profile. She suspected something would go wrong on this operation, and, like Ryan, she believed the mystery man from Paul's office would show up at some point. He'd overheard Paul's conversation with Joseph, just as she had while she'd been holding him at gunpoint.

As an insurance investigator, Emily had spent her fair share of time stalking thieves and crooks along the various waterfronts of the Atlantic and Gulf Coasts of the United States. She'd also traveled around the world, investigating shipping accidents and coordinating with various law enforcement agencies. Emily knew her way around the shady side of paradise, and it left her wondering how she could consider Ryan's work dangerous when she was often in tight spots herself.

She and Jennifer paused at the end of the yacht club building, beside the restaurant Paul and Diane had taken them to the previous night. After crossing the alley to the next building, they watched as Ryan exchanged the documents for Diane. As Ryan leaped aboard the yacht to go after Terrence Joseph, Emily saw a dark figure dart out from the shadows of a palm thicket and race down the dock past Paul and Diane. He scooped up the yellow box and sprinted back toward land.

Grabbing the umbrella from her friend's hand, Emily ran toward the dock. As the man approached, she swung the umbrella and clotheslined him, knocking him off his feet. The box skidded toward the edge of the walkway and fell into the water. When the man tried to rise to his feet, she whacked him again, placed the umbrella across his throat, and her knee on his chest to keep him in place.

Ryan ran up and knelt beside her. "You okay, babe?"

"I'm fine."

"Go help Jennifer," Ryan said. "I've got this guy."

Emily moved to where Jennifer was lying on her belly at the edge of the dock, trying to grasp the slippery yellow plastic case. Without the handle, it was difficult to lift from the water. Jennifer had pulled the box to the seawall, and they each grasped a side, but they had no leverage to lift it. Their fingertips barely had purchase on the slight ridges that ringed the case as they lay on their stomachs, arms fully extended.

Mango and Scott arrived, and Scott grasped Emily and Jennifer's free arms. They pulled against him for leverage while lifting the case. Together, the three of them pulled it up and set it on the dock. Emily picked up the case, and she and Jennifer followed Ryan, Mango, and Scott as they escorted the prisoner to the Viking.

While Mango and Scott tied up the man Emily had clocked with the umbrella, Ryan started the Viking's engines.

He asked her to cast off the mooring lines and, when she was back aboard, he motored them out of the bay and into the heaving Caribbean Sea. She stood beside Ryan, watching the radar, and giving him directions to a sheltered cove on a nearby uninhabited island where they could interrogate their prisoners.

She glanced over her shoulder at the mystery man. He was of medium height with short black hair, and he had a solid athletic build with a dark complexion. Despite the circumstances, she thought he had a kind face and was rather good-looking for a thief. It wouldn't take long for them to learn his name and his life story. There were three men aboard skilled at interrogation, and if they failed to get the information with a hammer, she and Jennifer could play the velvet glove.

The soft touch was the best way to start, she decided, and she stepped away from the helm to where their mystery man sat tied up on one of the built-in couches. Mango had duct taped his feet and hands together, but while they were secure bonds, she was positive that if they left this man alone for a few minutes, he could free himself with ease, just as he had back at Paul's office.

Mango and Scott were busy rolling Joseph's dead goons off the back of the yacht and hosing away the blood.

Emily sat beside their bound guest and asked if he wanted something to drink and if he was comfortable.

The man just glared at her.

"I don't know your story," she said, "but those three guys are all ex-Special Forces, and they know how to extract information. Now, you can talk to me or you can talk to those guys. Which would you like to do?"

"What do you do?" the man asked.

"I'm just here as eye candy," she said with a smile.

"You do it very well."

"Thanks." She flipped her hair over her shoulder. Ryan

liked to call it her Viking hair because he had once seen it in long braids and told her that all she needed was a horned helmet and a sword and she could lead men into battle.

Ryan pulled the throttles back, and the boat coasted forward. The heavy wave action had fallen away, and the big yacht rode easier on the calmer waters. He dropped the anchor and backed down on the hook before shutting off the engines.

Emily looked at the man beside her on the couch. "Like I said, it's them or me. I'm not sure where we are, but it's probably someplace where no one can hear you scream."

The man sat in silence.

"Do you work for Terrence Joseph?" she asked.

"Who is that?" the man responded.

"The guy we have tied up in the cabin," Ryan said.

"Let's start with an easier question," Emily said. "What's your name?"

The man stared at his hands.

"Okay, so you don't work for Joseph, but you want the documents that Paul has. Are you implicated by them?" Emily asked.

Again, the man remained silent.

"This isn't getting us anywhere," Scott said. "I say we use the dinghy to drag him around the bay with a rope tied to his ankles."

"You guys go see what you can do with Joseph," Ryan said to Scott and Mango.

The two men stepped down into the cabin while Ryan and Emily remained with their mystery thief. A moment later, a ghastly scream rose from the salon.

"That doesn't sound like fun," Emily said. Even though the scream had set her teeth on edge and she wanted them to stop torturing Joseph immediately, she knew it was necessary in the hope of loosening the thief's tongue.

Ryan raised the sleeves of the mystery man's T-shirt. Emily wondered what he was doing until she saw a tattoo on his right shoulder. He pulled the man's arm around so Emily could see it better. "This guy's a Venezuelan Marine, or used to be."

The Marine twisted his body to free himself from Ryan's grasp.

"Did you defect?" Ryan asked.

Another blood-curdling scream made Emily cringe. *What are they* doing *to that guy?*

"You hear that?" she asked the Marine, trying to keep her cool. "Now's not the time to play dumb because you're next."

CHAPTER NINE

The scream came again, and Oscar knew these people meant business. He had tortured men, too, and the men who'd captured him were clearly professionals. It was easy to see by their quiet demeanor and the quick way in which they had taken down their opposition.

The woman had surprised him by coming out of the shadows and whacking him with the umbrella. Even she seemed professional. There was only one who seemed bothered by the ordeal, and that was the second woman. He watched her out of the corner of his eye. She had her hands clamped over her ears and stood as far away from the action as she could get.

He looked around the boat, studying his surroundings and the people holding him hostage. It impressed him that the man had known he was a Marine based on his tattoo. Few Americans knew about the Marine units attached to the Venezuelan Navy. There were only ten thousand men and women serving in the Marine Corps, and they weren't well known, even among his own military community.

The man with the artificial leg came out of the salon and

leaned against the captain's seat. He had carried a duffle bag aboard the yacht, and Oscar suspected he was the sniper who had taken out Joseph's men. But from where? He racked his brain, thinking through the operation. These men were helping to rescue an old woman and aiding a money launderer, but whose side were they on?

He twisted at the duct tape around his wrists. Given the chance, he could break free, but there was nowhere for him to go. From the way the ship now rode quietly at anchor, he guessed they were in the lee of an island which blocked the storm-driven waves. Rain still streaked the windows, but the worst of the storm had passed.

Oscar looked Artificial Leg up and down. He was trimmer than the other men and seemed at home aboard the boat. What fascinated Oscar was the below-the-knee prosthetic on the man's right leg. It looked like something he had seen in the futuristic movies he'd watched before Chavez had taken over his country and outlawed American films.

"We need to talk to you, bro," Artificial Leg said to Ryan.

The two men went below, and Oscar glanced between the two women.

Again, the big blonde sat beside him. Quietly, she asked, "What do you want with Paul Langston?"

Oscar stared straight ahead.

"Why did you try to steal the box?" she prompted. When he said nothing, she continued. "They broke Terrence, they'll break you."

"I won't break," Oscar muttered.

"*Everyone* breaks."

"You're military?" he asked.

"No, but the guys are. Are things in Venezuela as bad as the news says?"

She's trying to butter me up. "Worse."

"Ryan spent six months in San Antonio Prison on Margarita Island."

Oscar's curiosity peaked. Then he remembered a wanted flyer that had gone around the military and police units, offering a reward of ten thousand dollars to anyone with information leading to the arrest of an American escapee. "He was the American who broke out with the help of a SEBIN officer?"

"Yes," Emily replied.

Oscar wondered why she was telling him this. Did she expect sympathy from him? The man she was helping was a convicted murderer and an enemy of his state. Oscar swallowed. *He* was an enemy of his state. Betrayed by the men he had served, they had left him to die in the jungle. They wouldn't hesitate to put a bullet in him, if given the chance.

"Why are you helping the smurf?" he asked.

"Ryan and I came across his burning sailboat and we rescued him and his wife. Then Joseph took Diane hostage in exchange for whatever is in the box you tried to steal. Paul might help criminals launder money, but he needed our help to save his wife."

Ryan and the two other men stepped into the cockpit. The tallest man in the trio had a thick blond mustache and shaggy hair. He had the Second Amendment of the U.S. Constitution tattooed on his right forearm in the shape of an AR-15 rifle, and his other arm was a sleeve of colorful tats. Among them, Oscar recognized a U.S. Navy SEAL trident.

"The gangster talked," Tattoos said. "Now it's your turn."

Oscar stared at Ryan. He didn't look like the formidable monster that the SEBIN—Venezuela's secret police—had made him out to be. The story he had heard was that the American had executed a man in front of a group of police and sailors, then laughed as he gunned them down. Staring right at Ryan, Oscar said, "You were in prison for executing a man."

"Yes, I was."

Oscar's voice turned venomous. "Tell me how it felt to shoot the policemen who tried to apprehend you."

"I didn't shoot any police," Ryan replied. "I shot a serial killer in the back of the head as we struggled for his weapon."

"I don't believe you," Oscar said.

"The SEBIN took me to their prison and tortured me for a month to make me confess to being a spy." Ryan hiked up the leg of his shorts and showed him where the cattle prod his interrogators had used on him had scarred the skin on his thigh. "I don't expect you to believe me, but I'm telling you the truth. Now, tell me why you're here. Why do you want the box of documents?"

Oscar leaned his head back and hooded his eyes. "Do you work for the U.S. government?"

"No," Tattoos said. "We're contractors."

"Mercenaries," Oscar spat.

"Remind me again why we're talking to this jackass?" Tattoos asked. He jerked a pistol from his belt and placed it against Oscar's head. "Tell me who you are."

Oscar kept his gaze fixed on Ryan. "Why did you work for the prison boss, Navarro?"

"I did what I had to do to survive," Ryan said. "I couldn't fight every man in there, just like you can't escape from this situation."

"Who are you after now?" Oscar asked. His skull ached where the gun barrel pressed against it.

"*I'm* asking the questions," Tattoos growled through gritted teeth.

"The documents in that box are proof of countless money laundering operations," Oscar said, tilting his head until it almost touched his shoulder. Tattoos moved with him, keeping the gun tight to his temple.

"And we're going to turn them and Paul Langston over to the U.S. government for protection and prosecution," Ryan said.

"You can't do that," Oscar pleaded.

"Why not?" Ryan asked.

"Because I need them," Oscar said.

Ryan motioned for Tattoos to remove the pistol, and Oscar rolled his neck to work out the kinks.

"This story better be convincing, bro," Artificial Leg said.

Oscar took a deep breath. He hoped that when he finished, these men would trust him as much as he trusted them right now. That was to say, he only trusted them as far as he could throw them, but they had what he needed. There was enough money in those bank accounts to fund a Third World country for many years, and he was willing to share some with these mercenaries if they helped him, because God knew he was going to get his fair share.

"My name is Oscar López, and I am about to tell you a story I've never told before."

CHAPTER TEN

Venezuela
Eight Months Earlier

There was nothing silent about the rainforest at night along the Orinoco River. The drone of mosquitoes sounded like a squadron of planes as they dive-bombed the Venezuelan Marines lying in ambush just off a dirt path at the edge of the river. Bullfrogs croaked and animals scrambled through the brush.

The team from the 8th Marine Special Operations Brigade lay in an L-shape along a curve in the trail as it bent toward the river. Towering trees flanked the riverbanks, and lily pads covered the water's black surface. In the daylight, the river was a glistening blue-brown color, carrying with it the rich minerals from the mountains in Colombia as it flowed north to join the Atlantic Ocean.

The Venezuelan government may have designated the Orinoco Delta as a national park, but it was a lawless place, fraught with drug runners and illegal gold miners. They blended in with the indigenous Warao people who had lived in the delta for centuries but now struggled to make ends meet, and many had turned to smuggling.

Tonight's mission was part of an ongoing operation that had begun almost a month ago when the team had broken up a major cocaine smuggling operation. The drugs that came down the Orinoco River were hidden in the delta, then moved to a passing freighter, which would take them to either Europe or to the United States.

After beating the bush, the team had captured a Warao paddling a canoe laden with cocaine beneath a load of *occumo chino*, a tuber vegetable that was a staple of the Warao diet. The Warao had guided the Marines to a farm ten miles deeper in the wilderness. They had raided the place but came up empty.

Another search led to the discovery of two men, both of whom had been trying to hitch a ride with a native on his boat. At first, the men had claimed to be tourists who had gotten lost in the confusing tangle of waterways, and that torrential rain had swamped their canoe and swept away their supplies. Under further interrogation, the men had cracked, giving the Marines the locations of ten pits at the farm they'd raided earlier, each dug six feet deep and lined with tar to make them waterproof. The pits had contained nearly ten tons of cocaine in small brown paper sacks.

Now, First Sergeant Oscar López rested his Croatian-made VHS-D assault rifle across his legs and checked his watch. He and Lt. Sosa, the leader of his fireteam, had agreed they shouldn't report the find at the farm but focus on capturing the next batch of smugglers and work the chain backward until they found the cocaine processing plants. With that in mind, they had lain in wait for another week, constantly wet, hungry, and miserable, but doing their part to combat the rising flow of drugs through their troubled country.

Oscar flexed the muscles around his ears, straining to enlarge them so he could hear better. A soft voice drifted on the humid air, and the clank of metal on metal signaled the arrival of the smugglers. The L-shape of the ambush meant crossing fields of fire and a backup team that would take over as the first leap-frogged out of the hot ambush site if things went wrong. The task tonight was capture, not kill, and if the smugglers wanted to escape, their only choice would be to flee into a river infested with swirling currents, crocodiles, and piranhas.

When Sosa gave the signal, the Marines raised their rifles in unison and stood, surrounding the smugglers and ordering them to surrender their weapons and their contraband. When one man made a move for his pistol, Sosa shot him. The rest laid down their firearms and put their hands in the air. The Marines then cuffed their prisoners and marched them to their staging area.

Sosa and Oscar moved through their captives, taking photographs and interrogating them. The third smuggler they spoke to told them that their leader, a man who sat calmly amongst the others, was Armond Diego, an assistant to the Undersecretary of the Minister of Defense, Victor Quintero. This stunned both the lieutenant and the first sergeant. They had gotten extremely lucky, and their bosses in Caracas would consider this a major victory for rooting out corruption in the government.

Lt. Sosa radioed the National Guard base in Guayana City where the Marines had set up an outpost to coordinate the drug sweeps through the Orinoco Delta. He informed them of their prisoner and asked for extraction. A few minutes later, he told his men to prepare Diego for transport, as another team of Marines was on the way to pick him up while

Sosa and his men remained in the field. A wave of grumbling swept through the tired and wet troopers.

Several hours passed before Oscar recognized the buzz of the high-speed outboards on their Guardian patrol boat. Mounted on the front was an M2 fifty-caliber machine gun and mounted on the stern above the engines were grenade launchers. Sosa ensured the flex cuffs on Diego's hands were tight and jerked the man to his feet. Two Marines stood guard over the prisoners while the rest lounged near a small fire, cooking a meal. Oscar smelled the roasting tapir his men had caught earlier in the day, and his mouth practically watered at the thought of its sweet, juicy meat.

Instead of accompanying Sosa to the patrol boat, Oscar shouldered his rifle and stepped into the jungle to take a leak. There was no need for him to be present for the prisoner handoff to their fellow Marines.

He had just gotten a steady stream going when the sound of the M2 firing shattered the night's stillness. Long tongues of flame belched from its muzzle, and red tracers ripped through the foliage, illuminating the macabre scene as the blistering gunfire cut down the Marines and their prisoners.

Oscar stumbled forward, trailing urine across his boots and hands, then tripped on a root and sprawled face-first in the damp earth. Rolling to his side, he tucked himself back in and zipped up his trousers. His breath caught in his chest as the grenade launcher made its hollow *thump*.

He covered his ears with his hands and opened his mouth as the grenade slammed into the ground and detonated, throwing mud, tree limbs, and human flesh into the air. Three more explosions immediately followed the first, each rocking the ground Oscar lay on.

Why were his fellow Marines firing on his team?

Silence descended on the jungle. The only sound he could hear over the ringing in his ears was the quiet burble of the outboards. He listened intently until he heard someone order the men off the boat and to put a bullet into the head of each of Oscar's teammates.

Slowly, Oscar crept under the foliage as gunshots rang through the trees. With each shot, his heart broke. Those men were his brothers. As he watched, the squad of assassins spread out in search of survivors. A lone male squatted and speared a chunk of tapir meat with his knife.

In the fire's glow, Oscar saw the face of the man who had led the attack and killed his own men. A man Oscar had once considered a father figure. The betrayal ate at his stomach, and Oscar lay under the thick, dripping leaves until the patrol boat had faded into the night.

Gradually, the sounds of the jungle came back, but Oscar didn't move from his hiding spot. He clutched his pistol to his chest, having lost his rifle during his fall and subsequent roll. After the adrenaline wore off, he dozed. A sound brought him out of a light sleep, and he held his breath, listening for what had awakened him. His gaze shifted around his limited view of the campsite. A shadow moved across the landscape, darted through the dead men, and cautiously approached the cold campfire. The spotted jaguar snatched the tapir from the ashes and darted back into the underbrush.

Despite the backdrop of horrific death all around him, Oscar smiled. He'd spent years in the jungle and had never seen a big cat, but thoughts of his men tempered his elation. Slowly, he crawled out from under the foliage. His hand found his rifle, and he holstered his pistol and stood. Walking forward with anger in his heart, he took in the scene. Bullets and grenades had shredded every man, and each had a hole in his forehead.

The raiding force had taken the drugs and Armond Diego.

Oscar gathered what little supplies he could find and

headed for Guayana City to confront the murderer. It took him several days to find a Warao with a boat to run him upriver. Oscar knew he couldn't show his face at the National Guard base. He needed to remain *una fantasma*—a ghost—so he could exact revenge on the government that had turned on him and his team.

The first person on the list was Sergeant Major Phillipe Mendoza, the man Oscar had seen by the fire.

———

Mendoza kept an apartment on the third floor of a five-story building that Oscar López had been to many times. The older Marine had guided him throughout his career, and Oscar couldn't believe that his mentor had sold out.

After casing the place, Oscar waited until two in the morning to scale a drainpipe to the roof of the building next door to Mendoza's place. A row of windows faced the rooftop he was on, and Oscar ran at the wall. He lifted his leg, jammed the toe of his combat boot against the brick wall, and grabbed the top of the concrete lintel above Mendoza's window. Once he got his feet on the sill, he used a slim piece of metal to jimmy the window latch, and then he opened the window and slipped inside the dark apartment.

He wanted to shoot Mendoza right where the man slept, but when he opened the bedroom door, he found the sergeant major sitting on the bed, holding a whiskey bottle in one hand and a pistol in the other. His face was drawn, and bags hung under his eyes. He looked like he hadn't slept since he'd murdered Oscar's Marines.

Mendoza took a swallow from the bottle. "I knew you would come. Your body was not among the dead."

Oscar trained his own pistol on Mendoza. "Why did you murder my team, Sergeant Major?"

"I had orders."

Oscar crouched by the bed. "Who gave them to you?"

Mendoza placed his hands against his head, cradling it between the gun and the bottle. "I don't know."

Placing the barrel of his pistol against Mendoza's forehead, Oscar said, "You have to know, Sergeant Major. Tell me who ordered you to assassinate my team."

The older man lifted his tear-streaked face. He dropped his gun onto the bed and reached for a cell phone on the nightstand. "I received this phone in the mail. It has pictures of my family on it. You know my wife and my children, Oscar. I could never let anyone hurt them."

"*Who* gave the order?"

Mendoza held up the phone for Oscar to see. He read the text message that told Mendoza his wife and children would die if he didn't kill Lt. Sosa's team and retrieve Diego and the drugs.

Oscar took the phone and scrolled through the text and photos. "If I get your family to safety, will you help me find the man who sent you this message?"

"Of course, my son. I will do anything to atone for my sins." Mendoza laid a hand on Oscar's shoulder. "If something happens to me, remember to celebrate the birthday of our beloved Marine Corps."

The first sergeant left the way he had come, stealing a motorcycle to make the eighteen-hour trek to Maracaibo, where Mendoza's wife and three children lived in a cramped two-bedroom house. When he reached the port city, he arranged for a smuggler to take Mendoza's family to Aruba. After seeing them off on the smuggler's boat, he returned to the sergeant major's apartment.

As he climbed through Mendoza's window once more, he caught a whiff of a dead body, and he found Mendoza sprawled on the floor, a gunshot wound to his head.

Oscar quickly scavenged the apartment for clues and found a wall safe. After trying several combinations, he racked his brain for the number Mendoza would have used. Reaching back in his memory, he recounted the conversation they'd had before Oscar had gone to Maracaibo. He punched in the birthday of the Venezuelan Marine Corps and the safe opened.

It contained bank statements from several accounts and two thick stacks of American currency—contraband in Venezuela. Mendoza had circled one of the account numbers in red. Oscar pocketed both the money and the bank records, then he wiped his fingerprints from the apartment and left via the window again, this time leaving it open.

Oscar rode the stolen motorcycle to Caracas and went in search of a black-market money lender he had met several years ago while stationed in the city. He asked if the lender could identify who had put the money into the account Mendoza had circled. The lender pointed him to a hacker who Oscar paid with the cash from the safe, laughing at the irony of the traitor's own money being used to find his blackmailer.

Several days later, the hacker sent a text to Oscar, asking him to come to his apartment. Convinced the police were waiting to arrest him, Oscar told the hacker to meet him at a busy café instead. Oscar scouted the location, and when he didn't see any police or military presence, he got himself a coffee. He sipped it until the hacker arrived. He was a slim youth, barely eighteen years old, with a wide smile and curly black hair that fell over his eyes. The boy dropped a folded scrap of paper on Oscar's table as he approached the counter. A moment later, Oscar rose from his seat and tucked the paper into his pocket. Sirens filled the air as he took a last sip of coffee. He sprinted up the street, not bothering to look back.

Oscar disappeared into the slums and made his way to where he'd left the motorcycle. He got on it and rode east out of the city. When he finally stopped to read the hacker's note, the only thing written on it was a post office box number in Road Town, in the British Virgin Islands.

Oscar crossed Venezuela to the tiny fishing village of Macuro and traded the bike for passage to Chaguaramas, Trinidad, where he stole a sailboat. Whoever owned the postal box was the next man in the chain of command.

Mendoza and his team were dead, and Oscar wanted revenge.

CHAPTER ELEVEN

Present Day

Ryan, Emily, Mango, Jennifer, and Scott sat transfixed by the Venezuelan's story. They glanced at each other before returning their attention to Oscar as he finished. Ryan had heard similar tales told by other military men in San Antonio Prison. They'd also tried to stop drug shipments, and either the drug cartels or troops loyal to President Maduro had ambushed them. Rumors swirled among the servicemen that the president had ordered his generals to help facilitate the movement of drugs through Venezuela and that his administration helped launder money for the drug cartels.

"Did you find out who owned the post office box?" Emily asked.

Ryan sensed she had built a rapport with Oscar, and he let her do the talking.

"Paul Langston," Oscar replied.

"So, you staked out the post office and followed Paul back to St. Thomas?" she asked.

Oscar nodded. "I followed him around for several days until he left on his sailboat. I thought he might be on his way back to Road Town. I went to his house and there were men there, tearing it apart. Then I followed them to his office, where they did the same thing. I stayed there because they left a watcher, and I thought maybe he would lead me to whoever Langston was working for. Then you guys showed up."

"And you want to find the person who ordered the deaths of your men by studying the bank records Paul kept?" Emily said to clarify.

"Whatever is in the box has to be a lead," Oscar said.

Ryan considered Oscar's efforts to help his mentor and to find his enemies. It was something he could definitely relate to. Oscar seemed like an honorable man who'd been wronged by his government. A government in bed with the Russians, the Iranians, and the Chinese as well as Colombian drug dealers and Cuban military leaders, if the reports he'd heard were true. Whoever Oscar was searching for could be a member of any one of those factions.

The U.S. embargos and sanctions against Venezuela were headlines across the Caribbean because Venezuela had, at one time, held treaties with all of them to provide oil and financial support. Now that the money had dried up and the oil had slowed to a trickle, it was up to other nations to step in and backstop the tiny Caribbean islands.

Ryan had also seen stories on the Internet about the U.S.'s hunt for Venezuela's corrupt politicians and former military leaders who had fled the country and taken billions of dollars with them, stripping Venezuela for their own survival. Another news headline had said that U.S. authorities had indicted President Maduro and members of his cabinet on charges of drug trafficking, money laundering, corruption, and narco-terrorism.

Oscar faced an uphill battle to bring his team's killers to justice. Whoever had ordered the hit must have plenty of political clout.

Oscar interrupted Ryan's train of thought. "I have answered your questions. May I ask some of my own?"

Ryan nodded.

"Who are you, and why are you helping the Langstons?"

"That's what we do," Ryan said. "We help people in need." Ryan then introduced the team using only their first names.

"Where are the Langstons now?" Oscar asked.

"They're supposed to go to a friend's house and we're to meet them when we finish here. I plan to turn them and the paperwork over to Homeland Security for their protection."

Oscar nodded. "May I have some water?"

Scott went to the galley and returned with several bottles of water. He handed one to Oscar, who opened it and took long swallows before he wiped his chin with the backs of his still bound hands.

"I want to look at those records before you hand them over," Oscar said. "If I can find a lead, I'll continue with my hunt, and you can do what you want with them."

"Why?" Emily asked. "The chances of you finding the real culprit are nearly impossible."

"I agree," Oscar said, "but I swore an oath of loyalty to my homeland; to defend the constitution and the entire population. If I do not follow through with this, that oath means nothing, and my men will have died for nothing."

"Why can't the troops there do something?" she asked. "Why not overthrow the government if things are so bad?"

Oscar shook his head sadly. "I wish it were that easy. The troops don't dare do anything. They are constantly watched. Their calls are monitored. Any person suspected of acting against the regime is immediately detained and questioned." He motioned toward Ryan. "Your friend knows what the SEBIN does to people they suspect are traitors. The prisons are full of dissidents." He made eye contact with Ryan. "I am right, am I not?"

"You're right," Ryan said. "They're full of people whose only crime was trying to survive."

"I asked you why you help the Langstons? Was it not because you felt some duty to care for those less fortunate, those who are weaker? We are military brothers." Oscar looked at each man in turn. "We may not have served the same country, but we defend our homelands, our families, our brothers. I don't ask you to take up my cause, and I don't ask you for help. I ask that you merely allow me to read those documents and continue on my way."

Oscar's plea was certainly charged with emotion. Ryan knew how he felt, having been in the man's shoes, chasing terrorists because it was a just and noble cause. He flicked open his folding knife and sliced the tape that bound Oscar's hands. "All right, Oscar. Let's see what's in the box."

The Venezuelan rubbed his wrists. "What about the man you were torturing downstairs?"

"He was afraid of needles," Scott said.

"Needles?" Ryan said.

"Yeah, I brought some new stuff to play with," Scott said. "The drugs put a person into a twilight state, slowing the connections in the brain. I dosed him up, and he fell asleep."

"What was all the screaming about?" Oscar asked.

Scott shrugged. "It took me three tries to stick him because he kept thrashing about. Mango had to practically sit on the guy's arm."

"Can we talk to him now?" Ryan asked.

"Sure." Scott led the way to the salon where Terrence Joseph lay bound and gagged on the sofa. His skin looked ashen, and his dreads hung over his face. Scott sat the kidnapper up and patted his face. "Wakey wakey, Terrence."

The gangster's head lulled on his neck.

"Come on, buddy. Wake your ass up," Scott said, slapping Joseph harder.

"Wh-what do you ..." Joseph heaved an enormous sigh.

"Tell me who you work for," Scott said.

Joseph licked his lips. "I'm my own playa."

"You sure are, buddy. Why did you try to kill Paul Langston?" Scott prodded.

"'Cause I'm gettin' paid."

"Who paid you?"

Joseph shrugged. "Got a phone call. Mon ... money in my account. To get the documents."

"Who wants them?"

"The man on the ph ..." Joseph's head lolled again.

Scott smacked the gangster's cheek. "Does this guy have a name?"

Joseph shrugged again. "He said to kill Paul and destroy the documents."

"How did you get paid?" Oscar asked, squatting beside Scott, and watching Joseph's sleepy face.

"Wire transfer. Playa wanted cash, but the man said no."

"Where's his phone?" Ryan asked.

"On the counter." Scott pointed to it.

Ryan picked up an Android smartphone and tried to open it. "What's the password?"

"Seven-eight-nine-one," Joseph recited.

Ryan unlocked the phone. "What's your username and password for the banking app?"

Joseph looked up and shook his head. "I ain't gonna give it to ya, playa."

Oscar grabbed a handful of the man's dreads and jerked downward. Joseph screamed as the hair tore free from his skin. Oscar threw the hair into Joseph's face. "Tell me or I'll do it again."

Tears ran down the gangster's face. "Okay, okay." He recited his account information while Ryan typed it on a note-taking app, then he entered it into the banking app's log-in fields. The app unlocked and he clicked on the checking account. A deposit of one hundred thousand dollars had come through several days ago. It stood out from the other smaller deposits, all of which were under ten grand.

"Who paid you?" Oscar demanded, grabbing another handful of hair.

"I don't know!" Joseph shouted. The pain of having his hair ripped from his scalp had sharpened his senses, but his brain was still slow to respond. "They paid me to destroy the documents, that's all."

"Why? You don't even know who's paying you, so why risk kidnapping Diane?" Emily asked.

"A playa gotta handle his business."

"I found a SWIFT code and an account number for where Joseph's payment came from," Ryan said.

Oscar stood and came to look over Ryan's shoulder. "We need someone to track it."

"Do you think Paul can do that?" Emily asked.

"I don't see why not," Ryan said. "Let's go ask him."

CHAPTER TWELVE

The sun hadn't risen yet when Ryan tripped the hook on the Viking and set the anchor on the floor of Turquoise Bay. The wind was still blowing, and the waves that rocked the large vessel in the unprotected waters made it a struggle to get the rigid hull inflatable dinghy into the water. Ryan had to make two trips to shuttle everyone between the yacht and the small beach on the narrow neck of land leading to Cabrita Point. It was barely two hundred feet wide, with a ribbon of tarmac separating the beaches of Turquoise and Muller Bay. Even shrouded in darkness, it was a beautiful setting.

Paul Langston met them with the van that Mango and Scott had left at the parking garage. Scott having tossed them keys as he passed Paul on the dock at American Yacht Harbor. The team climbed in and drove away, leaving the dinghy on the beach. Ryan called the Virgin Islands Police and told them where to find Terrence Joseph, who they wanted in connection with a string of crimes on the island. By the time they would find him, the drugs Scott had injected into Joseph should have worn off, and he'd have little to no memory of what had taken place during his short boat ride.

Emily sat beside Ryan in the van's rear, their backs pressed against the steel side, and they braced themselves with their hands to keep from bouncing around or falling over into the other passengers.

Five minutes later, the van stopped, and Paul shut off the engine at a rental home he'd quickly organized for them. Ryan popped open the latch on the back door and slid out into the cool morning. The rest of the crew disembarked and carried duffle bags into a ranch home set into a hill with a walkout basement. Tiled living spaces, a modern kitchen with granite countertops and stainless-steel appliances rounded out the home's interior, and the owners had furnished the entire place with cozy rattan furniture. From the back deck, they could see American Yacht Harbor across Vessup Bay. Using a pair of binoculars, Ryan surveyed the marina and checked on his sailboat.

"What now, Great Leader?" Mango asked, joining Ryan at the railing.

Ryan stifled a yawn. "I could use a nap."

"Me, too, bro, but Oscar is itching to get to work. He's already digging through Paul's papers."

"Let him."

"All I saw was a bunch of bank accounts and routing numbers."

"I'm sure Paul has a system to know whose money he was smurfing."

"Have you talked to anyone at Homeland about getting protection for the Langstons?"

"Not yet. It's next on my agenda—after a nap."

The two men walked into the living room where Emily and Oscar sat on the sofa, Paul's papers spread across the coffee table in front of them.

"Where's everyone else?" Ryan asked.

"They went to bed," Emily replied.

"Come on, Oscar. Let's get some shuteye," Ryan prompted.

The Venezuelan looked up from the papers. "I have work to do."

"It can wait. We need to sleep, or we won't do anyone any good. I'm sure you'll go cross-eyed looking at those if you don't get some rest."

"No."

"Let's do this," Emily said. "When we get up, we'll make copies, and Paul can explain exactly what he was doing. Without a guide, you'll never decipher these numbers."

"Okay," Oscar relented, gathering the sheets, and placing them back in the box. "But I keep the box with me."

"I don't have a problem with that," Ryan said. "We want to help you, and we're on the same side. Just don't screw me by taking off with the box."

"Scott is an impartial third party," Emily said. "We'll put the box in his room, and he can safeguard it."

Oscar glanced back and forth between them before reluctantly agreeing.

They carried the box to Scott's room and knocked on the door. He answered it in his boxers and a T-shirt.

"You're guarding the box," Ryan told him.

"Roger that." Scott took the box and pushed the door closed, and they heard the lock click into place.

Ryan put a hand on Oscar's shoulder. "Get some sleep, *amigo*. Tomorrow, we'll find another piece of your puzzle."

Oscar nodded. "Where do I sleep?"

Emily pointed to a door farther down the hall. She and Jennifer had worked out the sleeping arrangements when they'd first arrived. "You're at the end. Ryan and I are across from you."

They went into their separate rooms, and Ryan went to the sliding glass door that overlooked the pool patio and checked the lock. Then he removed his clothes and crawled into bed. Emily snuggled in beside him, and it wasn't long before he was sound asleep.

THE NEXT THING Ryan was aware of was the sound of running water.

He rolled over and looked out the door at the bright sunshine beating down on the shimmering water of the pool. Mango stood by a grill with tongs in one hand and a beer in the other, wearing swim trunks and an apron.

Ryan sat up on the edge of the bed and rubbed his head, then dug his palms into his eyes. After a moment, the fog cleared. His watch told him it was past noon. He'd gotten six hours of sleep, but he still felt groggy.

He heard the water shut off and, a few minutes later, a blow dryer turned on. Levering himself off the bed, he took his turn in the shower and, feeling refreshed, went to join the others on the patio.

"Where's Oscar?" he asked, sitting beside Scott at the patio table.

"Looking at the bank records," Scott replied, handing Ryan a beer from a small cooler.

"We need to copy them."

"Already done," Scott said. "Ashlee Williams put together a little kit for the Trident teams to use in the field, with cameras, a hand scanner, and a laptop. Anyway, I scanned everything this morning before I gave the box to Oscar. I also told him that if he tried to run, I'd put a bullet in his brainpan." Scott patted his concealed pistol and took a long pull from his bottle.

"Good. I wasn't sure how we'd copy them."

"As you know," Scott said, "we run across docs in the field all the time. It's standard practice to scan them."

Greg Olsen, owner of Dark Water Research, had stepped down from his post as president of the commercial dive and salvage firm and started Trident, a private military contracting business. He had teams working around the globe with both the U.S. government and the private sector. Ryan had worked with several of the teams on various operations, and Greg was always trying to bring him into the fold full time, but Ryan didn't want to live in Texas City. He preferred the anonymity of being an independent contractor, although he liked the title 'salvage consultant' better, a term coined by the infamous Travis McGee.

"Now that they're digital, it should make it easier to run a search of the docs," Ryan said.

"I thought about that last night, so after I scanned everything in, I ran a search for the numbers we retrieved from Terrence Joseph's banking app."

"Any luck?"

"Not yet. I didn't tell Oscar that I'd scanned the docs, so he thinks he's doing all the work."

"What do you think about helping him track down his boogeyman?"

Scott shrugged. "I'm due to hop back to the States tomorrow. I've got another op to run."

Ryan nodded. "I'm glad you got to come play in the sunshine."

"You know, when Jinks told me I was coming down here, I thought we'd be doing something like disarming a ship full of fertilizer and diesel fuel again, but this was a nice change of pace. The Caribbean is a helluva lot nicer than those little shitholes we've been in and out of in the Middle East and Africa lately."

"Yeah, that's why I don't work for Trident."

"If you ever put together a team just to work in the Caribbean, let me be the first to put in my resume."

"I'll keep that in mind," Ryan said.

Scott stood. "I'll be back. I'm going to check the computer dope."

Ryan remained seated in the shade of the patio umbrella. The smell of Mango's burgers wafted through the air, along with the scent of the flowering bougainvillea that surrounded the patio. Yeah, there was no way he was going back to the Middle East. The Caribbean was paradise.

Mango transferred the burgers to a platter and carried them inside to a table loaded with condiments and buns. The team helped themselves buffet-style, and Ryan sat beside Mango at the kitchen bar.

"What brings you back from the South Pacific?" Ryan asked between bites of his burger.

"We're moving back here. Our boat is in Florida right now. We'd just gotten to Key West when Jenn's mom called, saying her father was in the hospital. He had a heart attack, and we got there just before he passed."

"I'm sorry to hear that."

"It happens to the best of us." Mango shrugged. "Anyway, we heard you needed your ass saved again, and here we are. Plus, we're looking for a place to keep our boat. We want to run our charter business here in the Caribbean."

"Hitching a ride on the company dime, huh?"

Mango grinned. "I'm just a poor sailor trying to make a living."

"*Right.*"

Scott walked up to them and quietly said, "We have a match."

CHAPTER THIRTEEN

The three men walked to Scott's bedroom where the computer sat on the dresser, its screen flashing a match between an account Terrence Joseph had received money from and one logged in Paul's files.

Scott moved the cursor and another window appeared. "The SWIFT code is for a bank in Panama."

"Makes sense," Ryan said. "Paul told me he dealt with Venezuelans, and Panama is a hotspot for money laundering."

"So, what now?" Mango asked.

"We track down the owner of the account," Ryan said. "Whoever owns that account has information on Venezuelans moving money out of their country."

"Okay, but how does that help Oscar find the guy who ordered his team killed?" Mango asked.

"From what the news is reporting, the hierarchy in Venezuela is all connected," Scott said. "You just keep working up the chain until you find the person who ordered the hit on Oscar's team."

Mango asked, "What if he's just a smurf like Paul?"

"Let's talk to Paul," Ryan said.

They went back to the kitchen, and Ryan asked Paul to join them where Oscar was working at a dining table. When the men had assembled there, Ryan said, "Paul, tell us how the Venezuelans contacted you to move their money."

"I got a phone call. They knew I was an established money launderer, and they gave me an account number and SWIFT code where they had their money parked. Then they'd tell me where they want it to end up. Sometimes, that's a bank in another country with lax laws, or they want to purchase businesses to funnel the money through."

"What kind of businesses?" Mango asked.

"Do you know how this works?" Paul asked him.

"Vaguely," Mango said. "I know it's not putting money into a washing machine."

Paul shook his head and rolled his eyes. "You *good?*" His inflection implied, *are you done cracking jokes?*

"Yeah, I'm good," Mango said with a smile.

"It's like this," Paul said. "Laundering starts with what's called placement. That's where they place the dirty money in a legitimate banking institution. Sometimes it's just deposited in person with suitcases full of cash, or it's dripped in through small deposits. My job is to take that money and move it into other accounts via small transactions that won't raise no red flags."

"Like depositing over ten grand in a bank account," Scott said.

"Exactly. That raises a flag, and the bank has to report it. Once they park the money, then it gets layered. By that, I mean we set up shell corporations, so the transactions look like legitimate business deals. I do bank-to-bank transfers, or wire transfers, and the clients use the money to purchase assets like art, cars, houses, jewelry, diamonds—you know, stuff that's hard to trace and easy to move. That's called integration. Those assets are then sold via legitimate transactions on the open market, and the clients put the money back into the bank, all clean. Each step makes the money harder and harder to trace. Sometimes, they funnel it through legitimate cash, heavy businesses like strip clubs, car washes, gambling establishments, and parking garages."

"What about this account in Panama? Can you find out who owns it?" Ryan asked.

Paul shrugged. "It's probably a corporation."

"Can you dig into it?" Ryan asked.

Paul shook his head. "I just move the money. I don't know how to hack bank records. Besides, whoever set up this account probably has it encrypted or the records are exclusively on paper."

"What's your system here?" Oscar tapped the papers strewn across the table. "You must know names."

"Some I do, but most I don't. I move money for the New Jersey Mob, the Venezuelans, Colombians, and any other knucklehead who wants it shuffled around."

"How do you keep it straight?" Oscar asked.

"If you look at the paperwork, you'll see the originating account is followed by the accounts I moved the cash through. I like to call it my 'money tree.' The corporations branch out like tree limbs and I get a cut from the transactions, usually five percent."

"So, what names do you have?" Ryan asked. "Maybe we can narrow it down from them."

"None for what you guys want to know. Almost everything is done with codes. No one knows the name of the account holder unless you're the first guy the client talked to, and even then, the client may give you a false name."

Ryan rubbed his chin as he stared at the documents. "How did you know you were moving money for the Venezuelans?"

"Before Maduro cracked down on people moving money

last year, a lot of origination codes came from Venezuelan banks. Then they started moving money via Colombia or Panama. Basically, they'd put the cash on pallets and send it out of the country. They've moved billions of dollars offshore in the last ten years. I'm just a trickle in the firehose."

"This account has to be connected to a post office box or an address, right?" Oscar asked.

"Of course," Paul said.

"Then we stake out the box just like I did to find you," the Venezuelan stated.

"We could do that," Ryan agreed. "Can you get us any information on this account, Paul?"

"I'm not able to access the bank records. All I can do is pull cash from the account or put it in. If I'd set up the business, that'd be a different story, but youse guys are startin' at the root of my money tree." He tapped the paperwork. "This account is the first in the string."

The men fell silent, frustrated with the dead end.

After a few moments, Ryan said, "I need to make a call. I'll be back in a bit." He walked out onto the pool patio and used his sat phone to call Floyd Landis, his contact at the Department of Homeland Security. When Landis answered, Ryan explained Paul and Diane Langston's situation and asked if Landis could help secure protection for them. He left out any mention of Oscar López or their hunt for his team's killer.

"Let me see what I can do," Landis said.

"I'm putting them on DWR's plane to Texas City tomorrow."

"Let's not jump the gun, Ryan."

"They can't stay here. I saved Paul from being executed. *Twice*. He needs protection."

"Okay, put them on the plane, and I'll make some calls."

"Thanks, Landis—you're a lifesaver."

"I'll add it to the list of favors you already owe me," the agent grumbled.

"I knew I could count on you." Ryan ended the call and leaned against the chain-link fence at the rear of the property. The view of the harbor was spectacular: pale blue water washed onto palm-covered shores against a backdrop of wooded hills.

Emily came over and stood next to him. "I could get used to this."

"What, the view?"

"The view. The house full of friends. Being here with you."

Ryan put an arm around her and pulled her close. Closing his eyes, he took a deep breath. He was finally living the dream. He had a woman, a mission, a life. "Mango said that he and Jennifer are moving their sailboat here to run their charter business."

"Yeah? Maybe they need some extra crew?" Emily proposed.

Ryan grinned. "I don't know if I can take orders from a guy who was in the Coast Guard."

"I think you could make an exception."

"What are you saying, Em? Are you going to quit your job and stay here on St. Thomas?"

"I'm sure I can work remotely. What about you? Could you see yourself staying here?"

He gave her a kiss. "I can see myself anywhere you are."

"Gag me with a spoon," Mango said from behind them. "You two need a room."

Ryan grinned. "Shut up, RoboCop." He'd given Mango that nickname because of Mango's high-tech prosthetic leg. The manufacturer had made it from titanium and matched it to the contours of Mango's other leg. A special sleeve fitted with tiny sensors connected the nerves of his stump to servo motors and other electronics inside the metal shell, enabling the prosthesis to mimic the natural movement of his former leg and foot.

Mango had lost his leg during a boarding exercise in the Persian Gulf when he'd mistimed his jump from the Coast Guard's small craft to the freighter's Jacob's ladder, and his foot had slipped off the ladder rung. The two boats had collided, using his leg as a fender, and smashing it beyond repair.

Mango flashed him the middle finger. "Jennifer and I are going to look for boat slips. You want to come with us, Emily?"

She winked at Ryan. "Maybe we can find one with a house."

"What's she talking about, bro?"

"You don't want to know." Ryan gave Emily a kiss and swatted her on the behind as she walked away. Smiling, he pulled out his phone and dialed another number. The recorded message told him the number was no longer in service.

His next call was to Ashlee Williams at Trident. She answered with a curt and sarcastic, "Hello, *Ryan*."

He could hear the eye roll in the petite redhead's voice. Usually when he called her, he needed something from her, and she always gave him a sarcastic retort when answering the phone despite them being good friends. "How was the honeymoon?"

"It was *awesome*! Thanks for hooking us up with that place on Saint Martin."

"No problem. I just called in a few favors for you."

"It was the nicest house I've ever been in, and there was a maid waiting on us hand and foot. I didn't want to come home. But you didn't call me to ask about my honeymoon, did you?"

"Nope. I tried calling Barry Thatcher, but the number I have isn't any good." Thatcher was a hacker whose skills Ryan had used on a previous job. Although he'd never met the hacker in person, he figured he could make further use of his expertise right about now. "Do you have a current one for him?"

"He likes to change phones like other people change underwear." She read him the current number. "I'll send him a text and let him know you'll be calling."

"Thanks. Talk to you later." He hung up and waited a few minutes before dialing Barry's number.

Barry answered with a wary, "Hello?"

"Hey, Barry. It's Ryan Weller."

"Oh, *no*. What do you want now?"

"Come on, Bare. Don't be like that. I need your help again."

"Last time nearly cost me my business."

"This time, I just need you to tell me who the holder of a bank account is."

"Oh, is *that* all?" Barry said.

"Come on, bro, you know I'm good for the cash."

"Yeah, I know the company you work for is good for it, but I gotta look out for my other clients."

"How many do you have?" Ryan asked.

"*Fine*." The resignation was clear in Barry's voice. "Give me the account number."

"Before I give you the number, why are you so reluctant to help me?"

"I'm reluctant to help everyone but myself."

"In that case, consider helping me to be helping you. You'll get paid, and I'm sure while you're poking around in the bank account that I'm going to ask you about, you can skim a little off the top."

"Are you kidding? Just getting you this information could

get me killed if I know the kind of people you're looking for, Weller, let alone dipping into their funds."

"Then you'd better cover your tracks," Ryan said. "Oh, by the way, do you have a retainer fee?"

"Oh, *hell* no!"

Ryan gave him the account information. "Call me when you have something."

"Yeah, whatever." Barry hung up.

Ryan pocketed his phone. Guys like Barry were geniuses in their own right, and they had to be handled delicately. One wrong insult or perceived slight and you were permanently on their shitlist. Do not call; do not pass go; do not collect the needed information.

He went back inside and sat down at the bar to eat his now cold burger. When Ryan finished, he joined Oscar at the table. Scott was asleep on a lounge chair beside the pool, and Paul and Diane were watching television in another room. Only the hum of the air conditioner and the rustle of Oscar shuffling papers disturbed the silence in the room.

Ryan had spent the last few months with Emily practically glued to his hip aboard their tiny sailboat. Being alone helped to recharge his batteries. He fetched a beer from the fridge and went outside, where he stretched out in a chaise lounge and shut his eyes. Numbers swirled through his mind and, no matter how hard he tried to turn them off or push them from his mind with breathing exercises, he could not fall asleep.

He decided to walk down to *Windseeker*. After checking on Oscar, who was drinking a beer while still staring at the account numbers, Ryan told him he was going for a walk and that he was waiting on a call from his hacker contact.

The marina was less than three quarters of a mile from the house. Ryan enjoyed the walk in the warm sunshine, smelling the flowers that mingled with the salt air. The entire island bloomed with vibrant colors, either painted on the houses by their owners or splashed across the landscape by Mother Nature. She knew how to clothe her landscapes with unique colors and plants, and Ryan had always appreciated her splendor. He loved the Caribbean; the constant warm temperatures, the changes in the ocean's colors as it washed over the depths, and the contrast of the mountains clad in green vegetation against the yellow, white, or black sand beaches.

When he and Emily had left Trinidad, he'd expected to end up in Tampa, where Emily had an apartment and a job. He'd contemplated starting his own commercial diving business or partnering with Greg to run a division of DWR in Florida. Maybe he'd go to college. His mother had always wanted him to get a degree, and the G.I. Bill was there to pay the way. After all, he'd done thousands of push-ups in the mud to earn that opportunity.

Still, he hadn't been able to convince himself that living in Florida was what he wanted. With Mango and Jennifer now looking for a dock to start their charter business on St. Thomas, the option of him and Emily staying here with them was now on the table. Or had she planted the idea in his head with that pep talk at the fence?

He stopped at the marina office and asked about prices for a year-round slip rental. His breath caught in his chest when the man told him the amount. He shrugged and walked out to his boat.

After checking the mooring lines, he examined the cabin doors and hatches, looking for signs of tampering. When he saw none, he unlocked the door and stepped down into the aft berth. He inhaled, smelling the familiar odors of his boat.

With a beer in his hand, he retreated to the cockpit and sat on the bench, sipping from the bottle, one foot propped on the opposite bench. It was nice to be home, listening to the creak of the fenders against the wooden docks and feeling the gentle motion of the boat as sport and pleasure boats came and went past the mega yachts and sailboats.

Here he was, a boat bum living in paradise. The next best thing to being at a slip with shore power to run the air conditioner was being at anchor in a secluded cove with no one else around for miles.

"Speaking of no one else ..." he muttered to himself as he reached into the lazarette and retrieved a waterproof box. He opened it and pulled out a pack of cigarettes and a lighter. The first draw of smoke into his lungs was intoxicating, and he settled back into his perch, sipping beer, and puffing contentedly on the cigarette.

Nearly finished with both, his sat phone rang, and Ryan saw it was Barry. "Hey, bud. What's up?"

"Look, I got what you need, but it's really gonna cost you."

"Send it over."

"I don't think so, *friend*. This is some heavy-duty shit that you're in to, and my servers are still being pinged by guys trying to trace my trail. I want my money upfront."

"Okay. Where and how much?"

"You can bring me cash."

Ryan laughed at the absurdity of having to deliver cash to the hacker, wherever he was in the world. "I'm on St. Thomas, Barry."

It was Barry's turn to laugh. "I know. So am I. Meet me in a half-hour."

CHAPTER FOURTEEN

Ryan retrieved a stack of cash from a hiding spot above *Windseeker*'s engine to pay the hacker and locked the cabin door. He took a cab up the hill to the rental house and told the driver to wait while he went inside to fetch Oscar.

The Venezuelan lay on the couch with his arm over his face.

"You awake?" Ryan asked, nudging Oscar's foot.

Oscar lowered his arm.

"We're going to see my hacker friend. Apparently, he lives on St. Thomas."

"You didn't know this?"

Ryan led the way to the cab. "Nope, but he promised he has the information we need."

They climbed into the full-sized van, and Ryan gave the man the address. The driver put the van in gear and headed for their destination.

Barry's house sat in a wooded area at the western end of the island, surrounded by thick stands of trees and uncut brush. The narrow road ended at a stamped concrete driveway that sloped to the front of the dwelling. Ryan and

Oscar stepped through a metal gate set into an eight-foot-high fence that enclosed a courtyard filled with vibrant and well-tended flowerbeds. The sidewalk led to the rear of the property and a wide patio with an infinity pool overlooking the ocean. At the far end was a massive outdoor stone fireplace under a pergola.

Before the patio was another gated arch, and a chime sounded as Ryan walked under it. A voice came through a speaker, telling him to leave his pistol on the small table beside the gate. Ryan glanced up to see a video camera and wondered how the man had known he was carrying a gun.

He set his Walther on the table as the voice admonished him. "Ah, ah, ah—the pocketknife, too, Weller."

Ryan placed his CRKT tactical folding knife beside the gun. A shapely brunette in a blue bikini top and khaki shorts came out of the house. The first thing Ryan noticed besides her incredible body was the Walther CCP M2 in her hand.

At least she has excellent taste in handguns, he thought.

The brunette guided them to a spiral staircase leading up to the second-story porch. They followed her through a set of French doors into a large open room with windows all around, giving a 360-degree view of the surrounding property, even though the shades were partially drawn.

A man sat at a modern glass-and-steel desk with a single computer monitor resting on it. In the center of the room was a long table with a glass top. The hacker occupied the only chair in the room.

As his guests entered, Barry stood and walked over to the table. He was of average height and carried a few pounds of extra weight around his midsection. His black hair was spiked, and he had a leather cuff bracelet on his right wrist and a silver chain bracelet on his left. He also wore shorts, sandals, and a T-shirt that advertised a heavy metal band.

Barry motioned to Oscar. "Who's this guy?"

"Oscar López. He's a Venezuelan Marine." Ryan stepped over beside Barry and looked down to see his passport photo and details being displayed on the computer screen integrated into the table's glass surface. Oscar's picture was beside his, pinpointed with facial recognition nodals but with no name registered in the database.

Barry tapped a button and their pictures disappeared from the screen. "You got the money?"

Ryan pulled the envelope from his back pocket and tossed it onto the glass. "It's all there. But I'm sure you counted it as I walked in."

A smile ghosted across Barry's lips. He slipped the band off the money and laid the bills out in neat stacks until he'd fully accounted for every dollar, then gathered the cash into one large stack again and said, "Pleasure doing business with you." He handed the money to the woman, who stepped out of the room with it. Barry watched her go and smiled. "My business associate, Carmen."

"We're not done," Oscar said.

Barry winked at him. "Now that I have the horse, you can have the cart."

"What were you so worried about on the phone?" Ryan asked.

"Look, your number corresponds with an account at Citizens RBG, a boutique bank in Panama City. It's a ridiculously small firm with less than five employees, but they handle millions of dollars. It's a classic money laundering set-up." He tapped the screen and an image of a tall building appeared. From it, lines shot out in multiple directions, forming a spider's web. Barry manipulated the screen with his fingers and the image grew smaller as a map of the world appeared behind it. The lines bounced through every major city on the globe.

"What is this?" Oscar asked.

"This is the shitstorm I was telling Ryan about," Barry replied. "When I entered that account number into the bank's system, I tripped every trigger known to man. The bank's security features locked me out." He tapped the globe. "Those lines are people pinging my tracks."

"The question is, will they find you, *Señor* Barry?" Oscar asked.

"Hell no. I took my system offline as soon as I was done. I'm monitoring them through a server farm in Norway."

"You have servers here?" Ryan asked.

"Right now, they're air-gapped." Seeing Oscar's puzzled look, Barry added, "My computers don't have any wireless features. So, when I unplug the Internet, the computers aren't connected to the outside world. When I go live again, I'll fabricate a different IP address for somewhere in ... oh, I don't know ... say, Russia."

"You can do that?" Oscar said.

"Easy as pie."

Ryan pointed to the table where the spiderweb continued to grow. "How is this running if you're offline?"

"A magician never reveals his secrets." He smiled at Carmen, who had returned to stand beside the glass-topped computer table.

"Let's get back to why we're here," Oscar said. "The bank shut you out? I thought you were a good hacker?"

Barry fake laughed. "*Ha ha*. You think you're a wise guy, huh? Yes, the bank shut me out, and yes, I got back in, but the guys back tracing me will find me if I go at it again, and there's no way in hell I'll let them send a hit team after my ass."

"Any idea who set the tripwire?" Ryan asked.

The hacker held up a finger. "That's the interesting part. You'll want to talk to a lawyer who works for the bank and set up the account."

"What's his name?" Oscar asked.

"Vincente Emilio Valdez. I made a file for you with everything I could gather on him." Barry retrieved a manila folder from his desk. "I know you knuckle draggers think better with a piece of paper in your hand." He handed it to Ryan. "Our business has now concluded. You may leave."

Ryan tapped the folder against his thigh and eyed the hacker. "Keep your phone on."

With a frown, Barry said, "It'll cost you."

"How would you like to be neighbors, Bare?" Ryan asked. "I thought I saw a 'For Sale' sign down the road a bit."

The hacker's face blanched.

"Seriously, do you know a good realtor on the island?"

"Yeah," Barry mumbled. "Let me get her card."

Ryan took the business card that Barry pulled from a desk drawer, and Carmen escorted them back to the garden. Ryan put his gun back in its holster and returned his knife to his pocket. He rapped a knuckle against the thick garden wall. He guessed there was a full body scanner mounted inside the archway.

They rode back to the house in silence, finding that Mango, Jennifer, and Emily had returned.

Emily cocked her head as Ryan walked into the living room. "I know that look, Weller. Where are you going?"

"Panama."

"I'm in, bro," Mango said.

Ryan looked past him to Jennifer, who nodded her head. He didn't agree with her, but he'd talk to Mango privately. He left the folder with Oscar and stepped to the Langstons' bedroom. Paul was lying on the bed, watching TV.

"I need documents for Oscar. Driver's license, passport, that sort of thing. Do you know anyone who can do it?"

"There's a guy named Luis in Mandahl. I'll call him."

Ryan handed him his phone, and after Paul made the

introductions, Ryan told the man what he needed. After getting off the phone, he took a photo of Oscar and texted it to Luis.

"We'll have a full set of docs for you tomorrow," he told Oscar, then turned to Scott. "When is the plane coming for you?"

"Ten hundred."

Ryan nodded and stepped outside into the warm evening air. The sun was setting, and the boaters had put their toys away, leaving the bay looking like a flat mirror, reflecting the sky. He thumbed the call button for Greg Olsen.

Greg came on the line after two rings. "Let me guess. You need to borrow Scott for a bit longer?"

"No. I'm going to Panama. I'd like to ride on your plane when it comes to pick up Scott, but I need to leave later in the day."

"I don't see that being a problem."

"Good. I'll have Mango and three extra passengers with me."

"Want to tell me what this is about?"

Ryan asked, "Are you still in Bluefields?"

"Yeah, I'm stuck here, trying to cut through the red tape. It's like quicksand; the harder you work to get through it, the worse it gets."

"Better you than me, buddy. Can I borrow Rick and *Dark Water* when I get there?"

"See? You ask me stuff like that and you pique my curiosity. I want to know details."

"Big Brother has his ears on."

"I get that," Greg said. "I'll see you when you get here."

"Thanks again." As Ryan ended the call, Mango leaned against the fence beside him.

"I'm going with you," Mango said.

Ryan shook his head. "No."

Mango gripped the fence and leaned closer to Ryan. "I'm going with you. You need *my* help."

"That's what Rick and Oscar are for. You don't need to get involved in this."

Mango stared out across the bay, his jaw clenched, and his brow furrowed. "I'm already involved."

"Look," Ryan said, "you need to think about Jennifer and your business. You're out of danger now that the bounty is gone. Go and live your life."

"I *need* it, bro. I need the action."

"No. You don't."

"And neither do you." Mango turned and thrust a finger against Ryan's chest. "I'm going with you, whether you like it or not."

"*No*," Ryan said emphatically.

"You couldn't stop me from going into Mexico with you, and you can't stop me now."

Ryan closed his eyes and took a deep breath. He let it out slowly, picturing the flames burning through his anger and trying to ignore the tip of Mango's finger digging into his breastbone. "I promised Jennifer that I would end the bounty and that you would be safe after that. Don't make me a liar, Mango."

"You made yourself a liar by making promises you can't keep." The shorter man shoved Ryan hard in the shoulder and stalked into the house.

Ryan rubbed his face with his hands. He wasn't going to let Mango give up all the wonderful things he had just to run into a firefight because he needed the adrenaline rush. The sad thing was that he and Mango were two of a kind, and while Ryan was willing to put his ass on the line for the Langstons and Oscar, he didn't want Mango to do the same. He had a wife, a business, and ...

It was the same stuff Ryan wanted. What a knucklehead

he was for telling Mango not to do the very thing he was doing.

He walked into the house and looked around at the somber faces. It was always tough when friends argued, but it was more difficult when they did it in front of everyone. "Where is he?"

Jennifer pointed down the hall.

Ryan walked to the room and knocked on the door. "Open up, dude."

The door opened a moment later.

He entered the room, closed the door behind him, and sat on the bed. After rubbing his neck and making a few false starts, Ryan finally said, "I'm a hypocrite, bro. I'm telling you not to get involved, yet I'm sticking my neck out for a guy I barely know."

"Yeah. I get it."

"We've got the dream in our hands, man, and if we keep riding off into the sunset to chase bad guys, we're going to lose the dream or lose our lives. I know you're a solid operator, and there have been *so* many times I wished you were there with me, but I wanted to protect you and Jennifer at the same time."

"I get it, bro. I'm a one-legged man in an ass-kicking contest."

"That's not what I mean." Ryan paused. "Shit. 'Talk about your feelings,' Emily says. Well, I'm feeling this will turn sour. We're dealing with Venezuelans of the nastiest kind, and I know how they treat their prisoners. I just don't want you to have to go through the same shit I went through down there."

"It always goes pear-shaped, bro," Mango said, sitting beside his friend. "The best laid plans go out the window when the bullets start flying."

"And fly they will, Mango, because they already have.

Someone killed a Marine Special Forces team to keep their secrets, and we're over here poking the bear."

"That's why you need someone with my skill set. Someone who can reach out and touch them from a distance."

"Will that same person tell me he saved my ass again?"

"Of course. What are friends for?"

Ryan chuckled and shook his head at the running joke. "We fly for Panama tomorrow afternoon. Talk it over with Jenn and see what she says."

"Green light, bro. The ladies talked about it while we were out today. Apparently, I'm supposed to cover your sweet-looking six." He made air quotes around 'sweet-looking.'

"Never say that again."

Mango suddenly turned serious. "Sure. Do me a favor, though? Don't ever tell me I can't come along on a job. That's my decision, not yours."

"Agreed. I was just trying to keep you and Jennifer out of harm's way."

"I know, bro, and I appreciate it, but it's not necessary."

Ryan grinned. "If that's the way you feel, then let's go get a beer. We have a mission to plan."

CHAPTER FIFTEEN

Panama City, Panama

Ryan and Oscar waited in Vincente Valdez's twenty-first-story apartment. Through the floor-to-ceiling windows and sliding glass doors, they could see the Pan-American Highway stretching across the waters of Panama Bay to the suburb of Costa del Este, where Valdez worked for Citizens RBG. Both men wore gloves and thin balaclavas. They'd made a careful survey of the apartment, looking for safes or other places Valdez might have hidden paperwork, but neither man had found anything unusual. Undeterred, they waited for the lawyer to return home.

Arriving in Colón a week ago, they'd driven across the narrow Isthmus of Panama in a rental van and spent their time shadowing Valdez and detailing his movements. Now, they were ready to take him off the street and interrogate him.

Ryan checked his watch. Valdez normally returned to the apartment around seven in the evening, after having dinner.

"Hey, guys? We've got a problem," Mango said over their communications equipment. Each had a Bluetooth earpiece connected to Panamanian burner phones they'd bought with cash as soon as they'd arrived in the country. Mango and Rick were waiting in a Toyota HiAce minivan in the parking lot.

"What's the matter?" Ryan asked.

"Your boy has a lady friend with him," Mango said.

"Okay, everyone hang tight," Ryan said. "Let's let this play out."

Oscar gave Ryan a questioning look.

A few minutes later, the front door opened, and Valdez and his woman stepped inside the apartment. He didn't turn on the lights but pressed her against the wall as the door closed and kissed her deeply. Then they began tearing off each other's clothes.

Ryan and Oscar could have been standing in the middle of the living room with spotlights shining on them, and neither of the lovers would have seen them as they made their way to the bedroom. From his position behind the sofa, Ryan could see them making love on the bed.

"What's going on?" Mango asked.

"Valdez is getting a blowjob," Ryan whispered. "Do you want me to live stream it for you?"

"Actually, yes, get us a feed." Rick said. "We could use it as leverage."

Ryan pulled a GoPro camera from his pack and aimed it at the couple in the bedroom.

Twenty minutes passed before the woman got up from the bed, went to the bathroom, then gathered her clothes from the floor. As she pulled on her silky black underwear, Valdez shrugged into a robe and begged her to stay. She slipped the dress over her shoulders and settled it around her hips before he zipped it up for her. Ryan and Oscar remained crouched behind the sofa.

"I have to go, lover," the woman said as she kissed Valdez.

"Please stay, Maria," he begged. "I love you."

"You know I can't." She kissed him again and stepped out the door.

Oscar had a syringe of lorazepam in his hand and he glanced at Ryan, who held up a finger, telling him to wait. They watched as Valdez walked to the kitchen and drank a glass of water before heading back to the bedroom. As he passed the sofa, Ryan rose from his hiding spot, grabbed the lawyer around the waist, and covered his mouth with his free hand. Oscar jammed the needle into Valdez's neck.

The lawyer struggled for a moment before the drug kicked in. Ryan had ordered a low dosage so the man would be compliant but not completely knocked out. As Valdez sagged to the floor, he mumbled something.

Ryan leaned closer, prying Valdez's eyelids open. The dilated pupils stared back at him.

"Don't hurt me," Valdez muttered.

Oscar helped Ryan get the lawyer to his feet and they hooked his arms over their shoulders.

"Coming out," Ryan said.

"Roger that," Rick said. "The security cameras are off."

Valdez was closer to Oscar's height but weighed more than the fit Marine. He was in his late thirties, had thinning hair, which was going prematurely gray, and a wispy beard along his jawline. His mustache looked like something a prepubescent boy would have been proud to grow. What Maria saw in this guy wasn't visible to Ryan unless she was after his money.

They carried Valdez to the elevator and rode down to the second floor to avoid the lobby. When they exited the elevator car, the two men dragged their charge through the door to the stairway. Ryan flung the smaller man over his shoulder, and he and Oscar rushed down the steps and out the service entrance to the waiting van.

Mango had the side door open and helped Ryan lay the drugged man on the floor between the seats. They all climbed in, and Rick drove them across town to an abandoned farmhouse on the edge of the city.

Ryan and Oscar duct taped Valdez's ankles and knees to a chair, then wrapped more tape around his midsection, securing it to the chair back. Oscar pushed a wooden table against the lawyer's stomach, pulled his arms across it, and tied each wrist to a table leg.

Once they finished securing the prisoner, they set up a video camera to watch him before filing out of the room. While they waited for Valdez to come around, Ryan fast-forwarded through the video he'd taken in the apartment, found a profile and front view of the woman's face, and sent it to Barry Thatcher so he could use his facial recognition software to identify her.

Rick Hayes swatted at the cloud of mosquitoes buzzing his head, glanced around the dark jungle that surrounded the house, and shook his head. "You could have at least found us a spot with air conditioning."

To Ryan, his friend was a dead ringer for Telly Savalas's TV detective, Kojak, with his shaved head and stocky build. At five-foot-five and three quarters of an inch, he had a hint of a Napoleon complex. He could be boisterous, aggressive, and braggadocious, but the man had a right to be. He'd been an Army Ranger and then gone through EOD school, making him a member of a very elite club. When he'd left the Army, he'd gotten his pilot's license and flew tourists around Key West in a Robinson R44 helicopter before Greg Olsen had offered him a job at DWR. Like Ryan and Mango, Rick had jumped at the chance to get back into the action, and he had quickly become Greg's right-hand man.

"This is the best I could do," Ryan said. "Next time, I'll let you pick the interrogation site. Maybe down at the Holiday Inn so we can have a continental breakfast in the morning and the other guests can hear our prisoner scream through the walls."

Ryan didn't enjoy being out in the jungle either, and he hoped this would be over soon. Although he couldn't imagine Valdez would take long to crack as long as they came at the lawyer strong and convinced him they were more of an immediate threat than the people who controlled the money in the accounts he'd established.

The twilight sedation wore off, and Valdez finally awoke with a sudden realization that he was bound to a chair and table. His head snapped up and he swiveled it around, taking in the sagging floorboards, the leaking roof, and the broken windows. A curtain stirred in the faint breeze.

Ryan knew the smell of rotten garbage would make the man breathe through his mouth. He'd pulled his mask back on to help cover the smell, as had the rest of his team.

"He's awake," Oscar said, watching the camera feed on a tablet computer.

"Good," Ryan said. "Let him sweat for a little while."

They had planned to leave him until morning before beginning their interrogation, but another plan was forming in Ryan's mind.

First, he'd let Oscar do it his way.

CHAPTER SIXTEEN

It was close to midnight when Barry called Ryan back to let him know that he had identified the woman Valdez had been sleeping with. Her name was Maria Ortega, and she was the wife of a local baker.

"I can still use her for leverage," Ryan said.

"I doubt his partners at his bank would be happy that he's having an affair, but for your purposes, she needed to be the spouse of a drug boss or a politician."

"Yeah," Ryan agreed. "That would have made it easier, but he did tell her he loved her."

"I have a bad feeling," Barry moaned. "And when I get bad feelings, I charge more money."

"I'll let you know if I need your help," Ryan said, and he ended the call.

The men took turns standing guard while the others were resting in the van, but none of them slept well. Oscar nudged Ryan at four in the morning and asked if he was ready to get started.

Valdez raised his head off the table as they entered the

house. Ryan clicked on a powerful flashlight and aimed it right at the prisoner's face.

Valdez blinked and turned his head to shield his eyes. He licked his lips before asking hoarsely, "What do you want?"

Ryan walked behind him, leaned over, and wrote the account number on the table with a black marker. "Tell me who owns that account."

"I don't know."

"*Bullshit*," Ryan said. He pushed Valdez's face onto the table, grinding his cheek into the wood. "You set the tripwire on that account."

The lawyer remained silent, other than to grunt in pain.

Ryan let go of the man's head, but he didn't lift it off the table.

Oscar placed his hands on the table and leaned down to face Valdez. In Spanish, he demanded, "Who owns the account?"

Again, the lawyer was silent.

For the next twelve hours, they worked on Valdez, but he refused to answer any of their questions. Ryan suspected that whatever information they needed would be inside Valdez's office. Therefore, they needed to keep his face undamaged, but the rest of him was fair game if Oscar wanted to use him as a punching bag.

AFTER ANOTHER LONG night in the humid jungle, the team got together beside the open side door of the van and decided they needed to try another tactic.

"Anyone have any ideas?" Mango asked.

Ryan already had a list prepared for them. He laid it on the van's step. "First, we need to get a suit for Valdez, so he can escort me into the bank. Second, we need to snatch his woman. Once we have the information we need, we can release her."

"A hostage scenario," Rick mused, rubbing his head, which, like his face, was growing stubble.

"Let's use your 'lover boy' charms to lure her off the street," Ryan said to Rick. "If she's after Valdez's money, maybe you can flash some cash around and get her interested."

Rick rubbed his hands together. "Business is about to pick up. No," he corrected himself, "I'm about to pick *her* up." He laughed, then did a few pelvic thrusts to drive home the point.

"What if we tell Valdez we know who she is, and that we can get to her any time we want to?" Mango asked.

"That's good," Ryan said. He glanced at his watch, wondering if someone had reported Valdez missing. He wanted to get this done quickly and retrograde out of this situation before some poor kid stumbled upon their operation and blabbed to their parents or the police, but they still had work to do. "You and Rick get one of Valdez's suits from his place. Go in the back way in case someone is staking it out."

The two men nodded.

"On your way back, rent a helicopter so we have fast transport back to *Dark Water*."

"What about the van?"

"I'll call the rental agency and tell them where to pick it up," Ryan said.

"What else?" Rick asked.

"Just keep your eyes open. Valdez has been off the street for two days. Someone is probably looking for him."

"Roger that," Mango said as he and Rick climbed into the van.

"Wait a minute. We'll see if he takes the bait or whether

we need to snatch her." Motioning to Oscar, Ryan said, "Let's go."

Inside the house, Ryan placed his phone on the table and played the footage of Valdez fornicating with Maria Ortega. When the video ended, Ryan pulled up a picture of Maria that Barry had pulled from her social media account. She wore a short red dress and posed with her arms in the air in front of the large sign which spelled out 'Panama' in a park off Balboa Avenue.

"Her name is Maria Ortega," Ryan said. "Her husband owns a bakery in the old town. I know where she lives, and I know how she will die, unless you tell us what we need to know about this account number." He tapped the table where he'd written it.

"Please, *señor*. I can't. They will kill me."

Oscar pushed Ryan out of the way and got in the lawyer's face. "The men you're talking about have already killed my family. And I'll do whatever I have to, to get to them. I won't hesitate to kill your *punta*, but I think I might have a little fun with her first." His eyebrows danced deviously. "You know what I mean. And when I am done with her, I will come back for *you*." He pulled a knife from his pocket and flicked it open with a flourish. The *snap* of the blade locking into place made the prisoner jump. Oscar used the point to slice Valdez's forearm.

The lawyer screamed.

"Don't worry. That's just a flesh wound. I will continue to cut you until you tell me what I want to know." Oscar stepped back and wiped the blood from the blade with his finger. "But first, I will taste the blood of your woman." He turned and went out the door with Ryan on his heels.

"No. No! Wait!" Valdez sobbed.

Oscar grinned. "I should have cut you yesterday."

Valdez stared up at them with a pleading look on his face. Blood spilled from his arm and pooled on the table.

"Tell us about the account." Ryan tapped the number he'd written on the table.

"The information you need is in a safe deposit box at the bank," Valdez said.

"Give me the key," Oscar said.

Valdez shook his head. "I have to be there. It's my box, and they won't let you into the vault without me."

"Then you'll walk me into the vault," Ryan said.

"Just don't hurt Maria," Valdez pleaded.

Ryan left the room. He told Mango and Rick to go to Valdez's apartment and get his suit, then he went back inside and bandaged the man's arm.

During their study of Valdez's daily habits, they had spent plenty of time observing the bank that also housed his law offices. At only twenty-six-stories, the bank building was one of the smaller high-rises, and the architects had covered it with multicolored panels that reminded Ryan of urban camouflage. Surrounding the building were even taller skyscrapers filled with luxury apartments and offices.

Laundered money had built many of the buildings, and office space was cheap. Often, the offices and residences sat empty, but their records would show they were full. Shell corporations and money launderers like Paul Langston paid the rent for these fictitious tenants.

Going into an urban environment with high-rise buildings, pedestrians, and lots of vehicles always complicated an operation. At least tomorrow was Sunday, and the offices were closed. The only people they might have to deal with were the tenants on the upper floors or someone working overtime.

Ryan opened his laptop and studied blueprints of the P.H. Torre Banco Panama building that the architects had posted online. Open source access was very thoughtful of them, but the floor plans were blank, and the occupants would have created their own individual spaces. There was only so much information he could glean from pictures and blueprints. He wouldn't have a complete picture until he was inside the building with Valdez, and even then, there might be a surprise around every corner.

CHAPTER SEVENTEEN

The next morning, Ryan and Oscar threw a bag over Valdez's head and cut him free from his bonds. They had to carry him to the van, and they laid him on the floorboard between the two back seats. They hadn't allowed him to use the bathroom during his captivity, and he stank from soiling his pants. Mango rolled the window down and stuck his head out.

Oscar sat by the lawyer and, in a low growl, said to him, "Remember what will happen to you if you do something stupid." He laid his knife blade on Valdez's forearm and the lawyer nodded, fear etched across his face and in his terrified eyes.

Rick drove them on a winding route through the tangle of suburbs that surrounded Panama City. All four operators kept their heads on swivels, watching for a tail, but it was near impossible with the high volume of traffic. By snatching the lawyer, they had painted a target on their backs, and everyone fully expected to see action before leaving the country, although Ryan hoped it wouldn't go loud in the streets where civilians could be in harm's way.

Their next stop was a small house just off the Pan-Am Highway, a few miles from the interrogation hut. Rick parked the van in the driveway, and Ryan pulled the sliding gate shut on the fence to block the view of any onlookers.

Inside the house, they took turns showering and shaving before putting on clean clothes. Ryan dressed in slacks, a dress shirt, and a suit jacket he'd brought with him so he could accompany Valdez to the bank vault. The others had purchased similar outfits during the week, hoping to blend in with the lawyers, bankers, and diplomats that roamed the streets around their target.

"Where is Maria?" Valdez asked as they hustled him back to the van.

"She's at the bakery with her husband," Ryan replied.

"I want to speak to her. I want to make sure she is safe."

"No."

"I know how this works." Valdez planted his feet and fought to keep from being stuffed into the van again. "I have done hostage negotiations for the bank."

Oscar seized Valdez by the hair on the back of his head and wrenched backward, exposing his neck. He placed his blade against Valdez's carotid artery and growled, "Get in the van, *punta*. Your woman will have a rich, full life without you in it."

"I want proof of life," Valdez demanded.

Oscar was about to say more, but Ryan cut him off with a wave of his hand. He pulled Valdez's phone from his pocket and dialed the number stored in it for Maria. She answered tentatively, and Ryan put it on speaker.

"Maria, are you okay?" Valdez asked.

"I told you never to call me while I'm at work," she hissed.

Valdez glanced up at Ryan, who raised his eyebrows in an 'I told you so' gesture.

"I love you, Maria. I'll call you soon."

Ryan ended the call while Maria was still speaking. Oscar pulled his knife away from Valdez's throat and shoved him forward, and Valdez scrambled into the van. With Oscar and Rick keeping the hostage in check, Ryan climbed into the driver's seat, and Mango rode shotgun. They left the house and drove to a private airstrip near the port of Balboa on the Panama Canal, where Rick got out and headed for the hangar to make sure the helicopter he'd rented was ready to fly while the others headed for the bank.

After driving a circuitous route to lose any tails, Ryan pulled the van to a stop under the awning at the front entrance of Valdez's bank. Mango got out and opened the sliding door. Valdez stepped from the van and adjusted his suit jacket, buttoning the front as Ryan and Oscar did the same. Together, the three men headed for the door as Mango jumped in the driver's seat and pulled away in the van.

Ryan slowly let out a deep breath as they approached the security turnstile. He glanced around the opulent lobby as they strolled across the gray marble tiles that looked like three-dimensional boxes underfoot. A guard in a two-tone blue uniform stood by the security turnstile, and another had positioned himself by the bank of elevators.

As they passed through the turnstile, a buzzer went off. The security guard stepped forward, saying in Spanish, "Sir, we need to search your team."

Valdez pulled his credentials from his pocket. "These men are with me. They are my security detail."

"They're not allowed to carry firearms in the building, sir."

The lawyer moved closer to the guard and lowered his voice. "I've had several death threats recently. They're here for my protection, just as you are. Right, Manny?"

Manny rubbed his chin as he looked at Ryan and Oscar.

Ryan took a stab in the dark, figuring someone had been

checking on Valdez's whereabouts over the last few days. "Manny, have you seen any other men attempting to access Mr. Valdez's office?"

The guard cleared his throat, then nodded. "Yes. I was told *they* were his security team."

"They're the men I have received threats from, Manny," Valdez said. "As you can see, my security is here—with me."

Ryan nodded to Oscar. "This man will accompany you to the control room and retrieve any video footage you have of the imposters."

After glancing at the lawyer one last time, Manny motioned for Oscar to follow him and turned on his heels. Ryan and Valdez walked toward the elevators.

Ryan whispered, "One wrong move, and you're dead."

They stepped into the open elevator car and rode to the sixth floor.

"What's going on, Oscar?" Ryan asked into his Bluetooth earpiece.

"I'm reviewing the surveillance camera footage."

"Mango?" Ryan asked.

"Circling the block, bro."

"What about you, Rick?" Ryan asked.

"I'm finishing the preflight. I'll be in the air in ten minutes."

"Roger that. Step on it if you can." Ryan looked at his dive watch. They'd spent ten minutes getting through security and up to the bank.

When the elevator doors opened, the two men stepped out. They bypassed an empty reception area where the white marble desk bore the words 'Citizens RBG' in back-lit gold letters across its front.

Valdez used his keycard to unlock the heavy glass-and-aluminum double doors to the inner lobby. Ryan figured they were bullet resistant. The bank was a fortress, but the same invulnerability that made it hard to break into would also make it hard to escape from. A hard knot formed in Ryan's gut, and he had the awful feeling that Mr. Murphy of Murphy's Law was about to make things go pear-shaped. The plan was to get the docs and then take the van to the airport, but things were rapidly changing. The team had now split into four individual units, and Ryan didn't like it one bit.

On their left were three cubicles, and there were two more on the right beside the floor-to-ceiling windows. Now that they were inside, Ryan could see that the multicolored panels cladding the exterior were panes of glass set in an inverted subway tile pattern. In the distance, he saw the opposite view of the Pan-Am Highway bridge to Valdez's apartment across the bay.

Trying to lighten the mood, Ryan said, "I can see your house from here."

"Yes, you can. It's one of the reasons I chose this building for the bank's office."

"Let's open the vault."

Valdez hesitated. "I don't think you have anyone following Maria."

Ryan raised his eyebrows. "Do you want to take that chance?"

"Everything in this bank is being recorded. I promise you that whoever you're looking for will find you, and I pray they make your life a living nightmare."

"Sounds like fun and games to me, Vince. Just open the safe deposit box."

In his ear, Ryan heard Mango's voice. "Hey, bros. I think some new friends have just arrived. Four dudes wearing trench coats just entered the bank."

"What's your status, Kojak?"

"Ready to fly, squid."

"Get that bird in the air. Meet us at the open field up the road from the bank."

"Just get clear of the bad guys before I arrive. This flying tin can ain't built for a hot LZ."

"Copy that," Ryan said. With a kill squad coming, things had definitely gone pear-shaped.

It was time to implement Plan B, which was to retrieve the docs, fall back to the van, and meet the helicopter in a field less than half a mile up the road. Ryan wondered if he should develop a Plan C.

Valdez punched the digital code into the vault door keypad, then fitted his eye to the retinal scanner. A moment later, the locking bars retracted, and Valdez swung the thick steel door open. They stepped inside, and Ryan's eyes widened at the countless bundles of shrink-wrapped cash. He was here to retrieve documents out of a lock box, not rob a bank, but the thought crossed his mind.

Ryan took one of the safe deposit box keys that Valdez offered him, and together they inserted them into the panel in front of the box, turning them at the same time. Valdez pulled the box from its slot in the wall and carried it to a nearby table.

Oscar appeared in the vault doorway. "*Madre de Dios*," he murmured, upon seeing the cash.

"Did you get the video?" Ryan asked.

"Yeah. I erased the footage from today and took the entire surveillance system offline for the next twenty-four hours."

Valdez removed a file folder from the box and handed it to Ryan. "That will tell you what you want to know about the account."

Oscar stepped into the vault, scooped all the files out of the safe deposit box, and dumped them into a backpack while Ryan zip-tied the lawyer's hands and feet together.

"*Adiós, el cabrón,*" Oscar said to Valdez.

Mango's voice crackled in their ears. "The goons are heading up the elevator."

"Oscar," Ryan said, "you take the files and meet Mango outside. I'll hold off the goon squad."

CHAPTER EIGHTEEN

Before the Venezuelan Marine could argue, the elevator chimed, and the door slid open. Two members of the trench coat brigade stepped out, holding Tavor SAR rifles. Both trained their guns on the bank's entrance doors and depressed their triggers. The rounds slammed into the glass, crazing and fracturing it. The men concentrated their firepower near the door's handle, and soon the barrage of bullets had punched a hole in the glass large enough for them to reach through and open the lock.

"What's your protocol for a robbery?" Ryan asked Valdez.

"There's a panic button in my office. It drops steel barriers over the front doors, sets off the silent alarm, and locks the vault."

Ryan knew that if they pressed that button, they would be locked inside with no way out. He and Oscar squatted behind the vault door with their pistols drawn. While the door gave them some protection, it was only a matter of time before their position was overrun. They would have to figure something out—and fast.

"The stairwell on level five is being guarded by our new friends," Mango reported. "What's the situation up there?"

"We have the documents, but we're pinned down in the bank. Say the status of the building's security guards."

"Dead."

"*Shit*." Ryan ducked as another flurry of bullets pinged off the vault door.

"What do you want me to do?" Mango asked.

"Save my ass, bro," Ryan replied without hesitation.

"While you guys are down there screwing around, the cops are on the way," Rick said. "Holy shit, boys! They look like ants swarming a sugar cube."

Ryan closed his eyes and steeled himself to act. He lay down on the floor and braced his foot against the doorframe. He motioned for Oscar to take a few potshots through the gap between the vault door and the jamb. The Marine nodded and, without aiming, depressed the trigger on his Glock multiple times, which the Trench Coats returned with a firestorm of lead.

Shoving against the door frame with his foot, Ryan pushed himself out just enough to get a bead on the first man. He put two rounds into his chest and swung his pistol to the second man. Oscar was firing again.

The man Ryan had just shot regained his balance and tried to bring his gun to bear.

"What the hell?" Ryan muttered, before retraining his sights on the man's forehead and pressing the trigger again. This time, the man's head snapped back, and the Tavor slid from his hands as he fell to the floor.

By the time Ryan transitioned his sight picture again, Oscar had drilled the second shooter in the brain.

The two men scrambled forward and pilfered the long guns from the dead men. Ryan checked the rounds in his magazine and moved to the front door. He turned to look for Oscar, but the man had disappeared back into the vault.

"Where are you, Mango?" Ryan asked.

"Coming up the steps now, bro. Those dudes were wearing bulletproof trench coats."

"I know," Ryan said. A single gunshot rang out, and he turned back to the vault. He ran to the open door and saw Oscar holding his smoking Tavor. A bullet hole wept blood from the lawyer's forehead.

Oscar placed his pistol in the dead man's hand and, on his way out of the vault, shoved multiple bundles of cash into his backpack.

"I'm here," Mango said.

"Coming out of the vault," Ryan replied. He and Oscar ran to the reception area where Mango waited behind the desk, training a Tavor on the elevator doors. Instead of going down the stairs, Ryan rang for the elevator car. In a moment of silence, they could hear the faint wail of sirens.

"What's the plan here, boys?" Rick asked through the Bluetooth connection.

"Are you close?" Ryan asked.

"I'm just offshore."

"See that flat roof at the rear of our building?" Ryan asked.

The high-rise had a wide base which narrowed in the front at the eleventh story. It narrowed again in the rear on the eighteenth floor, and with each step in, there was a flat roof large enough to accommodate the helicopter if Rick hovered just off the edge of the building.

"Got it," Rick said. "Let me know as soon as you're there."

The elevator door slid open and, for a moment, the three operators stood staring at two more goons clad in trench coats, who were staring right back. Then Ryan shoved Mango out of the way and shot one goon point-blank in the chest before spinning out of the line of fire.

Mango slammed against the wall and lost his footing. Ryan hooked him under the arm, dragged him upright, and sped them toward the stairwell on the backside of the elevators. They banged through the exit to the sounds of automatic gunfire.

"Go," Ryan ordered, pushing his friend upward.

Mango started up the steps. Ryan turned back for Oscar but saw him entering the stairwell right behind him. Oscar sprinted past them as Ryan slowed to keep time with Mango.

"Five flights to go," Ryan said to both Mango and Rick.

"It looks like you guys robbed a bank," Rick said. "There're cops everywhere."

"Keep out of the area until we're ready," Ryan said.

"I know how an extraction works, Weller."

"Keep your eyes and ears glued on, anyway. Three flights."

Oscar was waiting for them at the eighteenth floor. "We need to go up one more."

"This is the floor we need," Ryan stated.

"Yeah, it opens onto a terrace, but the flat roof is one more floor up," Oscar reported.

Mango grabbed the rail and all three started up, huffing and puffing, sweat pouring off them despite the air conditioning. When they burst through the door to the nineteenth floor, they found an open office with long counters that held multiple computer workstations. They continued to the rear and entered a conference room. Oscar used the butt of his rifle to smash the lock on the French doors, and they stepped out onto a gravel terrace surrounded by a glass-and-steel safety railing. The flat roof occupied only half the space. The rest was open to a lower terrace one floor below that was surrounded by ten-foot-tall walls of glass.

A stiff breeze blew in from the ocean as Ryan walked

across the roof, glancing down at the moss growing between the brown pebbles. He leaned over the railing and saw the assortment of police vehicles that had surrounded the building.

"All right, Ricky. Show us some flyboy shit," Mango said.

"Roger that," the pilot said.

A moment later, a black Robinson R66 helicopter swooped in from the southeast, from over the Gulf of Panama, wove between the residential towers around the bank, and came to a hover with its starboard skid resting on the building's railing. Ryan shoved Mango into the helicopter and helped Oscar up next.

Just as Ryan grabbed for the helicopter's door, a hail of bullets shattered the glass railing next to him and Rick jerked the collective up, instinctively trying to protect the helicopter.

Ryan felt his stomach lurch as he grabbed desperately for the skid and missed.

CHAPTER NINETEEN

Ryan slammed into the railing and fell to the gravel, clutching his stomach. The gunmen switched their aim from him to the helicopter as Oscar returned fire with the Tavor he'd plucked from the dead goon in the bank.

"I'm coming back in," Rick called over the comms.

Still trying to catch his breath, Ryan said, "No. Get out of here. I'll make my own way out of the building."

He jumped up and ran toward the railing to the lower terrace, vaulted it easily, and dropped the ten feet to the grass-covered concrete below. Rolling with the impact, he came to his feet and pulled his pistol from its holster. He fired two shots into the door lock, slammed his shoulder into the door, and dove inside as the Trench Coats began firing at him.

"Get to the front terrace and I'll pick you up there," Rick said.

"Negative. I'll meet you later."

"How are you going to get out?" Mango asked.

"I don't know, but you guys need to leave before the police send another helicopter after you."

"Roger that," Rick said. "Stay safe, brother."

Ryan moved through the office and found the exit door. People who lived in the apartments above the twenty-second floor were now streaming down the stairs and jamming the elevators. He took a moment to drop his suit jacket and comms unit into a trash can before joining them.

As he made the turn down to the next level, he glanced over his shoulder and saw the crowd parting for the goon squad. He picked up the pace, screaming at people to move out of his way, but the goons didn't care if they wounded civilians as they raked the stairwell with bullets. The concrete acted like a funnel for both the people and the projectiles. Ryan heard ricochets singing off the walls above the cries of the injured. He kept running, trying to get through the crowd and away from the gunmen.

At the next exit door, he veered off to draw the goons out of the stairwell and prevent more casualties. The builder had broken this floor into four distinct office spaces, all of them empty. He tried the first door and found it locked, as were the rest. He smashed two of the glass doors and went through the second, hoping to separate the gunmen.

Squatting behind a desk where he had a view of the door, Ryan saw his plan had worked. The gunmen split up to search both the offices at the same time. Instead of shooting the goon who stepped into his office, Ryan retreated as the gunman advanced. Finally, he stopped with his back against the window of the last cubicle. He dropped to his knees and prepared to shoot as soon as his pursuer spun around the corner, but then he saw the gap under the desk, and he crawled through the opening.

On the other side, he paused and listened, holding his breath, and trying to quiet the beating of his heart in his ears. The gunman stopped abreast of Ryan and raised his weapon. With an evil smile on his face, the gunman swept the weapon back and forth, spraying the cubical where Ryan had just been with bullets and shattering the windows.

Ryan steadied his gun in both hands and shot the man in the head. He knew the gunfire would draw the second goon, and the man didn't disappoint when he entered the office and shouted for his companion. Before he could advance farther, Ryan dropped to his stomach, shot him in the foot, then put a round in his head when the goon bent over.

He went to the restroom, disassembled the pistol, and washed it with soap and water to clean away his prints before he buried it in the trash can. Carrying the magazine in his pocket, he went down a flight of steps and dropped it into another trash can, then made his way toward the building's exit.

The police had stopped the elevators, forcing everyone to take the stairs and leave through the lobby. When he stepped through the lobby door, he saw cops ushering the herd of people into a line, where they checked everyone's identification before they could leave the building. Glancing around, he saw no other way out, so he queued up and waited with everyone else.

The cop who asked for his identification was a sergeant in olive drab fatigues with a black armored vest and helmet. He sported an M4 rifle and a sidearm. Looking at Ryan's passport, he asked in English, "What's your business here, Mr. Parker?"

"I own a company called Maritime Recovery. I was looking to lease some space in the building."

"Where's your rental agent?"

"She didn't come with me," Ryan replied.

"Which space were you looking at?"

"It was on the twentieth floor. Although, after this fiasco, I don't think I want to rent here."

The cop wrote Ryan's passport information on a clipboard, then handed the little blue book back to him. "Your phone number, please?"

"Oh, yeah, hold on." Ryan dug a business card from his pocket and handed it to the cop, who recorded the details and handed the card back. If anyone bothered to call the number on the card, an answering service would take a message.

"Where are you staying in Panama City, sir?" the sergeant asked.

"The InterContinental Miramar on Balboa Avenue," Ryan answered as he scanned the lobby again for any sign of the gunmen.

"Very good, sir. If we have any more questions, someone will call you."

"Sure. Have a good one, Sergeant." Ryan walked out the door, positive there would be more questions than answers. He had a ton of them himself. Who did the gunmen work for? Had the rest of his team exfiltrated the area without incident? What was so important that the killers would risk so many innocent lives? He wouldn't get any answers if the cops threw him in jail, and there was no way in hell he was going to spend another minute in a Third World shithole of a prison.

Ryan walked outside and headed for a mall one street over from the bank. He knew he should run a surveillance detection route, or SDR. If there were gunmen in trench coats still chasing him, they probably had a handler directing them and plain clothes agents ready to trail him to his destination. Using an SDR, he could hopefully spot them before they saw him.

First, he needed to get his heart rate and breathing under control as the adrenaline ebbed. Stepping into a coffee shop, he ordered a cup of black coffee and sat so he could see out the window. No one seemed interested in him, so he stepped onto the sidewalk, still carrying the coffee, and headed toward a construction site. His goal was to check the cars to see if he could steal one, but on the way across the street, he heard a vehicle brake hard behind him and turned to see two men dodging around the hood of the stopped car, each holding a pistol. So much for an SDR. These guys were hot on his trail, and they didn't care who knew they were there.

Ryan threw away the cup of coffee as he sprinted up the street. Coming at him were two men on dirt bikes. He turned into the construction lot. The scorching sun had baked the dirt dry, and dust caked his pants and shirt as he dove and rolled between two parked cars. Behind him, the two bikers entered the lot and circled to find him. The foot patrol spread out to search through the parking lot. Ryan could see their feet when he looked under the cars.

Staying hunched over, Ryan ran to a scrap pile beside an unfinished parking garage that would form the base of the new skyscraper and grabbed a piece of rebar from it. As he turned to face his attackers, gunshots rang out, and the motorcycles spun and raced toward him. He hopped over the garage's low concrete wall and raced deeper into the unfinished structure.

The dirt bikes entered the garage, one roaring down the ramp to the underground levels and the other splitting off to search the upper stories. Ryan hid behind a thick support column and waited for the bike to come closer. As the rider sped toward him, Ryan gripped the rebar like he was Babe Ruth, calling his shot to center field.

At the last moment, he stepped out from behind the column and swung. The bar caught the biker in the chest and knocked him off the bike, which continued upright as Ryan stepped to the rider and delivered another body-blow with the rebar. He heard the motorcycle flop over and the engine rev while he whacked the rider again. The man lay still as

Ryan unbuckled his helmet and wrenched it off before he jerked the guy's pistol from his waistband.

With the helmet on and the pistol tucked away, Ryan ran to the bike, lifted it onto two wheels, and mounted it. He kicked it into first gear and spun it round, leaving a black rubber streak on the concrete as he headed for the exit. He tucked himself to the gas tank as he raced out of the parking garage, the boom of handguns echoing through the concrete canyons as he slid the bike sideways onto the street and twisted the throttle wide open.

During the week they'd spent trailing Valdez, he'd learned the main routes through town, and his team had established a plan to drive back to the eastern side of Panama, but as soon as he passed under the Pan-Am Highway and entered the tangle of suburban streets, Ryan was lost. He kept the throttle pinned as he weaved through traffic, always trying to aim north, knowing that eventually he would run into one of the two major arteries that paralleled the canal.

Soon, he had made so many turns he doubted anyone could have followed him. He slowed and pulled into a gas station. After filling the motorcycle's tank, he moved it to the side of the building, went inside, and purchased a laminated map of the country along with a bottle of water.

Back outside, he sipped water and studied the map. The original plan had been to exfil via Route Nine, but it was a toll road, which was not a problem in the rental van with a clean exit. But the op had gotten sloppy in a hurry, and he wanted to avoid the cameras at the toll booth. That meant taking a longer route, and once he had his bearings, he started the motorcycle and took off.

CHAPTER TWENTY

Route Three meandered through the mountains and villages along the canal. It was slow going. Even with multiple detours and stops to ensure he wasn't being followed, Ryan still made it to the outskirts of Colón in just under two hours.

When he crossed the newly opened Atlantic Bridge, north of the Gatún Locks and high above the Panama Canal, he knew he was almost home free. Fifteen minutes later, he parked the motorcycle in a thick stand of brush just off the road and walked the rest of the way to Shelter Bay Marina. He was hot and worried about the rest of his team. During the ride, he had stopped several times to call them, but had gotten no answer. He hoped it was because they had ditched their burner phones, and he'd tossed his into the canal as he'd crossed the bridge.

Stepping into the marina's mini mart, he paused for a moment to take in the air conditioning and realized just how sweaty and tired he was. After purchasing a bottle of water, he walked out into the heat and sat on the concrete steps, sipping the water, and looking at the boats moored in the marina.

Dark Water, Greg Olsen's blue-and-white Hatteras GT63, rode in her place at the end of one of the docks. Then he saw Mango come out of the salon, and relief swept over him.

After one last scan of the people along the wharf, Ryan walked down the dock.

Mango jumped out of the cockpit and embraced him. "Thank God! I didn't think you'd make it."

Ryan patted him on the back, and Mango let go. "Yeah, I'm here, but we need to get going."

"The boat is fueled and ready. All we need to do is clear Customs and we're gone."

While Rick and Mango cast off the lines and motored *Dark Water* across Limón Bay to Colón, Ryan took a hot shower and changed into clean clothes in the Hatteras's bunkroom. By the time he walked into the salon, they were pulling into the small marina near the port authority.

Two hours later and many dollars lighter from greasing the palms of slow-moving bureaucrats, they were back on the boat. Rick fired off *Dark Water*'s twin Caterpillar diesels and let them warm while Ryan and Mango cast off the lines. They eased out of the slip and idled through the maze of freighters anchored in Manzanillo Bay, waiting to transit the canal. When they hit the main channel, Rick threw the throttles forward, and they shot between the twin breakwaters of Limón Bay into the rolling Caribbean.

After passing the twelve-mile limit, Rick turned them on a northwestern heading that would take them directly to El Bluff, a tiny village marking the entrance to Bluefields Bay. At thirty knots, their destination was just nine hours away. In the meantime, Rick and Mango took the first watch on the bridge, and Ryan went below to find Oscar.

The Venezuelan had the file Valdez had given him open

on the table in front of him. Ryan fetched them both a cold beer before he sat down across from Oscar. "Find anything interesting?"

"The owner of the account is code named *El Armero*— The Armorer." Oscar spun the file toward Ryan.

He read through the paperwork. Under the original account, there was what Paul Langston had called his 'money tree.' The lawyer had set up multiple shell corporations and trusts, all owning a bank account in tax havens like Nevis, Malta, the Seychelles, or in the American states of Nevada and Delaware.

"It looks like a dead end," Oscar said.

Ryan closed the folder and leaned back in the settee, sipping his beer. There had to be a clue to the owner buried in the data, but they would need to dig into each business. Was there a link between the code name and the individual?

He opened his laptop and did an Internet search for the term 'The Armorer.' Most of the hits were for a female who played a character of the same name in a hit television series. He tried the Spanish version, and his computer automatically corrected the search to English, changing the meaning to 'gunsmith.' The lead article was about the eruption of the Nevado del Ruiz stratovolcano in Colombia, near the town of Gunsmith. The heat from the magma had melted the glaciers near the volcano's peak, sending mudslides and floods down to wipe out the village. None of his searches yielded anything useful regarding the man behind the money.

If they'd been able to extract the lawyer with them, they might have learned more from Valdez, but things had gotten out of hand. During the firefight, there hadn't been an opportunity to scrutinize the file and ask the lawyer more questions. And then Oscar had shot him in the head.

Closing the computer and leaning back in his chair, Ryan put his hands behind his head. "Each corporation has stockholders, directors—that sort of thing. If we can find one that will talk to us, we'll go from there."

"How do we do that?" Oscar asked.

"I think we need to call Barry."

Oscar rolled his eyes. "He's not my favorite person, but I wouldn't mind getting to know his associate."

"I think she's out of your league," Ryan said.

"If you can land Emily, I have a shot at Carmen."

"Touché, *amigo*." Ryan held out his bottle, and Oscar tapped it with his.

After taking a swig of beer, Ryan did some research himself. He woke up the laptop and started with the first Nevada corporation. Its address turned out to be a post office box in an obscure shipping and mailing facility that was nothing more than a storefront with mailboxes on every interior wall. The facility also offered a service where they scanned the mail and forwarded it to an email address, but there was no email address listed on the firm's incorporation documents. Using street view on a map application, he could virtually stand outside the office and, thanks to customers and the owner posting pictures of the business, he could also view the interior.

None of it gave him a clue as to who he was looking for.

The Delaware corporation was the same dead end. In researching the shell companies, he found that he could start his own company in these corporate, tax-friendly states for less than fifty dollars. Once he paid the money to an incorporation firm, they would assign a board of directors or managing partners, collect the mail, file tax paperwork, and anything else needed to keep the corporation current.

His next target was a P.O. box in Tortola, in the British Virgin Islands. He put the address into the Internet search bar and got eight pages of results, many of them dealing with the leak of the Panama Papers. The law firm Mossack

Fonseca had used the Tortola address to establish over six hundred thousand companies. Ryan let out a whistle of surprise and scrolled through the company names. Many were vague, and he wondered whether Mossack Fonseca had a division of people who did nothing but sit around all day and dream up company names. To him, it looked like one giant racket, especially when he saw the names Tea Kettle, Inc., or Harry Potter's Fortune.

Of all the things that baffled him was the fact that anyone who funneled their wealth through offshore corporations had to have complete trust in the lawyers and bankers that handled their affairs. The owners had to turn over control of the fictional companies to the lawyer, so it appeared that they were not the beneficiary of the houses, apartments, luxury cars, and massive bank accounts they owned.

While Ryan had an account in the Caymans with several million dollars in it, he had never trusted the bankers. He often checked his account balances, calculated the interest, and learned about the investments the bankers made for him. Sometimes, he had them explain an investment in substantial detail, so he understood exactly what was happening, and if it seemed over his head, he refused to let the bankers use his money.

After checking the Valdez file again, Ryan said, "Both the companies I've looked into are worth more than a million dollars apiece, and both are controlled by a trust called Rig Management."

"What does that mean?" Oscar asked.

"It means this is a spiderweb of a freaking mess, and I have no clue how to untangle it. As much as I hate having to go back to Barry, we're gonna have to."

Oscar groaned.

"My thoughts exactly." Ryan rose, went to the coffeemaker, and made a fresh pot before he poured it into a

Thermos. "I'm going topside. Feel free to take another crack at it."

Ryan stepped into the cockpit while Oscar pulled the computer in front of him. On the bridge, he found Mango at the helm and Rick staring through a pair of binoculars.

"What's up?" Ryan asked.

"Probably nothing." Rick handed him the binoculars and pointed to a speck on the horizon.

Ryan stared through the binos at another sportfisher, racing along behind them over a mile distant. "How long has it been there?"

"It fell in with us about thirty minutes ago."

"Do they have AIS?" Ryan asked, meaning the Automatic Identification System used to broadcast a ship's name, speed, coordinates, and a host of other information via satellite network.

"Negative," Mango said. "They're a small vessel like us and not required to have it."

"Or they turned it off," Ryan said.

"Maybe."

Ryan put the binoculars down. "How long do you want to stand watch?"

"I could use a nap." Rick yawned for emphasis.

"I'll take the helm," Ryan said.

"Thanks, man." Rick slapped Ryan on the shoulder and headed down the ladder to the cockpit.

Ryan watched through the binoculars again. The other boat was still a long way off and he couldn't make out any details about the vessel or who was aboard it. Where had it come from? Had it been in Colón or had it left from somewhere else? As far as he knew, there weren't any ports between Shelter Bay and Bocas del Toro, a good 150-mile run up the coast.

Then, as he watched, the fishing boat slowed and dropped

away. Ryan checked the radar and saw a few vessels far on the horizon, then he looked at the sonar and saw the long slope of the continental shelf, dropping from six thousand feet to nearly ten. It was the perfect place to catch enormous game fish, and Ryan would stop there if he were a charter guide, too.

For now, the threat had disappeared. He knew there was still plenty of action ahead of them as they searched for the man who'd given the kill orders for Oscar's team, but he didn't know if he could truly relax until this business was behind them.

They'd stirred the hornet's nest in Panama and attracted The Armorer's attention. Someone was willing to do whatever it took to keep their secrets, and now that Ryan had the bit between his teeth, he was more than willing to hunt them down.

CHAPTER TWENTY-ONE

During the run to Bluefields, Ryan had Oscar scan the documents they'd retrieved from Valdez's safe deposit box into the computer. Scott had left his Trident document kit with Ryan when he'd gotten off the plane in Texas City. Using the hand scanner, it only took a matter of minutes to run the device down one page after another and to have it appear as a PDF file on the computer. The technology impressed Oscar, and he said he had to use an ancient scanner-printer combination in his commander's office, which would have taken him hours to upload everything.

When Oscar finished, he called Ryan down from the bridge. Ryan encrypted the email and sent it to Barry Thatcher. A few minutes later, he received one from Barry, which included an outlandish price.

After reading it, Ryan whistled. "Oscar, how do you feel about parting with some of that cash you stole?"

"If it means that I find the killer, then yes."

"Well, it's going to cost a bundle."

With a shake of his head, Oscar said, "Your friend Barry is not cheap."

"No, he's not, but it will be worth it." Ryan went back to the bridge and sat behind the wheel, his feet up on the dash. They were miles from anywhere, and the vast Caribbean Sea rolled out to the horizon in every direction. He sipped coffee and thought about their next course of action.

Several hours later, Rick came up to the bridge to take the next watch. Ryan called Emily to give her an update on their location but told her little about what had happened in Panama, only that they were wading through the information they'd retrieved from the bank.

"When will you be back?" she asked.

"I'm not sure. We'll spend the night in Nicaragua and go from there. Barry is working on our file."

"Well, hurry back, sailor. I miss you."

"I miss you, too, babe. I gotta go. I love you."

"Love you, too," she replied.

Ryan hung up the phone and sat at the table, staring out the window at the setting sun. While it was nice to have someone waiting for him to return, he couldn't afford to get sentimental or let his guard down when he was operational.

It could only spell disaster for him and his team.

IT WAS LATE when Rick dropped anchor off Bluefields' municipal docks. The sportfisher they had seen earlier had not shown up again, nor had they observed any other vessels following them. All four men sacked out in *Dark Water*'s berthing compartments.

When Ryan awoke, it was broad daylight. After a shower, he climbed up to the salon. Rick and Oscar were already sitting at the galley island, eating bacon, eggs, and toast. Ryan poured himself a cup of coffee and scooped food onto a plate. Mango joined them, and when they finished breakfast, they unloaded the RIB from the *Dark Water*'s bow and headed for shore.

Not much had changed since the last time Ryan had been to Bluefields, and he doubted much would change even when they built the new port. The people wore either colorful clothes or blue jeans. Women carried their babes in wraps, and salesmen pushed carts loaded with fish, juices, and a variety of meats, vegetables, and fruits through the crowd while other vendors sold hot meals. As they walked up the street to the Oasis Casino and Hotel where Greg Olsen had ensconced himself in the top-floor suite, Ryan and Oscar each bought a freshly squeezed juice combination.

They found Greg Olsen, Shelly Hughes—Greg's girlfriend and chief operations officer for Dark Water Research—and a group of engineers poring over site surveys, location reports, and other data needed to make a comprehensive bid for building the new seaport.

Greg wheeled away from the table in his custom TiLite wheelchair and motioned them to join him in his other office, the master bedroom. Mango closed the door once everyone was inside, and they gave Greg a rundown of the last week's events in Panama.

"And you didn't get what you went for?" Greg asked when the story ended.

"We got a paper trail that stretches across the globe," Ryan explained. "I've got Barry Thatcher going through the docs."

"In the meantime, you also took a bunch of other files, right?"

"Yes," Ryan replied.

"What are your plans for them?" Greg asked.

"Nothing," Ryan said.

"Let's turn them over to Landis and Homeland," Greg said. "I'm sure they would love to get their hands on them."

"What about releasing them to the press?" Mango asked.

"Do you know a reputable reporter? Because I sure don't," Greg said.

"We could send them to the same reporters who handled the Panama Papers," Mango said.

"Let's let Landis handle it," Greg countered. "The government has been cracking down on money laundering and shell corporations for a while now."

"I'll pass them on," Ryan said.

"Give the hard copies to Landis," Greg ordered.

"Okay," Ryan agreed, not able to come up with a better idea.

"Now that I have you here, do you want to do some diving?" Greg asked. "I could use an extra hand for a few days."

"I don't have any of my gear, and we're in the middle of an operation."

"Your stuff is sitting over there in the corner." Greg pointed to a pile of dive gear. "They needed the room on *Peggy Lynn* for a new diver. Besides, it'll take some time for Barry to track down your shell corporations."

Ryan sat down on the bed beside Mango. "What do you guys want to do?"

"I do not want to stop this search," Oscar said. "This is *my* mission, and I will continue no matter what you do."

"If we have time off from this gig, I'd like to get my boat to St. Thomas," Mango said.

"Where is it?" Greg asked.

"Key West."

When Greg saw Rick's eyes light up, he said, "No, Rick. You're not going."

"*Come on*, man," Rick moaned.

"We've still got work to do here," Greg told him.

"I'm sick of this backwater country. I want to hop and

pop with Ryan and the gang."

"We could use him," Ryan said. "Even though he's a shit sailor."

Rick flashed Ryan his middle finger. "That's why I joined the Army, squid."

"Fine, Rick," Greg said with a sigh. "You can tag along."

Rick grinned and rubbed his hands together.

"I don't want to move a sailboat," Oscar said, crossing his arms. "We must continue our search for the man who ordered my team to be killed."

Ryan knew how he felt. If he could help Barry, then he'd be there with bells on, but the hacker hadn't called or asked for help. This mission—and the one before it—had required extensive satellite surveillance and hacking. Ryan knew enough about computers to do the basics, but he had no idea how to hack things. Perhaps it was a skill set he needed to learn. If he were to continue with this line of work, then he wouldn't need to rely on others.

Coming up with a compromise, Ryan said, "Let's give Barry time to work, and we'll move Mango's boat while we wait."

Oscar reluctantly agreed. The next morning, they flew to Key West, making a long bend out over the Gulf of Mexico to prevent them from flying through Cuban airspace. Once they landed, Ryan told Chuck to fly to St. Thomas. Chuck looked up with furrowed brows.

"Trust me," Ryan said. "Once Barry finds something, we're going to need you. I expect him to have a lead by the time we get there." He turned to Oscar and Rick. "This is your chance to go first class, otherwise we're in for a long, hard slog."

"If you don't mind," Rick said, "I think I'll go with Chuck. Us pilots gotta stick together."

"Whatever, grunt," Mango said, shouldering his bag. "Let's roll before the weather sets in."

CHAPTER TWENTY-TWO

Ryan shook hands with Chuck and Rick on the Key West tarmac outside the Beechcraft King Air. "I'll see you guys down there," he said.

He, Oscar, and Mango headed for the taxi stand to ride across the island. He knew the two pilots would find a party before the sun set on Mallory Square.

The trio's first stop was at a grocery store, where they stocked up on canned goods, fresh meat, vegetables, and beer. After stowing their purchases on Mango's Lagoon 52, *Margarita*, they topped off the boat's fuel and freshwater tanks. They had also decided to follow the fastest route. Known to sailors as I-65, the sixty-fifth meridian was a direct route south to St. Thomas.

Sailing past Fort Zachary Taylor, they made a left turn and headed northeast for the northern tip of Andros Island, then made their way to Spanish Wells on St. George's Cay, the last stop before the wild Atlantic. They fueled the boat again and started east, beating hard against the current and the wind.

Ryan had been right. It was a tough slog against gigantic

waves and gusting winds. When they were seven hundred miles off the coast of Florida, they turned due south.

Ten days after leaving Key West, they tied up at American Yacht Harbor, sunburnt and exhausted.

Emily and Jennifer met them at the dock. Ryan accompanied Emily and Oscar to *Windseeker*, ready for a long rest, while Jennifer stayed on *Margarita* with her husband.

In the *Windseeker*'s cabin, Emily told Ryan how she and Jennifer had been helping Barry and Carmen by making phone calls to various business entities and visiting the post office box in Road Town. It had been a fruitless trip because they couldn't tell who went near the box. She had put her investigator skills to use while Barry and Carmen tackled the online world. Ryan could tell they had learned something during their search, but she wouldn't tell him what it was. He fell asleep late, dreaming about the shoot-out in Panama City.

Morning dawned cool and windy as a storm front crossed the ocean from Africa. The weather service expected the storm to turn into a hurricane and track north into the Atlantic. Ryan hoped it didn't turn to the east, otherwise he and Mango would need to find a place to weather the storm aboard their boats.

When Ryan and the others gathered on the dock, they loaded into the rented van and drove across the island to Barry's place. Emily and Jennifer went through the garden without issues while Ryan, Oscar, and Mango tripped the metal detector. The hacker told them to come up to the office without leaving their sidearms on the table.

Barry and Carmen stood beside the flat-top computer table when the group walked into the office. Oscar placed several banded stacks of one-hundred-dollar bills on the hacker's desk and stepped back to let the man count the currency. Instead, Barry swept it into a drawer and walked back to the table.

"Emily says you have something for us," Ryan said.

"First, let me explain a bit about what we did, so you know what you're paying for."

Ryan didn't really care about the legwork the hacker had done, but he listened anyway, realizing he could learn something for the next job.

"We started with public records, searching for websites and email addresses. Once we found a web presence, we ran an algorithm to look for similarities. When the computer flagged something, I had Emily, Carmen, and Jennifer make phone calls or send emails. At some points, they were all on the phone, trying to connect with the signatories of the shell corps. Then we started mapping the network."

The hacker pressed a button on the screen and a diagram appeared. It looked like a pyramid, with lines extending off both sides to other entities. "The file you got from the lawyer assisted us greatly, but there was still a lot of research involved."

"What did you find?" Oscar asked impatiently.

Barry gave Oscar a brief glance of annoyance for interrupting him. "There are layers and layers of shell corporations and trusts, making this a giant puzzle. I'm not sure how Valdez kept track of it all. His files don't include any of the smurfing that Langston was doing, so the picture is even bigger than the network map I have here. What I can say is that it appears as if someone wired a considerable sum of money from a bank on the Crimean Peninsula to a bank in Switzerland before Valdez took over the accounts. Money comes from other sources as well, but *this* is the big one." He pointed at the bottom of the pyramid, representing the money from the Crimean bank. "It's the granddaddy of everything else."

"So how do we use this map to help us?" Ryan asked.

Barry minimized the network map and brought up a map

of the Caribbean. He pointed a finger at Grand Cayman. "Once a month, an automatic wire transfer from New Zealand puts the same amount into a bank on Grand Cayman. We backtracked the money through that entire jumble to Valdez in Panama, and it's funded by the original Swiss bank account."

"Where are you going with this?" Ryan asked as the hacker continued to ramble on about the technicalities of tracing the money.

Barry adjusted his leather bracelet, then tapped on a small box beside Grand Cayman. "So, the New Zealand payments go into a trust called Cayman Blue. The dumbasses named it after the house held in the company's name."

The box opened to show a single-story white stucco home with a white barrel-tile roof. In the back was a pool and steps cut into the rock down to the ocean. Next, Barry opened an Internet window which referenced an old real estate listing. Ryan and Oscar stood side by side as they scrolled through the pictures of the interior and exterior.

"Who lives here?" Oscar asked.

Barry grinned. "I'm glad you asked. I couldn't get a clear picture of anyone using a satellite view, so I ended up hacking the bank records. There's a debit card linked to the account, and four days ago, there was a withdrawal from an ATM in George Town."

Still smiling, he opened yet another file and displayed the photos taken by the ATM camera. "That is *Generalissimo* Esteban—"

"Rincone," Oscar finished.

"You know him?" Ryan asked.

"He was commanding general of the army until he disappeared about five years ago."

Ryan turned to Barry. "Is he The Armorer?"

The hacker shrugged. "I don't know. If you look at the network map, you'll see that Rincone's trust is an offshoot."

Ryan tapped the screen to reopen the network map and studied it. The Cayman Blue Trust was three layers deep from the original account. He wondered why the general was getting a payoff. "What do we know about Rincone?"

Carmen tapped the screen and opened the file they had accumulated on the general. "According to the U.S. Department of Justice," she said, "he's wanted on drug trafficking and money laundering charges. He's also wanted in connection to an oil price-fixing scheme."

Oscar had nothing to add.

Mango had been silent throughout the whole discussion until he said, "It looks like we need to go to Grand Cayman."

"Actually," Jennifer said, "there's a villa for rent less than a mile down the road from Rincone's place. We made reservations."

"For *when?*" Ryan asked incredulously.

"Next week." Emily grinned at him. "We're all going. Barry is staying here, but Carmen will provide us with on-site support."

"Okay," Ryan said. "I'll give Chuck a call."

"I forgot to tell you last night, but he and Rick went back to Nicaragua," Emily said. "Greg called them back on some urgent business. Rick didn't elaborate and I didn't ask."

"I know a guy who has a plane you could rent," Barry volunteered.

"Good, get him on the horn," Ryan said.

A few minutes later, he'd chartered a twin-engine Piper Chieftain Panther to fly them to Grand Cayman. While Ryan wanted to leave immediately, Jennifer and Emily told them they had other plans. They took Mango and Ryan to look at several houses either for rent or sale and talked about which marinas had the best amenities for the potential customers of their charter business.

While Ryan was more than happy to spend time with Emily and his friends, he kept thinking about the mission, hashing out a plan to grab General Esteban Rincone and extradite him to the United States.

The net was finally closing.

CHAPTER TWENTY-THREE

Grand Cayman

The Piper Chieftain touched down at Owen Roberts International Airport five hours after leaving St. Thomas. Once Ryan and the others were off the plane, the pilot refueled and took off on the return leg.

For probably the fiftieth time since leaving *Windseeker*, Ryan patted his pockets to ensure he hadn't left his pocketknife or anything gun-related in them. It was illegal to possess both firearms and knives in the Cayman Islands. He hoped the authorities wouldn't care about the CRKT tactical folder and Spyderco dive knife he'd packed with his scuba gear.

As they made their way through Customs, expedited by the private ground handling facility, a Customs and Border Patrol officer scanned their passports and checked their luggage. Once they were outside the air terminal, they boarded a shuttle to a car rental agency, where Ryan rented a

Jeep Wrangler and Mango received a Kia Sorento. With the SUVs packed, they headed across town.

Their first stop was a café across the street from the ATM where Rincone had appeared on camera. They ate a late lunch and kept a sharp watch on the surrounding crowds. Ryan noticed Oscar was especially vigilant and wondered if the Venezuelan wasn't telling him everything. If Rincone knew Oscar and spotted him, then the operation might be over before they got started and Rincone would go to ground again. If they let him slip away now, they had no other leads as to The Armorer's actual identity.

They couldn't afford for that to happen.

He leaned toward Oscar and asked in Spanish, "Is there something you're not telling me?"

"What do you mean?"

"Do you know this guy personally? Can Rincone recognize you, and if he does, will he bolt?"

"I have met him once. But it was during a Special Forces operation to stop smugglers along the Colombian border. I was in uniform, and I had my face blacked out."

Mango leaned into the conversation and said in hushed English, "What are we whispering about?"

Switching to English, Ryan said, "Oscar has met the general before, but he doesn't think Rincone will recognize him."

"He can stay at the house with me," Carmen volunteered. "We're already paired off. It would look weird if we didn't appear to be a couple."

Oscar grinned. "I would like *that* very much."

Carmen eyed Oscar with a look of disapproval. "*Se mira pero no se toca.*"

Mango asked what she had said, and Ryan, laughing, said, "'*You can look, but you can't touch.*'"

After they'd finished their meal, they drove to the villa

and checked in with the real estate agent. She gave them a tour, and everyone dropped their bags in their respective bedrooms. Oscar grinned at Carmen as he tossed his bag on her bed. She shot him a look that said, *I will kill you*.

The girls took the Kia to the local market and purchased food to last the next few days. Ryan went for a swim. While he had formulated a plan back on St. Thomas, he needed to recon the general's house to see if it would unfold as he'd envisioned. He waded out to chest-deep water, then pulled on his fins, mask, and snorkel. With his kit on, he struck out east toward the target's home, which was less than a mile away. The scenery below him was a spectacular reef, alive with colorful coral and fish. He also saw plenty of plastic trash, a common sight along the shores of every Caribbean island.

It didn't take long for him to make the swim to Rincone's house. As he floated in on the waves, watching the world beneath him, Ryan occasionally lifted his head to check Rincone's security and the access to the house from the sea. Ryan now saw there was only one way up from the water: the steps made of cemented rocks and coral he'd seen in the overhead photos. The stairs led up to a small seating area and then up to the pool deck. The cliffs on both sides of the steps looked to be a good six feet in height, and red mangroves grew thick along the clifftops and around the stone retaining walls that surrounded the pool patio.

Testing the security, Ryan swam slowly to the steps and sat on them to remove his fins.

"You need to leave, sir," a voice said from behind him, moments after he'd sat down.

Ryan turned and looked at a tall man wearing khaki slacks and a polo shirt. His sleeves were snug around his thick arms, and he had short black hair. His facial features told Ryan that the guy was from a former Eastern Bloc country.

"I said you need to leave, sir," the man repeated with more authority and a hint of a threat.

Putting on his best grin, Ryan said in a Southern accent, "Ah, shucks. This ain't 657 Old Robin Road?"

"No, sir. You're too far east."

"You mind if I walk on up to the road? I've been swimming a far piece, and I sure am tired."

"No, sir. I can't let you walk through this property, but if you swim west, you'll see another set of stairs. You can walk to the road from there."

"You sure are mighty nice. I'm Rufus Smith. I came down here on vacation. The wife wanted to get this secluded house, but not me. I wanted to stay over on Seven Mile Beach, look at them girls in the bikinis, you know what I mean?"

"Sir, you need to leave. *Now*." The security man reached behind his back.

Holding up his hands, Ryan said, "No need for getting out your shootin' iron, son. I'm a-goin'." He put on his fins and slid back into the water. The security guard watched him swim away.

Ryan found the steps the security guard had mentioned not far to the west along a narrow strip of beach. There was a walkway built into the top of the retaining wall and he leaned against the warm rocks, enjoying the view and the breeze blowing off the water. Having never been to the Cayman Islands before, all this was new to him, and while working in a tropical paradise, he liked to savor every moment he could.

That didn't mean he would let his guard down, though, because he was still visually searching for a way through the palms and shrubs between this property and Rincone's, and Rincone's man was watching him, too. He turned and appraised the tiny house set well back from the water and set to the side of the property closest to Rincone's. It looked abandoned, with its windows and door shuttered. Finally, he slipped on his fins again and swam back to his own villa.

Mango stood by the pool with a beer in his hand as Ryan walked up, holding his snorkeling gear. "Well?"

Ryan smiled. "We extract him by sea."

CHAPTER TWENTY-FOUR

The plan Ryan outlined for everyone was simple. They would have a team from Trident meet and equip Ryan, Mango, and Oscar with assault gear, including firearms. They would assault at night, from both the road and from the sea, surrounding the house and snaring its occupants. Once they had Rincone in custody, they would get him to the boat and extradite him to the United States.

"Sounds simple enough," Mango agreed.

Ryan summarized what he wanted everyone to do. Carmen was to hack Rincone's security system so she could turn it off just before the raid. Oscar was to go in with the road team and positively identify Rincone while Ryan accompanied the waterborne team. They needed a place for Mango to act as overwatch with a sniper rifle, and Jennifer and Emily would run a drone to search for any threats that might approach while the assault was underway.

With everything settled, he dispatched his people to find the best routes and positions to fulfill their roles. He then called Jinks at Trident and asked if the Samoan could send a team and put in place the logistics they would need to extract the former Venezuelan general. Jinks said he would begin as soon as they hung up, as he knew time was of the essence.

Ryan's next phone call was to Floyd Landis.

The DHS agent answered with a growl. "To what do I owe this honor?"

Ryan said, "General Esteban Rincone."

There was silence on the line, except for Landis clicking his pen in and out, a habit he had when he was thinking. The old agent probably had on his usual wrinkled suit with his feet up on his desk. Ryan knew the agent's steely blue eyes had a military hardness about them that matched his flattop haircut. He'd been on the receiving end of more than a few of the old Army Ranger's hard stares.

"Hello?" Ryan said.

"What do you know about Rincone?" Landis responded.

"He disappeared from Venezuela about five years ago. No one has seen him since the U.S. government indicted him for drug trafficking and bribery. The Venezuelans want him back, and the U.S. wants him to stand trial for his crimes. The State Department has issued a one-million-dollar bounty for him."

"So, why are you calling me about *him*?" Landis asked.

Ryan smiled. "Do I get to collect the bounty for finding him?"

"Are you telling me you know where he is, Ryan?"

"Yes. Do you want his address?"

"Why are you being so forthcoming, Weller? That's not like you."

"Because I'm going to snatch him, and I want to hand him to you when we get him back to the States."

"You get him, and I'll have a rendition team ready."

Ryan told the DHS agent his plan.

"Gitmo sounds like an excellent home for him," Landis said. "Plus, you're close to there."

"Sounds good. While Jinks is bringing a ship, can you send an agency plane to stand by at the George Town airport in case we need a fallback plan?"

"Yeah, just tell me when."

"Thanks. Can I ask one more favor?" Ryan asked.

Landis sighed, then said, "Name it."

"I'd like to have a Cayman Islands cop with the assault team. Just to make things kosher."

"I'll make a few calls. Can I have him call you on this number?"

"Yes. Thanks, Landis."

Before Ryan could hang up, Landis said, "The marshals put the Langstons in Witness Protection and they turned their documents over to the U.S. Attorney's Office."

"That's great news," Ryan said. "Thanks for getting them in."

"I'd add it to the list of favors that you owe me, but the papers should prove to be an intelligence boon."

Ryan chuckled. "Well, I'll owe you for helping with this one."

"Just bring Rincone in. That will be thanks enough."

Ryan ended the call and walked into the house. Carmen was on her computer, with Oscar hovering close by. Despite her obvious relationship with Barry, Oscar still had the hots for her.

Emily had a set of drone controls strapped to her torso and was using the joystick to maneuver it as she and Jennifer watched the screen.

After grabbing a bottle of water from the fridge, Ryan crowded in beside Emily and Jennifer to see an overhead view of Rincone's property. The man he'd spoken to was still on the pool deck, plus there was another guard near the front gate.

"Fly over that abandoned house beside Rincone's," Ryan said.

Emily manipulated the joystick and flew the quadcopter over the house he'd seen from the seawall. There was a low stone wall surrounding the property on three sides and a high white wooden gate across the entrance to the drive, which was just a sandy path leading to the house. The tiny structure with its shingled roof and tan stucco walls sat next to an empty lot that separated it from Rincone's place. Thick stands of mangroves and bushes heavy with yellow flowers grew in the lot, making sneaking through them a challenge. The rest of the abandoned house's yard was open, leaving little cover for either the assault team or Rincone's guards.

They spotted Mango walking along the road, scouting locations for his sniper hide. Ryan knew suitable spots were in short supply from his own reconnaissance of the area via satellite maps and his quick swim along the coast.

Ryan laughed as Emily buzzed Mango with the drone. He ducked, then ran after the quadcopter, swatting at it like it was a mosquito before using both hands to flip off the camera. Emily wiggled the drone back and forth, then raced it back to their house.

Mango again gave them the finger when he came in the door, then gave them his recon report. The only good perch was in a house two hundred yards to the west of Rincone's, and he didn't think the owners would let him post up there while they slept tight in their beds. Even if he could gain access, there was no guarantee he could cover the team effectively because of all the vegetation growing between the houses.

"We'll just have to do without," Ryan decided.

"When we take him offshore, what will be waiting for us?" Mango asked.

"I'm not sure yet," Ryan said. "Jinks is making those arrangements."

"If it's big enough, I could use it as a gun platform."

"Possibly," Ryan agreed. "We'll know more when Jinks calls back."

CHAPTER TWENTY-FIVE

While Jinks was preparing to deploy his team from Texas City, Ryan had Carmen look up the property records of the houses surrounding Rincone's. They were all held in trusts or shell corporations. She tracked several of them to their actual owners, who lived in either the States or Europe, and the owners used local real estate companies to rent the properties when not using them. The one she had the most trouble with was the house Mango had identified as the best shooting perch.

After a day of searching records, including real estate sales, property taxes, and tracing shell corporations, Carmen could find nothing concrete about the owners. Using drone and foot surveillance of the area, they decided from the activity and the accumulation of things around the house that the owners lived there, and they turned to other matters. Something nagged Ryan about it, but he couldn't put his finger on the problem. Maybe it was the lack of transparency or just the amount of obfuscation that people went through to hide who they were.

While Emily was making another pass over the house

with the drone, a car pulled into the driveway of their own villa, and a man got out. Even though he wasn't in uniform, everything, from his movements to his bearing, screamed 'police' to Ryan. He was of average height with a thick build, a round tan face, and close-cropped hair.

"That must be Whittaker," Ryan said. The two men had spoken briefly on the phone, and Ryan had given him the address for the rental house.

When Ryan answered the door, the man flashed a badge and introduced himself as Acting Superintendent Todd Whittaker.

They shook hands and Ryan invited him inside. "Thanks for coming, Superintendent."

Whittaker's voice was low and gravelly. "I'm here because my superior asked me to cooperate."

Ryan took him to the pool patio table, where they took seats under the umbrella with Emily and Jennifer. He showed Whittaker a photograph of Rincone and explained that they were there to extradite the general.

Whittaker looked through the sliding glass door at their computers and drone equipment. "You're not U.S. military or members of their law enforcement agencies. Are you bounty hunters?"

"We are contract employees of Homeland Security."

"This is highly unusual, to say the least, but my superior got a call, and here I am. So, how can I assist you?"

"I would like to bring a team from offshore, take the house, and send them and Rincone back to the ship," explained Ryan.

Whittaker nodded. "And you would like my help with what?"

"First, I can't bring weapons into your country without it being a felony, so I need your approval. Second, I need your cooperation to cordon off the roads. If something goes wrong, we don't want Rincone and his men to escape."

"I see."

"Rincone is a slippery devil, Superintendent," Ryan said. "The third thing I ask of you is to involve as few people as possible in this."

"Are you suggesting the Royal Cayman Islands Police Service is corrupt?" Whittaker asked.

"Everyone has a price, and Rincone has the money to pay it. I'm sure he has a couple of RCIPS men in his pocket."

Whittaker looked thoughtful as he rubbed his chin with the knuckle of his index finger.

"Getting Rincone off your island is in your best interest," Emily said. "If he's paying your men, you want that to stop."

"Yes, I do," Whittaker conceded. "I will mobilize the Specialist Operations department to assist you."

"What assets do you have?" Ryan asked.

"I will deploy two squads of the Firearms Response Unit to block the road and have the Marine and Air Operations units standing by. How soon will this take place? I will need time to gather my people."

"Let me make a phone call and I can give you an exact time frame."

"Please do," Whittaker said.

Ryan retrieved his phone and stepped inside to talk to Jinks. When the retired SEAL came on the line, Ryan asked him how long it would be before he and his team arrived in Grand Cayman.

"We're leaving Texas City right now," Jinks said. "The captain says twenty-eight hours at cruising speed; twenty-four if he can push forty knots all the way. We'll need to refuel once we get there."

"What the hell are you riding on that makes forty knots?"

"She's a fifty-seven-meter catamaran work vessel.

Normally, she delivers workers to oil rigs, but I commandeered her for this trip. I've got two twenty-foot RIB boats on the aft deck and a cargo container to house your prisoner."

Ryan stepped to the door and motioned for Whittaker to join him. When the Superintendent arrived, Ryan asked him, "Can you make expedited arrangements to fuel the ship at the Port of George Town?"

"I will have to make some calls, but yes, we should be able to do that."

Into the phone, Ryan said, "Head for the port, and I'll meet you there."

"Roger that," Jinks said. "I'll call you when we're close."

The call ended, and Ryan turned to Whittaker. "They'll be here between twenty-four and thirty hours, depending on weather and speed."

Whittaker nodded. "I want to go over your plan one more time, so I know where everyone will be."

They went to the kitchen, where Ryan spread a map of the island across the table. He pointed to locations where he thought the roadblocks would be most effective, and Whittaker asked about evacuating the surrounding homes. Ryan vetoed the idea; he didn't want to alert Rincone that anything was out of the ordinary, and the risk to innocents was minimal. With them hitting the house in the dead of the night, everyone should be at home, sleeping. But all the same, he was thankful Rincone had picked one of the more secluded spots on the island and not a high-rise penthouse in the heart of George Town.

After discussing some finer points of the plan, Whittaker left, promising to have everything ready in less than thirty hours.

Ryan walked down to the water and stood with his hands in his pockets. The ocean looked like a giant lake, stretching to the horizon, and he prayed the weather held for their operation. He went over the plan again in his head, working on details and trying to cover all the possibilities. He believed the plan was solid, but he also knew that Mr. Murphy had a habit of wrecking the best laid plans.

And on a night operation, Murphy always made an appearance.

CHAPTER TWENTY-SIX

Dark Water Research's catamaran workboat, *Amarillo*, arrived in George Town twenty-seven hours after Ryan and Jinks had spoken over the phone. Ryan, Oscar, and Mango met the vessel at the port and stood with Jinks, watching the fueling operation, until Acting Superintendent Todd Whittaker arrived.

In the cabin on *Amarillo*'s main deck, they met with the twelve other members of the Trident rendition team. Ryan knew some of them from previous missions. He shook hands with Scott Gregory and Aston Dent, a tall African American who had served with Jinks in SEAL Team Six. Even in his black battle dress uniform, or BDUs, he looked dapper. He would lead the landing party while Scott would go in with Oscar on the road team.

Jinks had pinned a map to a bulkhead, and they used it to decide on the placement of Whittaker's forces. With the plans complete, Whittaker departed, and the *Amarillo* pulled away from the dock.

The captain rounded the northwestern tip of Grand Cayman and stood the *Amarillo* fourteen miles out to sea, beyond the island's maritime limits, while the team prepared for their op. Once they'd performed final weapons checks and ensured their loadouts were ready, they relaxed for the next six hours. They would launch the raid at four in the morning when the guards would be sleepy and ready for their shift to end.

At three-thirty, the *Amarillo*'s captain moved her to within a quarter mile of the shore. The men unloaded the two RIB boats and raced toward Grand Cayman. Green Team, the land force, headed for Ryan's villa. They passed over communications earpieces to Emily, Jennifer, and Carmen so they could keep track of the action as it unfolded.

Ryan and Aston positioned their Blue Team boat just offshore and watched the Rincone residence through binoculars. Ryan radioed Mango, who was in position on the roof of the *Amarillo*'s bridge with an Accuracy International AT sniper rifle chambered in .338 Lapua. "RoboCop, do you see the guard by the pool?"

"I've got him," Mango replied.

"When I signal, take him out."

"Copy that."

Blue Team waited in the shifting RIB boat as Scott's Green Team moved up the road toward Rincone's.

Once they were in place near the gate, Scott radioed, "Green Team set."

"Copy," Ryan replied. "Hold one." He ordered the RIB driver to put the nose of the boat against the steps to Rincone's pool. Just before it touched, he said into the radio, "Now, RoboCop. Now, Green Team."

Mango fired, and his target folded over as the bullet struck him square in the chest. At the same time, Green Team cut the chain on the driveway gate and pushed it open. As Scott spun into the front yard, he shot the guard there with a three-round burst from his suppressed Heckler and Koch MP5.

"Green Team ready to breach," he radioed as his men stacked up behind him in a gun train at the house's front door.

Ryan, Aston, and the rest of their team ran up the steps, fanning out to cover the surrounding yard.

"Breach now," Ryan said.

Simultaneously, Scott and Aston blew the front and rear doors open with demolition charges. The two teams swept through the house with their bright tactical lights blazing on the foregrips of their MP5s. With quick efficiency, they dispatched the remaining guards and entered Rincone's bedroom.

They found Rincone in bed, disoriented from the noise and the light.

Oscar pushed his way into the room and nodded to Ryan. "That's him."

Scott and Ryan dragged the former Venezuelan Army general out of bed and secured his hands behind his back with flex cuffs. With a cordon of men spread out to guard the grounds, Ryan, Aston, and Oscar followed behind two of the team members as they marched Rincone outside and across the pool deck.

Just as they reached the stairs to the waiting boat, Rincone's head snapped to the side, and brains, blood, and bone erupted from his skull. The bullet that plowed through his head struck Bill Kirshen, the Trident operator on the other side of him, and both collapsed to the ground.

"*Shooter!*" everyone screamed.

"Where? Where the *hell* did that come from?" Scott yelled.

"He's in the house to the west," Mango replied. "The one I said would make a good hide."

"*Shit!*" Ryan screamed. "Green Team: get down there, *now*. Blue Team: rally to the boat."

A chorus of acknowledgments came across the net.

Aston ordered two men to stay with Kirshen while Blue Team climbed aboard their RIB and raced toward the house where the sniper had taken his shot from.

"What's going on?" Whittaker asked over the communications set.

"A sniper just shot Rincone," Ryan said. "We're going after him."

"We'll converge on the house," Whittaker said.

"No," Ryan yelled. "Stay at your post. I say again, *stay at your post*. Watch for anyone trying to leave the area."

"Copy," Whittaker replied.

The RIB driver ran the boat to the steps carved from the island's native rock and the team charged up them, spreading out on the rear lawn of the sniper's home.

An explosion came from the front of the house, and Ryan heard Scott order members of Green Team to guard the front gate before transmitting, "Green stacked and racked."

"Roger. Blue Team breaching from the rear."

Twin explosions rocked the house as the breaching charges shattered doorknobs and blew out ornamental glass. Both teams spilled in, laser beams flashing through the smoke left by the explosives in full repeat of the operation that had just taken place two hundred yards down the road.

"Scott, take the wing to your left," Ryan ordered as he spun toward the hallway on his left.

The teams cleared the house, but it was empty. The only sign that the sniper had been there was a shooting bench inside the upper room with a Blaser R93 rifle resting on it.

"Don't touch anything," Ryan ordered. "Everyone fall back to the boats. Whittaker, we need your forensics team in here."

They turned the sniper's hide over to the RCIPS, and Ryan, Mango, and Oscar gave all their assault gear but their handguns to the Trident team as they returned to the *Amarillo*. The three men walked with Scott Gregory to Rincone's house. They found Whittaker's Firearms Response Unit had taken up positions around the property, and Whittaker himself stood on the pool deck, looking at the dead bodies of Rincone and Bill Kirshen, who had bled out despite the best efforts of his comrades to provide medical assistance.

Whittaker rubbed his chin with his knuckle. "This was not how you expected things to go, was it, Weller?"

"No, sir," Ryan said, then thought, *Murphy, you bastard*.

"What do you want to do?" Whittaker asked.

"Have your CSIs look at the sniper hide, and do whatever investigation you need to with Rincone," Ryan said. "We'd like to get Kirshen back to his family as soon as possible."

"Can you take him back on your ship?" Whittaker asked.

Scott told them they could, and he radioed for the RIB to bring a body bag and a flag for their fallen comrade. Jinks was the first to get off the RIB. His face was ashen as he squatted beside Kirshen and looked beneath the blanket they had draped over him.

Ryan crouched beside Jinks and put a hand on his friend's shoulder. Together, they stared at the youthful face frozen forever in time by the sniper's bullet. Ryan hadn't known him, but it was still hard to lose a team member on a mission. He had to have been a first-class operator to deploy with the Trident teams, and that made him all right in Ryan's book.

After a few silent moments, the two men rose and laid out the body bag. They placed Kirshen gently inside and zipped it closed. The men who had come with Jinks helped lift Kirshen onto a stretcher before covering him with the American flag. One of the men was openly weeping at the loss of his friend, and it didn't help Ryan as he struggled to maintain his decorum.

He scrunched his lips together, fighting back his emotions, and helped lift the litter. They carried the stretcher silently to the water and waded out to the RIB. Ryan's throat constricted, and tears filled his eyes. No man should have to die for the sins of another, not when they'd won the battle and were on the verge of victory.

As the boat drove away, Ryan stood in the water, a cold ache in his gut and tears on his cheeks. Mrs. Kirshen had lost her baby boy today, and it was all because he had failed to prepare properly for the mission. He hadn't accounted for the possibility of a rogue sniper, and he would carry the blame for the rest of his life, adding Kirshen's name to the list of other men he'd lost in combat. Those faces haunted him, as did those of the men he'd killed.

Splashing water onto his face, Ryan smoothed back his hair and wiped away the tears. He could wallow in pity later.

Right now, he had work to do.

CHAPTER TWENTY-SEVEN

Ryan stepped out of the water and returned to the pool deck, careful not to drip water on the crime scene. He called Carmen and told her to join them at Rincone's house. He wanted her to look at the computers from both properties for a lead as to whoever was paying Rincone's trust fund.

Oscar stood in the kitchen with Whittaker. Ryan motioned for him to come outside, and the little Venezuelan marched up to him.

"How could you let this happen?" The anger was clear in Oscar's voice. "How are we going to find the person who killed my men now?" He started cursing in Spanish and smacked the pool's bar top several times.

Ryan understood why he was upset. He was angry with himself, but he couldn't change things. "I screwed up."

Jabbing a finger into Ryan's chest, Oscar screamed, "You're right. This is all your fault."

Ryan took a deep breath and said, "Yeah, it is. I should have secured that house and accounted for the sniper."

"There's no use in blaming anyone," Whittaker said,

joining them. "It happens to the best of us. We thought we had a solid plan, and things ended badly."

The men stood in a triangle, staring at each other. Ryan could feel the righteous indignation seething off Oscar. They had lost their chance to interrogate Rincone and find The Armorer. This entire operation seemed to be one screw-up after another.

They'd been chasing the tail of the snake by messing with these low-level players. Now, it was time to find the head and stamp on it. With that in mind, Ryan decided they wouldn't make a move until they knew for certain *who* the head of the operation was.

When Ryan told Oscar his new plan, the Marine wasn't happy, but he nodded in understanding. Too many men had needlessly lost their lives, thanks to this shadow organization.

The problem now was that the crime scenes were under the RCIPS's jurisdiction, and they were under no obligation to help Ryan or his team. In fact, the forensics unit had kicked Carmen off Rincone's computers and packed them away in cardboard cartons to take to headquarters. They'd done the same at the sniper hide.

"Will we get to examine the evidence?" Ryan asked Whittaker.

"I will have to speak to my superiors, but I'm sure we can arrange something," the superintendent said.

"I need access to those computers," Ryan said.

"That's not possible."

"Why not? You just said you could arrange it."

"My people will look at them and let you know what they find."

Ryan looked past Whittaker to Carmen, who had just come out of the bedroom. She'd had at least thirty minutes in there before the forensic teams had arrived. After shrugging, she shook her head and went out the front door.

A sense of hopelessness swept over Ryan. "Come on, Oscar," he said. "There's nothing more we can do here. I'll call you tomorrow, Superintendent."

The two men walked along the road to their villa. Neither of them said a word until they reached the driveway where Mango was leaning against a gate pillar.

He grinned at Ryan and Oscar. "Evening, gents. Can I see your papers, please?"

Oscar muttered something in Spanish as he brushed past him and went in the house.

Mango and Ryan closed the gate and went around to the pool. Together, they stood staring into the darkness of the sea.

"You can't blame yourself for this, bro," Mango said. "We all looked at that house and said it wasn't a threat."

"I should have known."

"You're not clairvoyant. None of us are. Chalk it up to Murphy's Law."

"Kirshen can't chalk it up to Murphy. He's dead because I screwed up."

Mango grabbed Ryan by the shoulders. "Dude, *you* didn't screw anything up. This was a clean op from the start. There was no way of knowing there was a sniper in that house. We all said it was good to go. Whatever pity party you're throwing for yourself is not helping anyone, most of all you."

Ryan cast off his friend's hands and backed away, shaking his head. "I can't do this right now." He walked down the steps and into the water. His boots and clothes were already soaked from carrying Kirshen to the RIB boat, so he didn't bother to take them off as he waded chest-deep into the warm water, trying to let it absolve him of his sins.

He heard a splash, and Emily waded up behind him. She slipped her arms around his waist and leaned her head against his back. Clutching her hands, he stared across the sea, which had taken on hues of orange and red from the rising sun. They stood like that for a long time, and when he finally felt her shiver, he turned, lifted her in his arms, and carried her to the steps. Inside, they took a hot shower together and climbed into bed.

Ryan's troubled thoughts visited him in his dreams. Kirshen's face floated in the ether with many others, calling to him for help. Help he could no longer give them; help he didn't think he could give to himself.

Then the dream changed to the recurring one of him being trapped inside a barracks in Iraq with enemy mortar shells raining down outside. A fire burned at his back and a wailing siren called for the EOD team to mount up, but the barracks door wouldn't open, no matter how hard he tried. When he held up his hands, they were skeletal fingers covered in blood.

His screams woke Emily, and she shook him to bring him back to reality. Ryan felt the shaking in his dream, but he couldn't stop staring at his hands. Corporal Jimmy Risk walked out of the fire, holding his neck wound, blood seeping out around his fingers. He placed his free hand on Ryan's shoulder and said, "You can't save us all."

The barracks door finally opened, and Ryan fell through it into bright sunlight, blinking his eyes and staring up into Emily's worried face. He sat up and saw the rest of the team, standing in the open bedroom doorway, concern etched on their faces. Hot tears burned down his cheeks, and he couldn't make them stop. Emily wrapped him in a hug, and Mango pulled the door closed.

When he finally calmed down, he fell back asleep and didn't dream.

By the time Ryan awoke again, it was late afternoon. He showered and went out to the kitchen, needing a cup of coffee to help clear away the mental cobwebs.

"He lives," Mango said.

Ryan gave him the middle finger as he waited for the coffee to brew. He poured it straight into a cup and drank it black, like the color of his soul. He swirled the coffee around the cup and understood why his friend Dennis Law, the old captain of the salvage vessel *Peggy Lynn,* had drank his coffee with a shot of Jim Beam. It took the edge off, and sometimes a man needed to relieve the ache in his chest. Maybe it wasn't that he didn't care, but that he cared too much.

Mango sat beside Ryan at the kitchen counter. "We've all been there, bro."

"I don't need your pity."

"It's not pity, Ryan. Every one of us has had nightmares about the shit we've done. Oscar relives the night they killed his team. I dream about boarding ships and shoot-outs in steel passageways. Jennifer has seen mangled bodies come into her ER. The one that gets her the most is the guy who wasn't wearing a helmet while riding his motorcycle. When he wrecked, the pavement ground away half his face."

Ryan shuddered.

"Yeah, bro, that's what I'm talking about. We've all walked a dark path, even Emily. You should ask her about the drug raid she was on when she was a sheriff's deputy, or some of the cases she's worked for the insurance agency. The point is, is that we all suffer from some form of PTSD. We're all screwed up in the brain, but we can't take it personally. Kirshen didn't die because of you. He died because the guy pulling the trigger didn't care about who he killed to take out his target."

Emily had once told Ryan about that drug raid, but he didn't know she dreamed about it. Despite Mango being one of his best friends, it angered Ryan that he had been prying into their private lives. Still sullen, Ryan snapped, "What makes you such an expert?"

Mango propped his prosthetic leg on a stool and pointed to it. "Because I've walked through the fire, bro. I've been where you are. You gotta surround yourself with good people and find joy in the work you do, otherwise you'll go crazy. We're here for you, brother. You don't have to carry this burden alone."

Ryan sipped his coffee, then set the mug on the counter. He leaned over it with both palms flat on the granite. Mango was right. He carried a burden that seemed to grow heavier with each mission. He had to find a balance between dealing with his inner turmoil and interacting with the world. One reason he had gravitated to commercial diving was that he didn't have to deal with people underwater. It was him against the elements, and if he made a wrong decision, the elements won. When he became irritated and combative on land, he was just a grouch who others didn't want to be around, but the people with him now had seen him at his worst, and they were still there for him.

Slowly, he nodded his head. "Thanks, Mango. I'm glad you're here, and I'm glad you keep saving my ass, because heaven knows I need it."

"We all need it at some point, bro. You just seem to need it more than the rest of us. And I've got a feeling that I'll get to do it again real soon."

CHAPTER TWENTY-EIGHT

Using his middle finger to scratch his chin, Ryan smiled at Mango. The two men bumped fists, and Ryan poured another cup of coffee before he went out to the pool where the rest of his friends had congregated.

Emily sat on a chaise lounge beside Jennifer. He stood behind her and ran a hand over her hair before he rested it on her shoulder. She put her hand on his and smiled as she looked over her shoulder at him. He gave her a kiss and whispered, "I love you."

She kissed his cheek and whispered back, "I know, baby."

He straightened and squeezed her shoulder, then walked over to Carmen, who was sitting at the patio table, working on her laptop. The sun pounded on him, and he stepped into the shade of the umbrella she'd positioned over her screen.

Looking up with concern, she asked, "Are you okay?"

"Yeah, I'll be fine. Did you get anything from Rincone's computer last night?"

She stared intently at the screen as her fingers danced across the keyboard. "No, but I had a feeling the police would take it, so I installed a backdoor. The police just booted it up. I'm accessing it right now."

Ryan smiled. Carmen was resourceful *and* hot. He appreciated her ingenuity. "When we raided the lawyer's office in Panama, Oscar took a bunch of files besides the one on The Armorer. Do you think there might be something useful in them?" he asked.

She shrugged. "Anything could help. Can you send them over to Barry?"

"Yeah. We scanned them before I sent the originals to my DHS contact."

Carmen looked up at him. "Why would you send them to DHS?"

"Because I work with them, and if they help take a few bad guys off the street, it was worth it."

She shook her head. "Don't be naïve, Ryan. There are two sets of laws in the world: one for the rich and powerful, and the other to keep the rest of us in line."

"Yeah, I know all about how the government works." He smiled. "Let me know if you find anything."

"I will."

Ryan doubted there was anything related to The Armorer in the files they'd swiped from Panama or he'd have sent them to Barry already, but they couldn't discount anything. Maybe they would help Barry flesh out the network map? He retrieved his computer and emailed the files to the hacker in St. Thomas, then called him to let him know what he would find in his inbox. They discussed how he should proceed, and, as always, Barry told him it would be expensive.

Ryan had just hung up the phone when Carmen called him back to the table. He and Mango walked over to see what she had found.

She turned the computer so the two men could see the screen as they sat beside her. "So, Rincone was getting payments from the trust that Valdez set up," she said. "There was also a significant cash infusion about two years ago. According to the records filed at the bank, Rincone claimed it was from the brokered sale of his yacht, and he had a receipt for ten million dollars. The bank tagged the records with a file that included the change in the yacht's title. But that's not the interesting part. The company who owned the boat before Rincone purchased it was Octavius International, and the signatory for both Octavius and the corporation Rincone set up for the yacht is a man named Marcus Syme."

"Is he our next target?" Mango asked.

"I don't want to go after any more low-level players," Ryan said. "We do the research and go for the king."

"You don't have to worry about Syme, anyway," Carmen said. "He's already in prison. The real story here is that I traced back the transactions for this yacht from Octavius to the Seychelles, then to the bank in Zurich that received the money from the account in Crimea."

"Do we know where *that* money came from yet?" Ryan asked.

"That, I don't know. I sent my network map to Barry, and he's integrating it into what we already have and running search algorithms on the files you sent him."

"Once again, we wait," Ryan lamented.

"Usually when we find a thread, it doesn't take long for the whole thing to unravel," Carmen said reassuringly.

"What about the sniper?" Mango asked.

Ryan leaned back in his chair, looking around at the rest of the team who had joined them at the table. "My guess is that someone was paying him to watch Rincone and take him out if he got picked up."

"How was Rincone's security being paid?" Oscar asked.

"The police took another computer from the sniper's house, but I don't have access to it," Carmen said.

"Whoever the shooter was, he was probably just a paid hitman," Emily said. "The only reason for us to go after him is to find out who paid him, or if you just want revenge."

"Who would want Rincone dead?" Ryan asked. "These are the options, as I see them." He held up his index finger. "The Armorer." He raised another finger. "And the Venezuelans, because he disappeared on them." Scrutinizing Oscar, he raised a third finger. "Unless you already know who The Armorer is, and you're working us to help take out his network."

Mango leaned toward the Venezuelan. "Tell me who The Armorer is so I can kick your ass."

Oscar held up his hands, palms out, and backed away from Mango. "I don't know who he is. Why would I have Rincone killed? His death has put us back to square one."

"Revenge," Emily said.

"Yes, I want revenge," Oscar confessed, "but I didn't hire an assassin to kill Rincone."

Ryan cleared his throat. "Well, buddy, it's starting to look like you're on a rampage. First, you killed Valdez in Panama, and now Rincone is dead."

"I didn't do it."

"You're looking pretty guilty, bro," Mango added.

"I'm telling you, I had nothing to do with it." Oscar backed farther away from the table.

"Give me your phone," Ryan said, and Oscar handed it to him, then stalked into the house.

"Carmen," Ryan said, "I want you to go through his search history and his call log."

Carmen hooked the phone to her computer and began working on her keyboard.

"What are we going to do with him?" Mango asked.

"He gets the benefit of the doubt, for now," Ryan said. "In

the meantime, I want to get into the sniper's house and look at the hide again."

"The cops still have it locked down," Mango said.

"Emily, can you get the drone up?" Ryan asked. "Let's see what they're doing."

It only took a few minutes for Emily to launch the quadcopter. She flew it along the coast, staying high to avoid being seen. The house looked much as it had after the assault. No one had covered the shattered doors, and the only cops they saw were sitting in a car, blocking the driveway. The same was happening at Rincone's house.

According to the drone footage, the island's shoreline was mostly rocky cliffs and a few sandy beaches. To get to the sniper's house, Ryan would either need to swim, walk down the road, or beat through the brush. He continued to study the drone footage and the online satellite map before deciding to walk along the clifftops and go through the brush.

Pulling on his tactical gear, he worked the boots to loosen the leather that had shrunk from the seawater. He left his pistol at the villa and took only his tactical folding knife. As he was preparing, Mango asked if he wanted him to go with him. Ryan told him no and asked that he keep an eye on Oscar. He wiggled an earpiece into his right ear so he could talk to Emily, who would continue to fly the drone while he was inside the house.

Once he was kitted up, Ryan headed east along the beach, having to beat through the brush where the cliffs met the sea. It was easier going than he'd thought, and many of the empty lots had barren spots along the cliff or small trails through the underbrush.

There were only four houses between the villa and his target. Three of them were empty, but at one three-story home, he had to wait until the couple sitting by the pool were looking the other way before he raced across the opening to the next stand of mangroves and wild palms.

The sniper's house had a pergola set off to the west with its own steps up from the water. A paver stone path led to the house, and Ryan followed it, staying close to the vegetation on the right side. He entered the house through the same door he'd helped to breach earlier that morning. Once inside, he paused and listened to the surrounding sounds. Besides the birds chirping outside, there didn't seem to be anything stirring.

Ryan stayed on the balls of his feet as he crept along the wide ceramic tiles, then up the stairs. Again, he paused to listen before walking to the sniper's room. He told Emily he was inside, and she reported that the police were still in their car by the gate.

In the room facing Rincone's house, Ryan studied the shooter's hide. There was a flat platform built four feet off the ground for the sniper to lie on as a perch. The height allowed for the downward angle of the muzzle and for the trajectory of the bullet to clear the ornamental concrete railing on the room's balcony. That morning, there had been a Blaser R93 rifle resting on its bipod and buttplate on the bench. The police had impounded it as evidence and dusted the room for prints, leaving black powder all over the room.

He checked the closets, under the bed, and beneath the small sofa. A nightstand held only the most generic items. Looking around, Ryan thought through how he'd have done things. The sniper had set up the rifle and the shooting bench exactly how he would have positioned them. Next, he would have wanted to place his bug-out bag close at hand, so all he had to do was throw it over his shoulder and bolt from the scene once he'd taken the shot.

But bolt to where?

He stood by the door to the balcony and surveyed the

surrounding property. Last night, the police had reported no vehicles passing through their roadblocks, and no boats had left from the shore because *Amarillo*, the Trident RIBs, and the RCIPS's Marine Unit had spotted no one racing away. All this meant that the shooter had stayed near the house, hiding in the thick underbrush until he could make a clean getaway. Ryan reasoned the sniper had to know that as soon as he pulled the trigger, the police would fixate on him. He wouldn't want to hide in the vacant lots between here and Rincone's because the cops had both houses and the lots between them covered, so Ryan figured he'd headed west.

After spending an hour searching the house, Ryan found no link to the shooter's identity and went outside to continue his investigation. At the northwest corner of the home, he made sure the police couldn't see him before dashing along the pool and crossing to the four-car garage. He slipped inside after picking the door lock.

The interior was cool and dark. Light spilled through the windows of the garage doors, allowing him an unobstructed view of the SUV and the minivan parked inside. He checked both before he walked through the two empty bays. Nothing caught his attention, and he slipped out the door, locking it behind him.

Back at the pergola, he checked for broken branches or bent vegetation, which would indicate if someone had passed through in a hurry. He completed two circles around the area before he noticed a narrow break in the mangroves. As he squatted by the opening, he saw a footprint in the dirt. He immediately recognized the tread pattern as that of a combat boot, similar to those worn by American servicemen.

"Did any of our guys check out the pergola on this property?" he whispered to Emily. He heard her ask Mango, then she told him no.

He stepped off the concrete walkway into the brush,

following the footprints along a faint trail. About ten feet from the road, he found an opening marked by narrow tire tracks, made by either a scooter or a motorcycle. He dropped to his hands and knees and looked up the trail. Through the narrow gap in the brush, he could see the elevated roadbed. Still in the down push-up position, he rotated his head to look both left and right beyond the clearing.

Something blue lay ten feet to his right. After marking the spot in his mind, he stood and pushed through the branches. The object he had seen was a plastic credit card, folded in half. He pocketed it and searched the area again before walking to the road. A barely visible mark of mud on the black pavement showed the sniper had turned right.

He probably headed for George Town so he could hop an airplane and get the hell outta Dodge, Ryan thought. *That's what we should do right now.*

"Can you see me?" Ryan asked Emily as he shook a branch.

"I see a branch moving," she replied.

"Can the cops see me if I step onto the road here?"

"It doesn't look like it. Just stay on the shoulder as you walk this way."

"Okay. I'll see you in a minute." Ryan moved out of the dense underbrush and walked through the grass along the side of the road toward the villa.

He was halfway there when a police car stopped beside him.

CHAPTER TWENTY-NINE

Ryan's heart jumped into his throat. Had the cops seen him come out of the brush? The car had come from the west, not out of the driveway behind him. Maybe they'd radioed for backup?

When the window slid down, Acting Superintendent Todd Whittaker smiled up at him. Ryan let out a long breath through puffed-up cheeks, feeling relieved that Whittaker hadn't arrested him.

"You must have slept in your clothes," Whittaker said.

Ryan looked down at his black outfit. A thin white line of dried salt marked where he had waded in the ocean. "Yeah, something like that."

"I want to talk to you after I check on my officers."

"Can you come by the villa?" Ryan asked.

"Certainly."

"I'll see you in a few minutes." Ryan began walking while Whittaker drove on.

When he got to the house, he showered and changed clothes.

A few minutes later, Whittaker pulled into the driveway,

and Ryan led him to the pool deck where the others were waiting.

"I'd offer you a beer, but you're probably on duty," Ryan said.

"Nothing for me, thanks. I wanted to come by and tell you the good news. The sniper rifle had a print on it belonging to a Randall Grasz."

"That's it? Just a name?" Mango asked.

"We caught him at the airport this morning," Whittaker informed them.

Ryan felt his mouth fall open. "You caught him?"

"We processed the rifle immediately, and once we had a print, we got a name and then used facial recognition to spot him."

"Can we talk to him?" Ryan asked.

"No. He'll stand trial for murder."

"What about giving us access to Rincone's computer?" Carmen asked.

Whittaker shook his head. "This is a RCIPS investigation now."

"Thanks for coming by, Superintendent," Ryan said, sensing they had nothing further to discuss.

Whittaker stood. "If you need anything else, don't hesitate to call. I believe you have my card."

"Yeah, I've got it," Ryan said as he ushered the policeman through the house, then watched from the front door as Whittaker got into his car and drove away.

Back at the pool, he found everyone clustered around Carmen and her computer.

Mango looked up as Ryan approached. "Grasz is a former Army Ranger."

"Shocker," Ryan said. "Let me guess, he spent time in the sandbox and has sniper training."

"Three tours in Iraq. Two in Afghanistan," Carmen said.

"And he leaves a print on the rifle and gets caught at the airport?" Emily questioned. "Something doesn't add up. I've been around you guys long enough to know how you're trained and how you think."

"You think someone set him up?" Jennifer asked.

"Maybe, or maybe he's not that bright," Ryan said.

"I'll go with 'not that bright,'" Carmen said. "The Army gave him a dishonorable discharge after they court-martialled him for trying to trade U.S. military weapons for a load of heroin that he wanted to ship back to the States."

"He may be dumb, but he's a decent shot," Ryan said.

Mango scoffed. "A monkey could have made that shot. It was two hundred and ten yards. Plus, he had collateral damage."

"At night, with a crosswind, and then he had to escape and evade. Speaking of which, I found this near the spot he kept his motorbike." Ryan laid the blue card on the table.

"Okay," Mango conceded. "He's had training, but he still killed Kirshen, and that pisses me off just as much as it does you."

Carmen picked up the card and unfolded it. "This is a prepaid access card." She immediately began typing on her computer.

"What are you looking for?" Emily asked.

"They load these things with cash, and because it has the Visa logo on it, it will work at ATMs. I should be able to hack it and track the transactions." She bent over her keyboard again and went back to work.

As they waited for Carmen to work her magic, Ryan got up and put on a pair of swim trunks. He waded out into the water with Emily beside him, and they pushed off the bottom, racing along the coast with quick freestyle strokes. She was a faster swimmer than Ryan and easily pulled away, but he kept at it, and when she was almost a full body length ahead, he grabbed her ankle and jerked backward. He stuck his tongue out at her as he swam past.

Emily pounced and pushed him underwater. She may have been a stronger swimmer on the surface, but underwater, he was in his element, and he could hold his breath for over five minutes. He pulled her under with him, and they tussled playfully before he let her go. She shot to the surface, and when he came up in front of her, she pushed his head back under.

When he surfaced again, he wiped the water from his face, and she splashed him. He tried to grab her, but she turned and raced back toward the steps to the villa. As she was wading through the shallows, he grabbed her around the waist and picked her up. Emily squealed and laughed as he threw her over his shoulder and walked up the steps.

She smacked him on the bottom. "Put me down, ya big galoot."

"Okay." He walked to the edge of the pool and leaned over, letting her fall into the water.

Coming up sputtering, she laughed, and Ryan glanced over his shoulder just in time to see Mango give him a push. He cartwheeled his arms as he fell in, making a big splash.

When he surfaced, he reached out to Mango. "Give me a hand, would you?"

Mango held up his hands and backed away from the pool. "No way, bro." He laughed. "You can get yourself out."

Ryan climbed up, sat on the edge, and watched his girlfriend float on her back. He enjoyed the joking and the comradery that came with working with his friends, and it was comforting to have people he could lean on when he felt like things were out of control. They understood him and the shit he'd been through.

He didn't understand why certain things triggered the horrible memories he tried to suppress, but they always bubbled to the surface when he least expected them to.

Mango was right; everyone had their cross to bear. How he dealt with his was up to him. He could crawl into a bottle or inject himself with a mind-numbing drug, or he could continue doing what he did best, pursuing the men who caused pain and destruction in the world and avenging those he had lost. He always felt at his best when he was on a mission.

Leaning back on his hands, he let the sun dry him as he thought about what a preacher had told him when he was in the Venezuelan prison. Learning to forgive oneself and allowing oneself to be forgiven was just the start, but the preacher had said only God could completely exonerate someone of his sins. God gave grace freely. One did not have to earn it. All he had to do was accept it.

Ryan closed his eyes, lifted his face to the sunshine, and told the universe to free him from his burdens. He imagined packing them into a garbage bag and hurling it off into space, never to come back again. He had to admit, he felt better.

Carmen interrupted his quiet meditation by saying, "I've got something."

CHAPTER THIRTY

Carmen's words were like a magnet, drawing everyone back to the table, including Oscar, who had come out of the house.

"What is it?" the Venezuelan asked.

"This card is linked to a corporate account belonging to Hotshots, Inc. in Miami, Florida."

"Who's the signatory?" Mango asked. "Charlie Sheen?"

Carmen looked up, puzzled.

"Never mind," Mango muttered, and Ryan chuckled at the reference to one of his favorite movies, *Hot Shots! Part Deux*, a ridiculous parody of nineties action movies that made him laugh every time he watched it.

Carmen rolled her eyes. "Anyway ... Hotshots put money on a whole bunch of prepaid cards. I hacked the issuing company because it was easier than cracking the username and password on this card."

"That's scary," Emily said.

"When we're done here, Barry and I will contact them and offer to fix their security issues, but that's a story for another day."

"What about the card?" Oscar asked, encouraging her to stay on topic.

"Hotshots, Inc is just a P.O. box number, but it traces back to another shell called Flamingo Services."

Ryan pointed to the network map, littered with boxes bearing company names and account numbers and arrows marking the flow of cash or assets between them. "Do you think the cards are connected to this mess?"

"I don't know," Carmen said. "We'll have to keep digging."

"There has to be a way to figure out where the money came from," Oscar insisted.

"That kind of money doesn't just appear out of nowhere," Ryan agreed.

"Unless you're printing it at the Federal Reserve," Emily said. "Remember those pallets of cash they sent to Iran?"

"It could have come from anywhere," Ryan said. "Drugs, oil, guns … It stands to reason that The Armorer codeword is literal. The man we're looking for probably deals in guns."

"Why would an arms dealer want to kill Oscar's team?" Mango inquired. "They were after drugs, not weapons."

"Maybe we've been looking at this the wrong way," Ryan said. "We've been chasing shadows when we should have been finding the head of the snake before it whips around and bites us again."

"What do you mean?" Oscar asked.

"Why didn't you go after the guy you picked up in the delta? What was his name?"

"Armond Diego," Oscar said. "He's an assistant to the Undersecretary of Defense, and he is under the protection of the SEBIN."

"So, he's a high-ranking member of the government, and he was helping to traffic drugs," Ryan said.

Oscar nodded.

At the mention of Diego's name, Carmen had begun

typing. When she stopped, she said, "Here's what I can find with a basic search. Diego has a degree from the Central University of Venezuela and a master's in social work from Columbia University. He's served in various government positions for the last twenty years. According to this source, Canada, the U.S., and Colombia have sanctioned him for serving in Maduro's cabinet."

"Too bad they don't have a network map for drug dealers," Mango complained.

"Why was he out in the jungle coordinating a drug shipment?" Ryan asked. "What are we missing here? High-level players don't muck about with the hired help."

"When we intercepted the drug smugglers, they were on their way to the farm we'd found in the Orinoco River Delta," Oscar said.

"I agree with Ryan," Mango said. "Why was Diego there? Did your friend know? The one whose family you helped?"

Oscar shook his head. "He was just told to rescue him and the drugs."

Ryan asked, "Do you still have any contacts in Venezuela?"

"A few," Oscar replied.

"What about someone you trusted in your chain of command? Someone you can talk to about Diego?" Ryan asked.

Oscar rubbed his forehead as he thought. "Colonel Mario Estevez runs the Marine Special Operations Command. I could call him."

"Are you sure he's not corrupt?" Ryan asked.

Oscar nodded. "I have known him since he was a young captain."

"Do you know him better than you knew your friend Mendoza?" Emily asked.

The Venezuelan's eyes narrowed as he glanced at her, then he looked away. Softly, he said, "I hope so."

CHAPTER THIRTY-ONE

There was something about the look that Oscar gave her and how he'd replied that made Emily believe he was lying. She hadn't liked this situation from the start, but she had given Oscar and Ryan the benefit of the doubt from the very beginning. The Venezuelan had told a fantastic and convincing tale of being ambushed in the jungle, but she had always felt there was something missing from the story. Yes, he could have gotten lucky by stepping away to relieve himself just as the boat with Mendoza's team had swept in to kill everyone, but the story made no sense to her.

She walked away from the table and stretched out on a lounge chair as the rest of the team talked about how Oscar would contact Colonel Estevez.

Oscar had said the boat had used grenades and heavy rifle fire to kill the team. She tried to picture the ambush of Oscar's team in her mind. Having worked investigations up and down the Florida coastline, she knew just how heavy the underbrush and mangrove swamps could be along a riverbank. As the ambush team had approached in the boat, they wouldn't have known how Oscar's team was dug in, where the drugs were, or even where the prisoner, Diego, would be. She knew enough about Special Forces to know that when they were in the bush, they didn't let their guard down, and if they suspected other forces were close, they wouldn't light a fire and have a pig roast. Admittedly, these were Venezuelan Marines who had been on patrol for a long time, but something still didn't add up. And to top it off, everyone Ryan and Oscar had gone after so far had turned up dead.

Sliding off the chair, she motioned for Jennifer to join her in the kitchen. She poured them each a glass of lemonade, then asked, "What do you think of Oscar?"

Jennifer thought for a moment. "He seems all right."

"You don't think something is off about his story?"

"Maybe, but we live with guys who are a little 'off.' I guess being in the military will do that to you. Why?"

"I've been trying to piece together his story about the ambush. It sounds too convenient." She leaned closer to her friend and put a hand on hers. "Can you do me a favor and keep him occupied while I snoop around?"

Jennifer cocked her head. "Okay. But be careful."

Emily looked out the patio doors to the team gathered around the table. "You go out there and keep him from coming inside. I'm going to search his room."

While Jennifer went outside, Emily went to Oscar's room. It was almost identical to the other rooms in the villa, decorated in tastefully bright Caribbean colors with matching fabrics for the curtains and the duvet. A small carry-on suitcase sat on top of the dresser, with the top open and leaning against the mirror. She rifled through it, careful to replace everything as she found it, but there was nothing unusual amongst his clothing. Next, she moved to the backpack sitting on the floor beside the bed.

She unzipped the main compartment and found his pistol,

extra magazines, and a large knife. It was all gear Scott had supplied Oscar with when they'd prepared to invade Rincone's house. Under them was a pair of cargo pants, a shirt, and a change of socks and underwear.

In the pack's front zippered pocket, she found Oscar's wallet. Flipping it open, she removed a *Carnet de la Patria*. It looked like a driver's license, with Oscar's picture in the bottom right corner, and above it was a QR code. Next, she pulled out a picture of a man in an old military uniform, followed by three credit cards. She laid them on the tile and photographed the fronts and backs with her phone. There was an assortment of currency, scraps of paper, business cards, and a picture of a beautiful woman with long black hair and smiling brown eyes. She snapped pictures of these, too, then placed it all back in the wallet as she had found it.

Rooting through the backpack's other pockets, she found the passport that Ryan had gotten for Oscar from the forger in St. Thomas and another credit card. This one was blue, like the one Ryan had found in the bushes.

Voices in the hallway startled her, and she glanced at the door before taking two more photographs and jamming everything back into the pack. She heard Oscar ask Jennifer why she was asking him so many questions when all he wanted to do was use the bathroom. Emily glanced around and knew that if the door opened, Oscar would catch her in the act. The window was out of the question. She couldn't get it open and climb out before the door opened.

The doorknob turned.

She dove under the bed, pulling the backpack into place and sliding to the far side of the bed. All she could see were Oscar's feet as he crossed the floor and stepped into the bathroom. He had left the bedroom door open and closed the bathroom one. Quickly, she got up and padded across the tile, thankful she was barefoot.

Jennifer gave a sigh of relief when she saw Emily come out the door. The two women went to the kitchen and retrieved their glasses of lemonade. As they returned to the pool area, Jennifer whispered, "Did you find anything?"

"I'm not sure," Emily said. "I'll check it out later."

CHAPTER THIRTY-TWO

It was late in the evening when the group returned from eating dinner at a local restaurant and Emily cornered Carmen before they went into the house. She showed her the photos she had taken of Oscar's things and asked if she could dig into the Venezuelan Marine's past.

As Carmen scrolled through the pictures, she stopped on the image of the blue card. "This looks like the card Ryan found."

"That's what I thought, too," Emily concurred.

Carmen emailed herself a copy of the photos, then handed the phone back to Emily.

"Did you ever get anything off his phone?" Emily asked.

"No. The only people he called was us. You didn't see a burner in his bag, did you?"

"No, but I got interrupted in the middle of my search."

"I'll look at this stuff and talk to you later." Carmen headed for her bedroom.

Emily found Ryan and Mango sitting by the pool, drinking beer. She debated telling them about her suspicions. Her investigator instincts told her there was more to Oscar than met the eye. It was her job now to steer Ryan in the right direction, so Oscar's possible treachery didn't blindside him.

She had seen Ryan lose it after Kirshen had died, and while she knew he had a closet full of ghosts, she'd accepted it and wanted to help him in any way possible. If Carmen had a bombshell to drop about why Oscar carried around a prepaid card that might be connected to the same account as the sniper, she wanted her man to be unfazed by the news.

After helping herself to another glass of lemonade from the fridge, she went out to join them and sat down on the end of Ryan's lounge chair.

"When you guys were in Panama, how did Oscar act?" she asked.

"What do you mean?" Mango asked.

"Did he make phone calls to someone you didn't know or try to do things secretly?"

Ryan gave her a quizzical look. "Where are you going with this?"

She debated with herself about telling him of her clandestine visit into Oscar's room. "How much do we really know about Oscar? The two men you went after died before they could tell you who The Armorer is, and Oscar looks like the common denominator."

Mango raised his eyebrows and looked at Ryan. "She makes a point, bro."

"Yeah. It's not the first time we've talked about that."

"Have you checked him out?" she asked.

"When I asked Landis for help with the Langstons, I also had him check on Oscar, but there wasn't much other than that he was a Venezuelan Marine. That part fit with what he'd told us, and I figured he needed help to avenge his team."

"Why do you trust him?" she pushed.

Mango also looked quizzically at Ryan.

Ryan stared into the night for several moments before he answered. "I've walked a mile in his shoes."

"Because of Greg?" Emily asked.

"No."

"Then why?"

Again, he was silent, and she could see something was weighing heavily on his mind. He took a drink and closed his eyes, then let out a sigh. She couldn't tell if it was in annoyance or resignation.

Eventually, Ryan said, "I've been betrayed and left for dead by someone who I thought had my back. I know how he feels and right now, he needs us to have his back."

She could see there was much more to the story that he might never tell her. While Emily wanted to know everything about Ryan's mysterious statement, she continued to press on about Oscar. "What if he's working for the same people as the sniper who shot Rincone?"

"Then why involve us?" Mango asked.

"Because he hit a wall in St. Thomas," she said. "We had the documents he needed, and he told us a fanciful story to get us to trust him when, all the while, he's been playing us."

"Who is he using us to hunt?" Ryan asked.

"The people who have crossed The Armorer," she said.

The three of them clammed up when they heard the door to the patio open. Emily saw Carmen come out of the house. She wore a silk robe that fell to her knees, and her dark hair hung long and loose. She motioned for Emily to join her on the far side of the pool.

Emily glanced at Ryan, who was staring at the ocean, almost oblivious of his surroundings, but she knew from experience that he was aware of everything that was happening around him. She rubbed his leg and went to join Carmen.

"I ran the details of that card you found in Oscar's backpack," Carmen whispered. "It came from the same batch as the one Ryan found, but it's never been used and still has twenty thousand dollars on it."

Emily felt her heart sink. Ryan trusted this guy, and now she thought she had proof that he was in bed with The Armorer. She glanced over her shoulder and saw Ryan watching them. With a wave, she motioned him over. He stood and walked around the pool, giving Mango the finger. It was such a crass gesture.

"What's up?" he asked and sipped his beer.

"I found a prepaid card in Oscar's backpack that came from the same batch as the sniper's," Emily explained.

The news didn't seem to faze him. "I know. He took it from the safe deposit box when we grabbed the docs on The Armorer. Has he used it?"

"No," Carmen said.

Ryan chuckled. "He probably can't figure out the password." He stared at Emily for a long moment. "Why were you in his pack?"

"I'm an investigator. I go where my head says the next lead will be."

After another long moment, he nodded. "Okay. I understand why the guy is suspicious to you. What else did you find?"

Emily showed him the pictures she'd taken with her phone.

"His Fatherland Card identifies him as Oscar López, and he *was* a Marine," Carmen said.

"What's a Fatherland Card?" Emily asked.

"It's the card that looks like a driver's license. The *Carnet de la Patria*," Carmen said.

"So," Ryan said, "Oscar is who he claims to be, and now that we're done witch-hunting our friend, we can get back to figuring out who The Armorer is, right?"

"I just want you to be careful," Emily told him. "This entire thing is predicated on him telling you that he lost his team, and I think we need to verify some facts."

"I think some of those facts are being born out in front of us because every time we get close to someone with more information about The Armorer, that person ends up dead. Whether or not Oscar is telling us the truth, The Armorer is laundering a serious amount of money out of Venezuela and is killing people to keep it a secret."

"Whoever he is, he has to be involved in the oil industry or drugs, irrespective of his code name," Carmen said.

Ryan tapped his empty bottle against his thigh. "Why don't we ask Oscar in the morning?"

"Do you really trust him?" Emily asked.

"He's trying to avenge his team and that's something I understand," Ryan said.

Emily shook her head. Ryan hadn't said that he trusted Oscar, and that confirmed her suspicions. There was much about Oscar that they didn't know, but for now, she would trust her instincts about him, and her gut told her that Oscar wasn't who he said he was.

To discover the truth, she'd have to keep digging.

CHAPTER THIRTY-THREE

Ryan spent most of the night tossing restlessly in bed. He'd gone down this rabbit hole based on a story that Oscar had told them. When he'd first appeared on the scene, he had been trying to steal a box of documents from Paul Langston. If he was working for The Armorer, then why was he so eager to find the person who had paid Terrence Joseph to kill Diane and Paul? Wouldn't he already know? If that were the case, was Oscar backstopping his story and using Ryan and his friends to hunt down the men who The Armorer believed would talk about his business?

Were they unwitting pawns in Oscar's game?

He got up early and made coffee. As he sipped his first cup of the day, he decided he needed to know more about Oscar and his background before they continued the hunt for The Armorer. He went upstairs and picked up Emily's phone. She had shown him the pattern she used to unlock the screen, and he swiped his finger over it. He smiled when the phone opened to a selfie of them cheek-to-cheek in the cockpit of *Windseeker*. She was a beautiful woman, and he was punching way above his weight class by dating her.

Opening the photos she'd taken of Oscar's personal items, he slowly scrolled through them. He wondered if Carmen had checked the other credit cards as well as the prepaid. He stopped at the faded picture of Simón Bolívar in his dress uniform. From his time in Margarita Prison, he knew that Venezuelans were proud of their heritage and often carried a portrait of the country's founder. On the back of the photo was a set of numbers that could have been a lock combination or a credit card pin. The scraps of paper contained notes about the investigation. He stopped on the picture of the woman. Who was she to Oscar?

He needed more information on the mysterious Venezuelan man that they were helping. Thinking back to when he and Oscar had met Barry at his house on St. Thomas, he visualized the computer screen Barry had open, displaying his and Oscar's pictures. The hacker had plenty of information about Ryan, but none about Oscar. In fact, Barry had been quick to swipe Oscar's photo off the screen and move on to the banker, Valdez.

Ryan went to Carmen's room and stepped in without knocking. She was under the covers with a sleeping mask over her eyes. He sat on the bed and shook her shoulder. Carmen stirred and lifted a hand to remove the mask.

She had a puzzled look on her face. With sleep and disdain in her voice, she asked, "What do *you* want?"

"When Oscar and I came to your place on St. Thomas, Barry had been running a facial recognition scan on us. What did he find out about Oscar?"

Carmen rubbed her eyes. "What time is it?"

"Five-thirty. Tell me about Oscar."

She let out a sigh and pulled the mask down before rolling over. "Talk to me when the sun's up."

He threw the covers off her to encourage her to get out of bed. Carmen snatched the covers before they got below her waist, and Ryan turned away when he saw she was sleeping in the nude.

"What the hell, *pendejo*?" she hissed. "Get out."

"I'm sorry," he said. "I didn't mean to ... *Shit*, I just need to know what you learned about Oscar."

"Fine." She sat up and pointed at the door. "Get out, and I'll be downstairs in a minute."

Ryan closed the door behind him and went to the kitchen. He poured another cup of coffee and walked outside. Ten minutes later, Carmen joined him at the patio table with a mug of tea. Her hair was wet from showering, and she now wore a T-shirt and a pair of shorts.

She sipped her drink but wouldn't meet his gaze.

"I'm sorry," he said again, sincerely.

"Okay, stop, Ryan. Don't be pathetic. You had a good look. Now let's get down to business."

He nodded, and she launched into her story. When Ryan and Oscar had walked into the garden at Barry's house, the security system had taken photos of them with its hidden cameras. They had matched Ryan's photo with those from his military service, U.S. passport, and his North Carolina driver's license, which she told him had expired over a year ago.

Oscar, on the other hand, was an enigma. There was no record of him in the databases they had rapid access to, including the FBI's Next Generation Identification system.

"Did you look further?" Ryan asked.

"No," Carmen said. "You vouched for him, and that was good enough for us."

"What about now?"

She smiled mischievously. "I'll need to have a good look, just like you."

"Oh, come on. How long is this going to last?"

"Not much longer. I just like to see you blush," Carmen said, laying a hand on Ryan's.

He knew his face was crimson, but said, "How did you access the NGI?"

She pulled her hand from his and waved it dismissively. "*Please*. Barry and I are hackers."

"Have you looked at the other information Emily retrieved from his kit?"

"I sent everything to Barry. We'll have to wait and see what he comes up with. By the way, this place is nice, but I'd like to sleep in my own bed. How long are we going to stay here?"

"We can go back to St. Thomas. There isn't anything else we can do here."

"Good. I'll go pack. You get us an airplane."

"Wait," Ryan said. "What about his phone? You looked at it yesterday."

"The only calls on it were to you guys."

"What do think would happen if we emptied the prepaid card that Oscar took? Would it trip an alert somewhere?"

"Maybe," Carmen said. Her phone chimed as she stood. After reading the message, she turned the phone for Ryan to see. "Barry emailed me a video from a bodega in Miami of the guy who bought the prepaid cards. His name is Webster Griffin."

Mango, who had just come outside with a cup of coffee, huddled with Ryan and they watched the video several times.

"Want to go to Miami?" Ryan asked Mango.

"Sure," he replied with a shrug.

"Before we do that, we need to have a talk with Oscar." Ryan stood and maneuvered Mango away from their hacker. "Here's how we'll do it."

CHAPTER THIRTY-FOUR

Ryan and Mango walked into Oscar's room and found him sitting on the edge of the bed in his boxer shorts, his cell phone in his hand.

The Venezuelan looked up from the tiny screen. Mango sat beside him, and Ryan pulled a length of cord from behind his back. He looped it over Oscar's neck and pulled it tight. Oscar's eyes went wide, and he immediately pawed at the rope.

As Ryan placed his knee in the smaller man's back, Mango put a strip of duct tape over Oscar's mouth.

"Stop struggling and this will be a lot easier," Ryan said.

They shoved him face down on the bed and secured his hands and ankles with flex cuffs, pulling off his underwear as a form of humiliation. Next, they sat him in a straight-back chair that they pulled away from the writing desk, and Ryan wrapped the cord around Oscar's torso and the chair back.

Oscar struggled against his restraints and tipped the chair over backward. It slammed into the floor, and Oscar's head bounced off the tile with a *thud*. He groaned and his eyelids fluttered, but he didn't pass out.

"Let's get him upright," Ryan said.

When Oscar was vertical again, Ryan said to him, "I'm going to remove the tape, and you're going to answer our questions."

Oscar nodded; his eyes still dull from the blow to his head.

"Good." Ryan ripped off the tape. "Let's start with an easy one." He showed him the photo Emily had taken of the woman in Oscar's wallet. "Who is she?"

"My wife. She's dead."

Ryan glanced at Mango with raised eyebrows. Then he asked Oscar, "Why did you order the hit on Rincone?"

"I didn't."

"Come on, bro," Mango said. "You killed Valdez, and you had your sniper kill Rincone."

"*No!*" Oscar shook his head. "I mean, yes, I killed Valdez, but we'd already gotten what we needed. We needed Rincone alive. You're the one that didn't account for a sniper."

"Why take the money from Valdez's vault?"

"Because those rich assholes can spare a few dollars."

"Do you know who The Armorer is?" Mango asked.

"I'd never heard of him until we got the papers from Valdez."

"I think you've been jerking us around and getting us to do your dirty work," Ryan said.

"I swear, I'm not," Oscar pleaded. "I just want to know why they killed my team."

"Why do you have *this*?" Ryan held up the prepaid card. He had lied to Emily about Oscar finding it in the vault with the cash, and he was pissed that Oscar had it.

"I found it in Rincone's place, and I took it, just like the money from the bank vault."

"Why didn't you bring it to us right after you found it?"

"I wanted the money off it."

"How did you know there was money on it?" Mango asked.

"There are thousands of cards like that in South America. Drug dealers use them to send money from the States instead of using cash. No one looks at a credit card."

"You're a greedy little pig," Ryan said. "I don't think you're telling us the truth. I think you concocted that story about being ambushed. I think you're tracking down and eliminating anyone The Armorer thinks will talk about his business."

"No, I *swear*! Let me talk to Colonel Estevez. He'll corroborate my story."

Ryan walked to the bedroom door and opened it. Carmen stepped inside. She walked over to Oscar, who tried to cover himself with his bound hands. Ryan knew Oscar had a crush on the woman and wanted to use her to humiliate the man. He hadn't told her that Oscar would be naked, and she paused just inside the door. She glanced at Ryan, who motioned for her to hurry up and do her thing.

Carmen squatted in front of Oscar and used an app on her iPhone to copy his fingerprints. Then she took a photo of his face.

Ryan reapplied the tape to Oscar's mouth before he and Mango carried him into the bathroom and set him in the tub. "We'll be back for you soon. You better get your story straight between now and then."

Oscar shouted something behind the tape, but the two men walked out without acknowledging him.

Outside the bedroom, Mango turned to his friend. "I hope we're doing the right thing."

"We need to be more careful. If he is who he says he is, then we'll apologize and move on with the investigation."

"And if he's not?"

"Then we get back to our lives."

"Then why go to Miami?" Mango asked.

"That's a good question," Ryan said. "Let's see what Carmen comes up with first, then we'll make that decision."

Mango nodded. "It's been fun playing detective again, but I'd like to get back to St. Thomas. Jennifer and I want to get our business started again."

"Say the word, and you can be done," Ryan replied.

"Someone needs to stick around and save your ass."

With a smile, Ryan said, "Again, and again, apparently."

"And *again*." Mango smiled. "Come on. I need another cup of coffee."

The two men went downstairs, refilled their mugs, and stepped out onto the patio. Carmen sat at her usual seat under the umbrella at the table, typing on her laptop. Emily and Jennifer sat across from her.

"What's going on?" Emily asked.

"We're verifying Oscar's story."

"What about Colonel Estevez?" she asked.

Ryan went back to Oscar's room and retrieved the man's backpack. He emptied the contents onto the table but found nothing more than what Emily had already discovered. If he wanted independent verification of who Oscar was, then they needed to do something other than biometric scans. He had to talk to someone who knew Venezuela and had connections there. As he racked his brain for who he could talk to, one name kept coming to the surface: Tomás Navarro, the *pran*, or gang leader, of Margarita Prison.

Retrieving his sat phone from his own backpack, Ryan dialed a number he had memorized more than a year ago.

A man answered the phone on the other end after three rings. "Who is this?"

"Daniel, this is David Brockhoff," Ryan said, using the alias the missionary had known him by in prison. Shortly before Ryan himself had been imprisoned, Daniel Torrance had gone to Venezuela on a mission trip, during which the SEBIN had locked him away, claiming he was an American spy. While Ryan had escaped from the prison on Margarita Island, Daniel had languished there, with the Maduro regime refusing to negotiate with the U.S. for his release. Despite Ryan asking Landis to intercede on the missionary's behalf, the DHS agent hadn't been able to secure Daniel's freedom.

"David, how are you?"

"I'm well," Ryan said. "How are you?"

"I've been better."

"How's the ministry going?"

"Not well," Daniel replied.

"Any news on when they'll release you?"

"After Silvercorp tried to invade, Maduro ordered the SEBIN to interrogate all American prisoners again. He cut off the Red Cross visits and all petitions for our release."

"I'm sorry." Ryan felt guilty for having left the man in prison while he was walking around free.

"It's not your fault," Daniel said. "Although the SEBIN interrogated many prisoners after your escape, including me."

"I didn't mean for you to get involved." Now he felt bad for calling Daniel to ask a favor.

"To what do I owe the honor of this call?" Daniel asked.

"I was wondering if I could speak to Papa?"

"You're a brave man. I will speak to him for you. Call me back in an hour."

"Thanks, Daniel. Is there anything you need?"

"I need to get out of here," Daniel said curtly.

"I've spoken to several of my government contacts on your behalf. They all told me it would be difficult to secure your release, but they're still working on it."

"Thank you, David. I'll talk to you soon."

Ryan ended the call and looked around the table at the inquisitive faces staring back at him. "I have to call back."

He glanced at his watch, stood, and left the table. The memories of his days in prison had come flooding back, and he needed a few minutes alone to deal with the raw emotions. He walked down the steps to the sea. The water always had a soothing effect on him.

Before he had a chance to take a deep breath and push back the demons, his phone rang. He saw it was Daniel and answered before it could ring a third time. "Hello?"

"Brockhoff, if you were here, I would kill you," Tomás Navarro said in Spanish.

"Good to talk to you, too, Papa," Ryan replied, continuing the conversation in the *pran*'s native tongue.

"What do you want?"

"Have you heard of Armond Diego?" Ryan asked.

"He is a low-level government official."

"Really? I heard he was the assistant to the Undersecretary of Defense and involved in a shoot-out that killed a team of Marines."

"I am unaware of that."

"Who can I speak to that would know about it?"

"No one will talk to you, Yankee spy."

"That's why I called *you*."

"What will you do for me?" Navarro asked.

Ryan glanced around to see if anyone was near him. He didn't want them to overhear this conversation. Yes, they all knew he'd been in a Venezuelan hellhole, but he wasn't about to tell them about the things he'd done to survive. He lowered his voice, even though he saw he was alone. "I did some wicked shit for you. Doesn't that earn me some goodwill?"

Navarro laughed. "No, that went out the window when you escaped without me."

"It wasn't by choice," Ryan lied. "They were taking me to the Helicoide, and I saw my chance to escape."

"You think you can lie to me, David? I know you had outside help, maybe even from the SEBIN. So, what will I get for helping you?"

"You told me once that you were loyal to your country and its people, not the politicians."

"I did, and I still am," Navarro said.

"The politicians who run your country are as corrupt as any there have ever been. They're siphoning billions of dollars out of the economy and crippling it in the process. The information I'm asking for will help put a stop to that."

"*Patriotism*, David?" Navarro chuckled. "You know me better than that."

"How's your connection to the Aztlán Cartel doing?" When Ryan had worked for the *pran*, the cartel had been one of the prison's main pipelines, moving drugs off Margarita Island and bringing back food, clothing, medicine, and money.

"I heard there was a *gringo* who destroyed the cartel's drug labs and helped assassinate the leader."

"And who do you think did that?"

Navarro was silent.

"*I* did, Tomás. My friends and I went to Mexico and destroyed the cartel because they put a hit on me. I'll come back down there and slit your throat while you're sleeping in your bed beside your little *punta*. My gift to you is to let you live."

"Such threats. I always knew you were a man after my own heart. Why don't you become my man in America? We could make a fortune together."

Ryan gritted his teeth. He wanted to tell him it wasn't ever going to happen, but he figured he could catch more flies with honey than with vinegar, so he smiled and lied. "You help me; I'll help you."

"There's the man I know." Navarro laughed. "I have your

number. I will call you when I need your help. Now, Diego worked for a man named Victor Quintero, the Undersecretary to the Minister of Defense. He established many of the drug routes through Venezuela, and he pushed the minister to purchase vast quantities of military hardware from the Russians to prepare for a U.S. invasion."

"Would he ever go into the field?" Ryan asked.

"Quintero? No, he would never soil his hands. That is why we have subordinates."

"Did they have a route through the Orinoco River Delta?"

"I've heard Quintero's associates have been smuggling both cocaine and illegally mined gold through the delta to ships that stop just offshore."

"What about an ambush on Marines working in the delta?"

"No. But it wouldn't surprise me if they ordered the Marines wiped out for interfering with one of their drug routes."

"Do you know of a Colonel Mario Estevez?" Ryan asked.

Navarro snorted. "I did battle with him before I was arrested. He is a member of the Army Special Forces."

"Does he work for the drug smugglers?"

"He's an honest man. I have never heard of him taking a bribe. He certainly wouldn't take one from me."

"Last question, Papa. Do you know a man code named The Armorer?"

"I am sorry, David. I do not know that name."

"Thanks, Tomás. Do me a favor? Take care of Daniel."

"He causes no trouble as a man of God. No one messes with him except the soldiers. You know I have ordered it so."

"*Gracias* and *adiós*, Papa." Ryan ended the call.

He had more pieces of the puzzle. Now, he just needed to fit them together.

CHAPTER THIRTY-FIVE

After Ryan recounted his conversation with the *pran* of Venezuela's infamous Margarita Prison to his friends at the patio table, Mango asked, "Do you suppose The Armorer is Quintero?"

"I don't know," Ryan said.

"What about Oscar?" Emily asked. "Does any of this exonerate him?"

"No. I only confirmed that his contact, Estevez, is a straight arrow," Ryan said.

"How long are you going to leave him tied up?" Jennifer asked.

"Have you drained his prepaid?" Ryan asked Carmen.

"Yes, but there's been nothing so far. My guess is that they give these cards out as payment and don't track their usage."

"Are we still going to Miami to check out the buyer?" Mango asked.

"Yes," Ryan confirmed. "There's more to this than just Oscar. Speaking of which, what else have you found out about him, Carmen?"

She nervously drummed her fingers on the table. "Uh ... Venezuela put an Interpol Red Notice out for him."

"When did they issue that?" Ryan asked.

"Yesterday," Carmen replied. "They want him in connection to the murder of Rincone. They claim he's now working with an opposition group, killing former members of the Venezuelan government."

"How convenient," Emily said. "If Superintendent Whittaker sees that, he'll come looking for Oscar."

"We need to get out of here," Mango said.

"I have the name of a guy who flies cargo around the Caribbean," Ryan said. "I'll call him and arrange a flight for this afternoon. Everyone, get packed."

The group dispersed to get their bags, and Ryan glanced at Carmen when she didn't move with everyone else. "What's wrong?"

"They put a Red Notice out for you, too." She turned the computer so he could see the screen.

Ryan stared incredulously at it, but it made sense. The Venezuelans wanted him for murder and escaping prison.

He grabbed his phone and called the pilot, who told him to be at the airport in two hours.

Ryan hurriedly packed his kit and then packed Oscar's. When he finished, he stepped into the bathroom and peeled the tape off Oscar's mouth. The Venezuelan glared at him.

"There's an Interpol Red Notice out for you. They claim you killed government officials. I'm going to cut you loose, and you're going to shower and get dressed. We're leaving in a few minutes."

"Screw you," Oscar said. "I trusted you, and this is how you treat me? You tie me up like I'm a common criminal."

"I'm sorry. You gotta see how this looks. The circumstantial evidence points to you being involved in something other than what you've told us."

"And *now?*"

Ryan sliced off the flex cuffs. "We're getting out of here and you're going to call Colonel Estevez. Once we talk to him, Mango and I are going to Miami to track down the guy who bought the prepaids."

Oscar looked puzzled as he rubbed his wrists. "You're going to continue the investigation?"

"There's a lot more to this than a few Marines dying in the jungle."

"I've been telling you that all along." Oscar stood and set the chair outside the tub before pulling the shower curtain closed. "I won't forget this, Weller."

"No, I don't suppose you will," Ryan said as Oscar turned on the water. He'd be pissed off, too, if his 'friends' had tied him to a chair and left him. That said, Ryan had apologized and the only thing he could do to make up for it was to find The Armorer, but right now, they had to get out of the Caymans.

When Oscar was downstairs, the group piled into the rental vehicles and drove to the airport. They cleared Customs and were on their way to the plane when three RCIPS vehicles slid to a stop, boxing them in.

The officers jumped from their vehicles and surrounded Ryan and his friends.

"Hands in the air," Whittaker shouted from behind a car, his service weapon aimed at Ryan.

Slowly, the team let their bags fall as they lifted their hands into the air.

"This ain't good, bro," Mango said.

Ryan glanced at Emily. She met his gaze. Behind the steely resolve in her cornflower-blue eyes, he could see the fear.

"What's this about Whittaker?" Ryan demanded.

"You're under arrest. Now shut up and get in the car."

One by one, the group got into the police cars, and the officers drove them to a detention center complex on Fairbanks Road.

At the prison, the cops separated them by gender and took them to different buildings. Ryan sat on the narrow wooden bench beside Oscar and Mango. He looked at the grim faces of the other two men and figured he looked the same. He had no desire to look at the world from behind bars again. He had to figure a way out of this.

Whittaker motioned for Ryan to come over to the desk.

"What're the charges?" Ryan asked.

"Possession of a firearm and multiple knives, aiding and abetting a fugitive, and murder."

Ryan gulped. His body seemed to freeze at the last charge. Murder? He hadn't killed anyone. When he found his voice again, he asked, "Who'd I kill?"

"A man named Billy Ron Sorenson."

Ryan's body shook with a chill. He had left Venezuela and the grizzly struggle with the serial killer behind him. Like a specter from the past, it was now back to haunt him.

"*Who?*" he managed to say, his throat constricting around the word as he thought about going back to the nightmare that was the prison on Margarita Island.

"Interpol has issued Red Notices for both you and Oscar López."

"What about everyone else?"

"They're facing firearms charges."

"Even the girls?"

Whittaker nodded.

"Come on, man. We worked together on the Rincone operation. You know I'm connected to Homeland Security. Why would I have a Red Notice for killing someone?"

"By law, I have to detain you for extradition."

"Are you really going to send us to Venezuela?"

"Yes." Whittaker stood and walked into another office.

"What about my phone call?" Ryan shouted.

CHAPTER THIRTY-SIX

The Cayman Islands prison guards came for Ryan in the middle of the night. They shackled his hands and feet and led him to an interrogation room. He hadn't been to sleep yet, and he was both tired and wired. The adrenaline had shot through him as soon as the guards had called his name. Now, he rubbed his eyes and forced himself to focus. The midnight interrogation technique wasn't new to him, and he tried to clear his mind of doubts and clutter. It wasn't easy on account of the guards leaving him in a warm, quiet room, and before long, his head drooped, and his eyes fluttered shut.

It was then that the interrogation room's door slammed open, startling Ryan back to reality. His heart hammered in his chest. When Acting Superintendent Todd Whittaker walked in, Ryan breathed a sigh of relief and opened his mouth to protest his innocence. The superintendent cut him off with a wave of his hand and sat down across from Ryan. He placed a cup of coffee and a file folder on the table and opened the folder.

Whittaker explained that possessing an unlicensed

firearm in the Grand Caymans carried a seven-year sentence if he pled guilty. If the court convicted him and his friends, their punishment would be ten years in prison. Ryan didn't want his friends to serve any amount of time.

"You allowed us to carry those firearms for our protection," he protested.

"I made no such declaration," Whittaker said. "As a matter of fact, I'm thinking of charging you with the murder of Esteban Rincone."

"I'd like my phone call," Ryan said.

Whittaker closed the file and clasped his hands in front of him on the table. "Here's the deal. I'm going to put you in a cell with a friend of yours, Randall Grasz. You talk to him, and ring for me in the morning." With that, the superintendent stood and left the room with his folder and coffee.

Ryan leaned back in his chair. Had this all been a ploy for Whittaker to put him in the cell with the sniper? He didn't have long to ponder the question, because the guards came in and escorted him to Grasz's cell. As he waited for the guards to unlock his shackles and open the cell door, he looked through the bars at the man stretched out on the bunk. He was short and wiry, with shaggy brown hair. There was nothing distinguishable about him; a true gray man who could blend into the shadows, except facial recog had taken away the shadows.

The guard pushed Ryan into the cell, and Grasz looked over at him before returning his gaze to the ceiling. Ryan suspected Grasz wouldn't give him information easily and had no idea how to approach him. Surely Grasz had seen him through the sniper scope before shooting Rincone?

"What are you in for?" Ryan asked, starting with an easy question.

Grasz rolled over to face the wall.

Ryan sighed. He might as well dive right in. "I heard you

got your training in the Rangers and then joined Special Forces. What I want to know is, who paid you to shoot Rincone?"

Grasz remained silent.

"I found the prepaid card you left in the bushes. That was sloppy work. Sloppier still was getting caught because you left your fingerprints on the gun. I know the Army trained you better than that. So, who set you up?"

More silence.

"There's more to this story than just you shooting a retired general. Someone is taking out their money laundering network, and *you* are now part of that. Rincone was going to lead us up the ladder to the mastermind."

The sniper shrugged. At least he'd responded. They were making progress.

Ryan knew Grasz had trained in counter-interrogation techniques. It was safe to assume that if one took on the role of a hitman, he would eventually spend time in prison or die from a bullet. Ryan couldn't promise Grasz a path to freedom or even leniency, but he needed information.

"Someone paid you with a prepaid debit card. So, how did they contact you?"

Grasz rolled over and stared at Ryan. "It doesn't matter. You take out a cog, and another will take its place."

"That's true, but if you jam the cogs, the machine stops working," Ryan replied.

"The machine *never* stops working. You stop one part, and another starts. There are a million Rincones out there. What's one more dead Venezuelan?"

"What if I told you that the person at the top of this mess is killing military members to achieve his objectives? He took out a team of Marines in the Venezuelan jungle, and a friend of mine was the lone survivor. He wants revenge."

Grasz sat up and heaved a lengthy sigh. He rested his

elbows on his knees. "I got an envelope with directions and two prepaid cards in it. One had my normal fee on it, and the other was for expenses. I was to set up in the house and instructed to kill Rincone if someone tried to snatch him. I did my job. I'm sorry your operator died. He moved at the last second. Shame, too. But that's life. If Rincone was involved in killing your friend's team, then he's paid the price."

"Who contacted you?"

"Who cares? I got the money and the target."

"Have you ever heard of a guy named The Armorer?"

"Nope." Grasz stretched out again and put his hands behind his head. "I don't know who *you* work for, but you've got some pull to get in here to see me, just to find out I don't know a damned thing."

Either Grasz had told him everything or he hadn't told him anything. Ryan couldn't be sure which and figured the sniper would take whatever else he knew to the grave. Lying back on his own bunk, Ryan closed his eyes and listened to the sounds of the prison. He would stay awake until the cops took him to a different cell. He didn't trust the sniper, and after asking all the questions he had, he wondered if Grasz might give his handlers a two-for-one special and try to silence him as well.

As he lay in the dark, Ryan tried to lock the pieces of the puzzle together in his mind. This had started on a lonely jungle trail with the arrest of a government official. The only reason to wipe out the team was so that no one knew of Armond Diego's involvement.

Diego worked for Undersecretary of Defense Victor Quintero. Rincone was a general, so he might have known Quintero. There were rumors that the Venezuelan government and its military were neck-deep in drug smuggling. The money Ryan and his team had been chasing could have come from the drug cartels. The entire drug system from street dealers to the Colombian bigwigs seemed to be awash with cash to spare.

"Hey?" Ryan said to his cellmate.

Grasz rolled over. In the low light, Ryan could see the whites of the man's eyes glowing, giving him a sinister appearance.

"Tell me if these names mean anything to you." Ryan watched him closely, but it was hard to see the man's expression. He said them slowly, pausing for effect between each one. "Armond Diego. Vincente Valdez. Oscar López." Something behind Grasz's eyes shifted. Ryan continued. "Paul Langston. Victor Quintero."

The sniper remained unmoving. He could probably lie in that same position for days on end, not moving a muscle, waiting for his prey to appear.

"Someone paid you to take out Rincone," Ryan persisted. "Those same people took out a lawyer in Panama, tried to kill a money launderer in St. Thomas, and now you're next. Do you think you'll get to live to a ripe old age in jail? They'll come for you because you were dumb enough to get caught, or they set you up to fail. You're a dead man either way."

Slowly, the sniper unfolded himself from the bunk and sat on the edge again. "They planted my prints. I never handled the gun without gloves."

"Who else was in the house?" Ryan asked.

"Two local guys."

"Do you know their names?"

"Bob and Ron. I think they were Jamaicans by their accents," Grasz said. "All I had to do was get to the house and take the shot. They provided the weapon and secured my shooting location."

"You didn't ask any questions?"

"I'm not Johnny Carson; I can't put a white envelope to

my head and guess who sent it. Inside, there were instructions, two prepaids, a passport, and a ticket from Atlanta to here. That's it."

"No return ticket?"

Grasz shook his head.

"That doesn't bode well for you, does it? I bet your new friends are face down in the mangroves right now."

"Probably." Grasz laid back down. "Just remember, if I die in prison, me and Jeffrey Epstein will have something in common. We didn't kill ourselves."

CHAPTER THIRTY-SEVEN

The next day, Ryan, Mango, and Oscar went before the magistrate. Ryan was thankful that Whittaker had declined to press charges against the women. The men pled guilty to possessing illegal firearms, and they each paid a three-thousand-dollar fine. After Ryan used his DWR corporate credit card to pay the fees, Whittaker escorted them from the courthouse to the airport.

On the way, Whittaker told Ryan he'd been right. The two men had talked privately before Ryan had gone with Mango and Oscar to the courthouse. A tourist couple from Portugal had discovered two dead bodies while they were walking through an abandoned housing development near Rum Point on the northwestern side of the island. The dead men were members of a Jamaican cartel that smuggled drugs and weapons into the Caymans, and their prints matched those taken from the sniper's house.

The police van pulled up beside the airplane Ryan had originally scheduled his team to leave on the day before. As they disembarked the van, the pilot came down the airstairs of the CASA C-212 Aviocar twin-engine turboprop. With a grin, he said, "I didn't know the police ran a delivery service."

"It's like Uber but with guns, bro," Mango said.

The pilot laughed and introduced himself as Zeke Williams. He was an independent carrier, flying a route around the Caribbean and based in Puerto Rico. The high wing plane had six passenger seats and a sizeable cargo area packed with bags and boxes. Ryan knew the plane by its military designation, the C-41A, and had made several parachute-training jumps from the rear ramp during his time in the Navy.

Once the passengers had strapped in, Zeke took off for their first stop in Jamaica.

An idea was formulating in Ryan's mind about getting his pilot's license. If they stayed in the Virgin Islands and continued to do operational activities for Dark Water Research and Trident as an independent salvage consultant, he would need a faster way to get around than by sailboat or by relying on private and commercial airlines. Emily had also talked about working remotely for Ward and Young, continuing to do insurance investigations. He could be her private pilot, and that thought put a smile on his face.

She nudged him with her shoulder. "What are you grinning about?"

He put his arm around her and kissed her forehead. "I'm happy to be alive and free."

"Do we need to worry about your Interpol Red Notice?" she asked.

"I'll need to file a dispute via a lawyer. Whittaker thought there was an excellent chance of getting it dropped because the Venezuelan government has a history of issuing Red Notices on people they have personal vendettas against."

"What about Oscar's notice?" she asked.

"We'll have to fight it, too."

"Will it show up every time you go through Customs?"

"Unfortunately," Ryan said. "I'll call Landis and talk to him about it."

THEY MADE several stops along the way, eventually landing in St. Thomas close to nightfall.

Barry was there to meet Carmen. After giving her a hug, he trotted over to Ryan. "I have some stuff I want you to see."

"Can it wait? I need to take a shower and get some sleep."

"Sure. Sure. Yeah. No problem. Can you come over to my place tomorrow afternoon?"

"I'll call you when I'm on my way over."

Barry left with Carmen, and Ryan called Landis to tell him about the Red Notice. Landis called St. Thomas Customs and spoke with the agent in charge, who allowed Ryan and Oscar to check in without hassle. It was good to have friends in high places.

Using a convenient taxi, Emily, Jennifer, Mango, Oscar, and Ryan rode across the island to American Yacht Harbor and crashed on their respective sailboats. Oscar stayed in the V-berth on *Windseeker*, where Ryan could watch him. While he still had his suspicions about the Venezuelan, he was back to trusting that he was legit. Hopefully, when he saw Barry tomorrow, Ryan would know for sure, as the hacker had done a deep dive into Oscar's history using the fingerprints and photo Carmen had taken of him on Grand Cayman.

Oscar was still understandably angry about Ryan and Mango tying him up when he told them that all they needed to do was ask for his cooperation.

As Ryan stood in the marina's shower, letting the hot water pound his body, his brain pulsed with names. Diego.

Quintero. Valdez. Rincone. Langston. How did they fit together? Diego. Quintero. Rincone. Valdez. Langston. Who was the mastermind? Obviously not Rincone, Langston, or Valdez. Two of them were dead, and the third was in witness protection. That left Diego and Quintero.

The epiphany of where to focus the hunt was short-lived when he heard an automatic weapon going cyclical outside the bathhouse.

CHAPTER THIRTY-EIGHT

Ryan jerked on his shorts over his wet body, forgoing toweling off in his hurry to get outside and see who was shooting, and at what. He dashed toward the exit and felt more than heard the bullets slam into the concrete wall of the bathhouse. Dust sifted down through the shaft of sunlight coming through the transom window above the door. He hadn't brought a gun with him to the shower, and now he was regretting it.

Dropping to the concrete floor, Ryan crawled back toward the shower to put a second layer of block between himself and the shooter. The rounds continued to pockmark the outer wall, but they hadn't broken through the inner layer of the block. Over the barrage of fire, Ryan heard sirens.

Suddenly, the bark of a pistol answered the roar of automatic fire, and the shooting stopped.

"Ryan!" Mango shouted. "You okay, bro?"

Ryan scrambled out of the shower stall and ran outside. Mango was kneeling over the dead body of Terrence Joseph and a still smoking M4 rifle.

"Who shot him?" Ryan asked.

"I did," Mango said. "I dropped my gun in the water."

Ryan glanced around at the people now appearing on the walkway. "I'd ask if there were any witnesses, but ..." He trailed off as several police officers rounded the corner.

The police ordered them to put their hands up and step back from the body. As they did, Mango muttered, "This is getting to be really old, bro. You need to sort this shit out."

"You ain't kidding," Ryan agreed.

Ryan smelled something burning and glanced over his shoulder to see thick black smoke pouring out of *Windseeker*'s cabin doors. Soul Patch had aerated her hull with multiple rounds.

Emily appeared in the cockpit, her hair wet and her clothes covered in soot. There was blood on her shirt and hands.

Ryan bucked against the cops. "That woman's been shot! She needs help."

He broke free and raced toward the smoking boat. Emily had disappeared into the cabin again. When he reached *Windseeker*, two police officers were right on his heels and followed him down the steps into the cabin. Flames danced and flickered along the galley countertop as they drew life from a severed propane tank and feasted on the decades-old wood that adorned the cabin. The interior felt like an oven, baking them on high.

Oscar lay at the base of the steps, half his head blown off along with multiple gunshot wounds to the chest and torso. Ryan surmised that Joseph had caught Oscar as he was entering the cabin and unloaded the entire magazine from his automatic rifle into the boat before turning his attention to the bathhouse.

"Grab him," Ryan ordered the cops, and they hooked the dead man under his arms and hustled him out onto the dock. He turned to see Emily trying to douse the flames with a fire extinguisher. For a second, he paused and glanced around the cabin's interior. His heart ached. His home was on fire, and his girlfriend was fighting a losing effort to douse the flames. There were so many memories, keepsakes, and possessions going up in flames. Yet the only one he cared to grab was the big blonde.

He snatched her around the waist and hauled her toward the cabin door. The engine was between the forward and aft cabin hatches, and the surrounding walls blazed brightly. His skin felt like it would peel off him. The cops were shouting for them to come out, but Emily struggled to keep fighting the fire.

"We gotta go, babe!" he shouted. He shoved her up the ladder, and together they tumbled onto the deck.

Ryan pushed Emily over the lifeline into the water between *Windseeker* and a Viking sportfisher and fell in beside her. Together, they swam across the channel to the next set of docks. Two men helped them onto the dock, and the couple stood dripping wet, watching their home burn to the waterline.

Heat shimmered off the boat in waves, blistering the fiberglass of the surrounding boats. The wood interior was ready fuel for the fire and fiberglass burned quick and hot, meaning whatever efforts they made to extinguish the flames would be pointless, other than to save the nearby boats from damage. The boat was a total loss, along with everything in it.

People rushed from the nearby marina office and restaurants to fight the fire and cut loose the boats docked beside *Windseeker*.

Emily threw her arms around Ryan and buried her head into his bare shoulder. She shook as she cried, and an anger burned deep inside of him at the vile evil of the men who had so little regard for either life or property that they were willing to destroy everything to keep a few dollars in their pockets.

"Are you hurt?" he asked as he gripped her tightly.

"I don't think so," Emily replied.

"You didn't get shot?"

"No. Whoever shot Oscar caught him just as he came down the ladder from the cockpit. I was in the galley and ran to the V-berth. When the shooting stopped, the engine was smoking. I went to help Oscar, but he was already dead, so I tried to put out the fire. A bullet must have cut through the propane line." She pressed her forehead to Ryan's chest and hugged him tight.

Ryan's heart still ached. Not only had his boat burned, but his girlfriend had witnessed a brutal execution. Although his boat was a total loss, it didn't matter to him. Emily was safe. Everything else was replaceable.

As he held her close, he glanced up the dock to where the cops had congregated around Joseph's body and had cordoned off the area with caution tape. Mango was speaking to a short, black woman in a uniform who was taking notes in a spiral-bound pad.

Jennifer came down the dock and wrapped her arms around Emily and Ryan. Gently, she said, "Come on, sweetie. Let's get you cleaned up."

Emily peeled herself away from her boyfriend, and he followed the two women up the dock to the shore. Before they could continue to Jennifer and Mango's catamaran, the female cop stopped them by saying, "I need to speak to you."

Ryan stopped, swatted a mosquito that landed on his bare chest, and said, "Give her a minute to clean up, will you?"

The police officer nodded, and Emily and Jennifer continued to *Margarita*.

"Can I go in the bathhouse and get my shaving kit and clothes?" Ryan asked.

The detective nodded to another cop who stood by the bathhouse door, and Ryan went inside to collect his kit. He pulled on his T-shirt and remembered the cable-knit sweater his mother had made for him. When he was chilly, it was nice to pull it on and think about her at home in North Carolina. He should call her. He hadn't talked to her in a while, and he usually tried to call her at least once every two weeks.

With the boat gone, maybe it was time to go home. Emily wanted to meet his family. He wondered if Oscar's violent death and the fire aboard his boat would make news Stateside.

Ryan had his answer when he stepped out of the bathhouse, holding his shaving kit and towel. At least three people were photographing his burning boat and Joseph's body with long lens cameras while the coroner did his work.

A woman rushed over, pushed a digital recorder under Ryan's chin, and demanded, "Sir, what happened? How did the boat catch on fire?"

He wanted to brush past her but paused to make a statement. "Two men died because of senseless violence, and I lost my sailboat. Terrence Joseph was a thug and a drug dealer who was recently released from prison, where he should have been rotting forever. I feel no remorse for him."

Ryan turned to walk away, but the reporter grabbed his arm. "How do you know Joseph?"

"He's just a local thug who got what was coming to him. You live by the sword; you die by the sword."

With that, he walked over to where Mango stood with the police officer, who introduced herself as Detective Johanna Smith. Ryan flicked his damp towel over his shoulder and shook her hand.

"I hate to see a man's home burn down," Smith said. "My condolences."

"Thanks." He turned to look at his boat. The volunteer

firefighters had extinguished the flames and were using water hoses to cool the hulls of the neighboring boats. They'd pushed some away from the docks closest to *Windseeker* and had tethered them on long lines.

"Do you have a place to stay?" the detective asked.

"With me," Mango said. "My wife and I live on that Lagoon 52 over there." He pointed to the catamaran tied to the end of a pier.

"I need you to come down to the station so I can get statements from each of you," Smith said.

"Are we under arrest or just persons of interest?" Ryan asked.

"Witnesses," Smith replied. "And you are the owner of the boat that burned, yes?"

"Yeah." Ryan nodded.

"Come tomorrow morning." She handed a business card to both him and Mango. "Nine a.m."

"Yes, ma'am," Ryan said.

"I'll see you in the morning," Smith said.

Tapping the card against his leg, Ryan watched the detective squat beside the coroner. He grabbed Mango by the arm and headed for the Lagoon. "You need to scrub that GSR off your hands."

Once they were aboard *Margarita*, Mango went straight to the sink and scrubbed his hands with soap and water to remove the gunshot residue and unburned powder that had blown onto his hands when he'd fired his pistol. Then he threw his clothes in the washer with white vinegar and detergent and took a shower to cleanse the rest of his body.

Jennifer was in the salon and Emily had just come up from showering in a head of the aft stateroom in the starboard hull. She wore a pair of Jennifer's pajama pants and a T-shirt that read *MJ Charters* over a stylized picture of the catamaran under full sail. It reminded Ryan of the T-shirts and polos he'd collected while he bounced around the Caribbean. They were all gone. At least Emily had most of her clothes and possessions in her apartment in Tampa.

Ryan walked back to his smoldering boat and spoke with the volunteers who had put out the fire. He thanked them and helped pull the other boats back to their slips. The boats closest to *Windseeker* had blistered fiberglass and smoke damage. He gave his insurance information and his phone number to their owners. His insurance company would not be happy with him.

When he returned to *Margarita*, he retrieved a beer from the fridge and went out to the aft deck. Taking a seat in a chair, he lit a cigar from Mango's collection. As he held the lighter to the tobacco, he remembered the Zippo inscribed with the U.S. Navy EOD logo that Greg had given him after pirates had shot his other sailboat out from under him. Every item was replaceable, but each held sentimental value beyond its dollar amount. He and Emily had escaped without major burns, although the heat had singed his eyebrows and hair. Sniffing, he caught a whiff of acrid fiberglass smoke clinging to him.

He needed a shower and, more than anything, he needed to find out who had paid Terrence Joseph to perform the hit on him and Oscar. That bastard had made it personal now, and Ryan was gunning for him like a laser-guided missile.

CHAPTER THIRTY-NINE

Before meeting Barry at his home, Ryan took Emily shopping. They both needed new clothes, and he picked up two new cell phones. He quickly filled a bag with shorts, T-shirts, and underwear. He realized he needed to put together a go-bag, because, like everything else, it had burned up on the boat. While there were several stores that would have what he needed on St. Thomas, replacing his guns would have to wait until he returned to the U.S.

He had to go to Barry's house, and he had promised to stop by the police station. Ryan left Emily and Jennifer to continue their shopping while he went into a discount store, where he bought a roll of duct tape and a paring knife. He used the tape and cardboard from the knife's blister pack to make a sheath and tucked the knife into his waistband. At least he had a weapon if things got out of hand.

After hailing a taxi, he rode across the island and got out at a crossroads near Barry's home. When the taxi disappeared around the bend, he set out on foot. He was sweating heavily in the humid heat by the time he had walked the mile to the hacker's house.

The metal detector tripped when it sensed the knife, but Barry let him through the gate regardless, and Ryan went up the back steps to the office. Carmen opened the door for Ryan and gave him a hug.

"I'm sorry to hear about Oscar," she said. "The news said it was a drug thing."

"The shooter was a local thug. Mango took him out before he could kill anyone else."

"Forget about that," Barry said. "I've got good news."

"I could use some," Ryan remarked, walking over to where the hacker stood beside his glass-topped computer table.

Barry tapped the touch screen, and a grainy video began playing. A man appeared on screen at a convenience store counter and paid cash for a stack of prepaid cards.

"That's Webster Griffin, but he's known on the street as Pops," Barry said. "He's got a rap sheet but hasn't been arrested since he got out of prison about fifteen years ago after doing a stint for armed robbery. He's been a bit of a ghost ever since."

"What about his parole officer?" Ryan asked.

"He did two years of parole. After that, it's anyone's guess, but you know how these things go."

"Yeah," Ryan said. "Prison is a criminal college. Any idea who *Pops* is affiliated with?"

"He's a low-level errand runner for anyone willing to pay him," Barry said. "Anyway, he buys two hundred prepaid cards a week. He spreads them out across three different stores, but this one seems to be his favorite."

"What does he do with the cards?" Ryan asked.

"Unfortunately, I don't know yet. I've had a tough time cracking the Miami-Dade traffic cam system. For some reason, our Internet has been spotty and, for the last week, we've had rolling blackouts, even though I have a generator. If the substations and Internet relays aren't powered, I have to rely on satellite Internet, and it can be slow."

"Have you had these problems before?" Ryan asked.

"Once in the past two years since Carmen and I moved in here."

Ryan's hackles rose. Barry had told him that whoever was behind the money had set on him like a pack of wolves when they'd started investigating Valdez. Maybe The Armorer had discovered Barry's location and was actively working to subvert the investigation.

The computer screen went black, and Barry tapped it. "Dammit! Not again."

Glancing around the room, Ryan saw the lights had also gone out. "How long does it take for the generator to kick in?"

"Less than two minutes," Carmen said.

Ryan moved to the window and pulled back the shade just enough for him to peek out. He saw a man dressed all in black hop over the garden wall and drop into a crouch, swinging an MP5 submachine gun around to shoulder it.

"You got any guns around here?" Ryan asked.

"Just Carmen's, and its downstairs. Why?" Barry asked, stepping over to join him.

Ryan jerked the hacker out of the shooter's line of sight and turned to see Carmen reaching for the doorknob.

"Don't!" Ryan ordered.

Before she could ask why, a bomb went off outside.

Ryan shoved Barry to the floor and dove on top of him. They landed beside Carmen, who had fallen as the house shook.

"Is there another way out of here?" Ryan barked.

Barry grabbed Carmen's hand, and they scrambled toward the desk. Ryan hoped they had a plan other than to cower under the desk as armed men assaulted the house.

The hacker shoved the office chair out of the way and lifted a trapdoor. He helped Carmen down the ladder and went down after her. Ryan was about to descend when the office door flew open. Drawing his paring knife, he stabbed the breacher in the shoulder, and a flashbang grenade fell to the floor. For half a second, Ryan stared at the pin in the man's hand before diving headfirst through the trapdoor.

He grabbed the ladder rung to arrest his fall, but his legs were still above the lip of the hole when the grenade detonated, and the flash singed the remaining hair from his legs as he tumbled down the ladder, landing on Barry and Carmen. All three of them fell to the tiled floor in what Ryan recognized as a bedroom before his head struck the ground and he saw stars.

Barry and Carmen wiggled out from under the salvage consultant and grabbed him by the wrists, dragging him into the darkness.

RYAN CAME to several moments later, with Barry patting him on the cheek and telling him to get up.

Rolling onto all fours, Ryan shook his head. He ran a hand over his temple and felt a lump forming there. He drew in a long breath and opened his eyes as wide as he could to focus them, but all he saw was black. Then the ground shook again, and dust rained down from the ceiling.

Still on all fours, Ryan put his head in his hands. "What was *that?*"

"I just blew the charges I'd set to destroy my equipment. I may have been overzealous with the C-4."

"I told you it was too much," Carmen hissed.

"Yeah, yeah, yeah. We're safe, aren't we?"

"*Where* are we?" Ryan asked.

"This is an old wine cellar that I had dug out to make into a panic room."

"How do we get out?" Ryan asked.

"No worries," Barry replied. "During the excavation, we found an old sea cave. We'll go out that way, but you'll have to do some climbing."

Carmen kneeled beside Ryan and gently touched his head. "Can you stand?"

"I think so."

She hooked her hands under his armpit. "Grab the other side, Barry."

After a moment of fumbling in the darkness and kicking Ryan in the shoulder, Barry did as she instructed, and they helped Ryan to his feet. The larger man swayed, and Carmen took a firm grip on his arm.

"Am I blind," Ryan asked. He didn't think he was, but he couldn't see a damned thing.

"No," Carmen said with exasperation. "Barry didn't charge the emergency batteries, *again*."

"Hey! In my defense, we never come down here."

"But you're *supposed* to check them once a month," Carmen shouted.

"Be quiet," Ryan hissed. He had heard something.

In a quieter voice, Carmen said, "It's probably the rats."

"Oh, *great*," Ryan moaned.

"Or the snakes," Barry said. "They like to hide in here because it's cool."

"Just shoot me now," Ryan moaned.

"Come on, lean on me," Carmen said. "Barry, you go first."

Barry moved forward, but Ryan couldn't see anything, so he held on tightly to Carmen with one arm and kept the other out in front of him. About fifty feet later, they came to a corner, and light spilled through the tunnel. When they rounded the bend, Ryan saw a tangle of vines covering a small entrance. Coiled up in a crook of the rock, just as Barry had said, was a snake.

"Don't worry." Barry reached down and picked up the two-foot-long reptile. "It's just a garden snake. It's not poisonous."

No matter what type of snake it was, Ryan hated them. The only good snake, in his opinion, was a dead one. He felt the adrenaline rush through him at the mere sight of the reptile in Barry's hand. While he wasn't afraid of much, snakes were at the top of the list. When he was young, he'd gone fishing with a friend, and they'd come across a cottonmouth with a frog wedged in its throat. His buddy had poked the snake with a stick, laughing that it couldn't do them any harm because it had a mouthful already, but when the snake lashed out at the stick, Ryan had taken off running.

Now, he wanted to run again as Barry held the snake out with both hands.

"Get that *thing* away from me," Ryan growled, leaning back far enough that Carmen had to struggle to keep him upright.

The hacker took a step closer to Ryan, who drew back.

"*Barry!*" Carmen hissed. "This is not the time to be fooling around."

Barry tossed the writhing snake behind them and pushed through the vines. Ryan followed him onto a ledge about twenty feet above the ocean, which crashed in waves onto the massive boulders below. They walked along the ledge until it ended, then scaled the last five feet to level ground.

The three of them sat and listened to the crackle of the fire Barry had sparked with his explosives. Far in the distance was the sound of sirens.

"How far are we from the house?" Ryan asked.

Barry pointed to their left. "It's about thirty yards that way."

They couldn't see it through the thick underbrush and trees, but they could hear running vehicles and shouting men.

"Do you have transportation?" Ryan asked.

Barry stood and brushed the dirt from his bottom. "Come on."

They trudged along a faint path to another property, pushing aside branches and bushes. At a garage door, Barry keyed in a number on a security pad, and the door lifted silently along its tracks. Inside sat a two-door Jeep Wrangler. When they were all in, Barry started the engine.

"What's your plan?" Barry asked. "Carmen and I have our own way off the island."

"Take me to where I can grab a cab and then email me all the data on that Griffin guy."

"I already sent it," Carmen said.

As Barry drove, Ryan called Mango. When he answered, Ryan told him to get ready to sail and explained the attack on Barry Thatcher's home. They needed to get away from St. Thomas and regroup.

"We'll be ready in an hour," Mango said.

"Good," Ryan replied. "I'll see you soon." He ended the call and leaned forward between the front seats. "What are the chances that your exfil route has been compromised?"

"They didn't find the Jeep," Barry said. He pulled to a stop at the taxi stand in front of the airport terminal.

Ryan got out of the back seat. "We're leaving on Mango's boat. If something happens, call me, and we'll wait for you."

"Thanks," Carmen said as Barry pulled away.

Ryan took a taxi across the island. Halfway there, his phone rang. "What's up?" he asked when he saw Carmen's caller ID.

"Our boat has disappeared," she said. "We're heading your way."

"What do you mean, disappeared?"

"Like, it's not there. And there are two *really* sketchy-looking *pendejos* hanging around the dock."

"Get to the American Yacht Harbor as fast as you can," Ryan told her.

"We will. See you soon." Carmen hung up, and Ryan kept watch out the cab's rear window. He couldn't see any tails, but that didn't mean they weren't there or that someone wouldn't be waiting at the yacht club for him. St. Thomas was turning out to be more dangerous than he'd bargained for, and he'd left a trail of death and destruction in his wake.

Instead of going straight to the marina, Ryan had the cab driver drop him at the ferry terminal parking garage that he'd scouted before rescuing Diane Langston. He paid the cab fare and milled about with the other ferry passengers while he watched for tails or suspicious activity.

Their adversaries in Panama and those at Barry's house hadn't been shy about making themselves known, so Ryan was sure no one was following him when he walked into the marina store. Fortunately, he'd had his wallet with him when he went to the bathhouse to shower, so he had his credit cards and some cash. His shoulders dropped as he realized his stash of cash had gone up in flames. After asking about his and Mango's boat fees, he laid his credit card on the counter, paid both their bills, and arranged for them to dispose of his burned-out boat hull. As he was signing the receipt, he saw Barry and Carmen pull into the parking lot.

He met the hackers at the Jeep and helped them carry their bags. No sooner had they set foot on the dock than Mango started the motors. Emily and Jennifer cast off the lines, and they held the boat in place as Carmen, Barry, and Ryan climbed aboard. Moments later, they were motoring away from the dock.

Emily found Ryan in the cockpit with Mango. The first

thing she noticed was the nasty knot on his temple that was turning black and blue. "What happened?"

"I fell through a trapdoor when Barry's house came under attack."

"Who attacked it?" Mango asked.

"I don't know. The power went out and I looked out the window in time to see a commando come over the wall. Then all hell broke loose as they assaulted the house." He went on to recount the story in detail.

As they exited Vessup Bay, Ryan told Mango to steer to port and follow the island around to a westerly heading. Then he entered a route for San Juan Bay Marina in San Juan, Puerto Rico, into the GPS plotter.

"Why are we going there?" Mango asked.

"We can get a direct flight to Miami. All of us. We're not splitting up the band," Ryan said.

Mango and Emily agreed.

Ryan fished his cell phone from his pocket and checked his email. The last one he'd received had been from Carmen, and it contained the information about Pops Griffin and his card-buying spree. He finished reading, then dialed Scott's phone number.

When the former SEAL answered his phone, Ryan explained about Webster Griffin and their need to surveil him. Scott quickly agreed to meet them at the Miami airport with gear bags and weapons for him and Mango, and the two men had a brief conversation about vehicles, manpower, and priorities before Ryan hung up.

"What's the plan?" Mango asked.

"We'll follow this Griffin character to his drop and work our way up the chain."

"As Yogi Berra said, 'It's like déjà vu all over again,'" Mango quipped.

"You're not kidding." Ryan ran both hands through his

hair, careful to avoid his newly formed goose egg. "This thing has more moving parts than a Swiss clock."

"I guess we'll see what happens when the machine stops," Mango said.

"That's easy," Emily replied. "The owner of the clock sends in a hit team."

"Ain't that the truth," Ryan said. "There's something we're missing that I can't pinpoint. Normally, we can figure out who the head of the operation is, but this guy has buried himself under layer upon layer of paperwork and shell corps, so he seems like he's untouchable."

"Something will break loose," Mango said. "It always does."

CHAPTER FORTY

During the sail from St. Thomas to San Juan, Ryan and Mango took turns at the wheel. It was during one of his brief stints away from the bridge that Ryan dialed the voicemail box for his satellite phone that had burned on his boat, intending to forward the calls to his new phone.

There were several messages, each several seconds long before ending. The last one contained nothing more than a phone number spoken in heavily accented English, and Ryan had to replay it several times to interpret what the caller had said. He recognized the +58 country code from his time in Venezuela. Glancing around the salon, he saw Barry and Carmen had their heads buried in their laptops and Emily and Jennifer were outside on the trampoline.

He retreated to the aft deck where his sat phone had a clear view of the sky and sat on a small sofa. Dialing the number that the mystery caller had left on his voicemail, he put the phone to his ear.

When the man on the other end answered, Ryan said, "*Buenos dias.*"

In Spanish, the other man replied, "Who is this?"

"You called my sat phone." Ryan recited the number for the man. Now that he had a decent connection, the man wasn't as hard to understand, especially when speaking in his native Spanish.

"I was told to call that number if I couldn't reach Oscar. Who are you, and what has happened to Sergeant López?"

"Oscar is dead."

"How did he die?" the man asked.

"Who am I speaking to, and why did Oscar tell you to call me?"

"My name is Mario Estevez."

Ryan straightened and felt his heartbeat increase, instantly recognizing the man's name. He was finally talking to Oscar's contact in Venezuela. "Are you Colonel Estevez of the Venezuelan Army Special Forces?"

"Yes."

"Can you speak freely?" Ryan asked.

"I can."

"You know that Oscar's team was ambushed and killed, right?"

"Yes," Estevez said.

"After he left the jungle, Oscar tracked a bank account to a money launderer in the U.S. Virgin Islands. That's where I met him. We worked together to find a man with the code name of The Armorer."

"I don't know that name," the colonel said.

"Did you know General Rincone?"

"I did. He defected."

"He's dead, too. So is a lawyer in Panama City named Valdez," Ryan said.

"I don't know Valdez."

"What about Armond Diego and Victor Quintero?" Ryan asked.

"Diego is dead. He was shot in the back of the head, along

with his wife and children, in his home in Caracas. The news is reporting that an opposition group is responsible for their deaths, but that is not the case. Victor Quintero has fled the country, and he's practiced a scorched earth policy on his way out the door."

"Where did he go?" Ryan asked.

"Where all rich Venezuelans go when they leave—Miami."

"You're telling me that Victor Quintero defected to the U.S. and is living in Florida?" Ryan demanded.

"Yes. He left a month ago."

Ryan pondered this for a moment as he digested the information.

Estevez interrupted his thinking. "Quintero has plundered our treasury and robbed Venezuela blind with his transactions with the Russians. He was Venezuela's principle armorer for more than a decade. Now, he is selling himself to the U.S. government. He is a traitor."

"And he's eliminating anyone who has any dirt on him."

"Exactly."

Ryan closed his eyes, focusing on what Estevez had just said. He had called Quintero Venezuelan's principle armorer. *The Armorer*. It fit. It had to be. If he could tie Quintero to the guy purchasing the prepaid cards in the U.S., they could confirm that Quintero was The Armorer.

"In our search through banking records, we found a Swiss bank account tied to multiple shell corporations," Ryan said. "One of which was supplying General Rincone with a monthly stipend. Do you know anything about that?"

"Quintero was well known for overpaying for military hardware and receiving kickbacks from suppliers," Estevez said. "The worst deal we discovered was for five thousand shoulder-fired missiles that he purchased from the Russians in anticipation of an invasion by the United States. He overpaid by millions of dollars. If I had to guess, he was paying Rincone to keep quiet."

"Oscar told me that officials in the Venezuelan government are protecting drug shipments through their country. Is that true?"

"Sure," Estevez said. "That is the truth. Your government has placed a bounty on Maduro and his officials for just such a reason."

Ryan's mind raced to make connections. Barry had said that money had come from a bank on the Crimean Peninsula. The Russian military could have funded the account in Crimea and wired it to Switzerland for Quintero. Even if he could see all the connections, he would have a tough time proving them in court or even to his DHS handler, Landis, who always wanted an overwhelming avalanche of evidence before moving in on a subject. If Quintero was now a pawn in the chess match between the United States and Venezuela, it would complicate matters even further.

"*Hola?*" Estevez said.

"I'm sorry, Colonel. I was thinking. Are you somewhere safe?"

"Nowhere is safe, but I am in Colombia. I am training members of the opposition." He let out a sigh. "I, too, am a defector from my beloved country, but there is much work to do. We must replace Maduro for our country to move forward."

"Good luck, Colonel," Ryan said.

"I hope you get that *bastardo* Quintero. He has done much to harm my country and my people. Avenge him for myself and for Sergeant López."

Ryan gripped the phone tighter, both feeling and hearing the emotion in Estevez's words. "I will, Colonel."

The call ended, and Ryan laid the phone onto the sofa beside him. What Estevez had said made sense. Every path they'd been down had led to either a dead end or a dead body. If they were all connected to Quintero, then he was certainly cleaning house. He was just coating the walls with blood instead of fresh paint.

Back in the catamaran's salon, Ryan sat beside Carmen. "Can you find me any information relating to the Russians selling a shipment of five thousand shoulder-fired missiles to Venezuela?"

She looked at him with a puzzled expression, then shrugged and began typing. Ryan looked over her shoulder, and within a few seconds, she had dozens of hits to her search terms. "What do you want to know?"

"Who are the principles, and where the money from Venezuela went."

"Give me some time, okay?"

"Yeah. No problem." Turning to Barry, Ryan asked what he was working on.

"I'm trying to figure out how those mercenaries found my house and who they were." He looked up to face Ryan with determination and anger in his eyes.

"Are you having any luck?" Ryan asked.

"I'm going through security cam footage and the other data I'd uploaded to my servers in Norway. I don't know how they found me, but I'll figure it out. Then I'll make them pay."

Ryan's eyebrows rose. He was seeing a vindictive side to Barry that he hadn't seen until now. The hacker's gaze flicked away from Ryan to share a moment with Carmen before returning to his laptop screen.

"Keep digging, both of you," Ryan said.

"I booked us on a flight from San Juan to Miami, like you asked," Carmen said.

"Good girl. She's a keeper, Barry."

He didn't look up from his rapid typing, but mumbled, "I

know."

Ryan stood and went up to the bridge, where Mango had his feet propped on the wheel and was strumming his flattop. He told Mango everything Estevez had said, and they tried to link him with all the deaths they had seen over the last couple of weeks. Neither of them had any concrete connections, but both agreed that, taken as a whole, he was the most likely mastermind. The best course of action was to track the prepaids and hope they led to Quintero.

It wasn't long before Carmen joined them on the bridge and stretched out on the sunpad just aft of the navigation station. She lay on her stomach and rested her head on her hands as if she were going to sleep.

"What did you find out about the missiles?" Ryan asked.

Without opening her eyes, she said, "Quintero was the Undersecretary to the Minister of Defense for the last ten years. He was involved in buying everything from tanks to jet fighters from Russia. He purchased the five thousand missiles. The military likes to put them on display, and there are pictures all over the Internet of soldiers and civilians holding them, including a nine-year-old girl. But without sending someone into the ministry building in Caracas, we won't be able to look at the purchase records because everything is on paper. Which is smart for them."

Ryan blew out a long breath through puffed-up cheeks. Another dead end. If Oscar hadn't shot Valdez, they could have asked him who The Armorer was and saved themselves countless hours of work, but now both Valdez and Oscar were dead, along with dozens of mercs and former Venezuelans. He wondered if Grasz was still alive in the Cayman prison.

An hour later, Barry stepped onto the bridge. He had four beers clasped between his fingers and handed one each to Carmen, Ryan, and Mango. "I've got bad news."

"What is it?" Ryan asked.

"I identified one of the men who came over the wall at my house as Mike Thornton. Guess which PMC he worked for."

"The infamous Russian group Wagner?" Mango asked.

"Academi?" Ryan asked, referring to the new name of what used to be Blackwater, one of the most famous PMCs in the world.

"Both of you are wrong." Barry took a sip of beer. "He worked for Trident."

It took Ryan several long seconds to formulate a thought beyond *what the hell?*

Mango beat him to the punch. "No way. Greg didn't send guys after you."

"I used facial recognition and that led me to his military file and his employment record at Trident. That means one of two things. Either you assholes attacked my house and are using me or"—he held up a second finger—"someone falsified Trident's records."

"There's one way to find out." Ryan reached for his phone and dialed the number for Jinks at Trident's headquarters in Texas City. The phone rang three times before Jinks came on the line, and when Ryan told him about the attack on Barry's house and how the facial recog scan had led back to Trident, Jinks was just as incredulous as Ryan and Mango had been.

At Ryan's request, Jinks typed Mike Thornton into the Trident database and found a file labeled Foxtrot Team. Inside was the employment record for every assaulter on Barry's home. Jinks echoed Ryan's earlier thought. "What the *hell?* These guys don't work for us. I've never heard of them."

"Then you've been hacked, and you're being set up to take the fall," Barry stated.

"There are employment records, pay receipts, mission briefs, and training records. These hackers were thorough," Jinks said.

"Wipe it all," Ryan said. "And get Ashlee to set up a better firewall."

"Roger that."

Ryan hung up and pocketed the phone. "How is one man able to execute operations all over the world and orchestrate sophisticated cyber-attacks at the same time? This dude has *deep* pockets."

"Or he has help from a foreign government," Mango replied. "If Quintero was in bed with the Russians, maybe they're trying to cover their tracks. He could spill the beans about all kinds of hinky shit going on in both countries."

"Whoever it is," Barry said, "they're doing everything they can to stop you from finding out who The Armorer really is. I'm ready to get off this crazy train."

"You and me both, bro," Mango said. "Jenn and I are supposed to be opening a charter business in St. Thomas, and now I'm probably *persona non grata* there. We need to be done with this shit so we can go back to our daily lives."

Ryan agreed with both men, but he also knew his daily life was just filler for between missions. It was becoming clearer to him that he was no longer a reluctant participant in chasing bad guys, but a person who actively ran toward danger because he felt the need to protect others.

Right now, he needed to protect the people on the boat with him. Whoever they were after was one step ahead of them and seemed to know every move they were making.

CHAPTER FORTY-ONE

Miami, Florida

After clearing Customs at Miami International Airport, Ryan and his team stepped outside the terminal to get a ride to a rental car company. As they stood on the sidewalk, waiting for a shuttle bus, a Ford Explorer pulled alongside the curb and the window rolled down.

Scott Gregory grinned at them from the driver's seat. "What's up, punks?"

"I thought we were meeting at the hotel," Ryan said.

"Things are moving fast. I need to talk to you."

Ryan glanced over his shoulder at the rest of his troops. "You coming, Mango?"

"I'll help get the rentals and meet you at the hotel."

"I'll go with you," Emily volunteered. "I've been on plenty of stakeouts."

Without another word, Ryan opened the door for her to get into the back seat of the Explorer and climbed into the passenger seat beside Scott. He buzzed the window up as Scott pulled away from the curb, merging with the airport traffic.

"What's going on?" Ryan asked.

"We've been tailing your boy, Pops. He's been all over the map." Scott checked his mirrors before continuing. "He bought prepaids at two other stores, and he makes regular stops at a horse track and a strip club."

"Cash-heavy businesses that would be easy to launder money through," Ryan said.

"Yeah. I brought you a present. I figured you'd want it before you got back to the hotel. Check the glove box."

Ryan opened the glove box and found a pistol inside. It was in a Kydex holster and had a magazine in the mag well and two more in a magazine holster. He had expected one of his favored Walther PPQ M2s, but instead drew out a Springfield XD-M Elite Tactical in flat dark earth. He gripped it with both hands and aimed the sights at the footwell, keeping the gun below the window.

"She's got one in the pipe and twenty-two in the mag," Scott said. "She's my new go-to gun, and I figured you'd like it, too."

"It's nice." Ryan screwed the thread cap off the end of the barrel and inspected the threads. "You got a suppressor?"

"It's in a bag in the back." Scott glanced in the mirror. "There's a gun in there if you want it, Emily."

"No, thanks. I'm good for now," she replied.

Ryan slipped the holster inside his belt on his right hip, pulled his shirt down over the butt, and hooked the spare mags on his left side. "What's Pops doing when he makes his stops?"

"He meets with various individuals," Scott said. "I've seen him hand off a paper bag to one of his contacts at the track, but I don't know what was in it."

"Have you checked his car?" Emily asked.

"Got a tracker on his old school Cadillac. That's how we're watching him. He has a regular route, so we'd be conspicuous tailing him even if we used multiple cars. We just don't have that kind of manpower."

"How many guys *do* you have with you?" Ryan asked.

"Me, Jinks, and Rick Hayes."

"I thought Rick was still in Nicaragua."

Scott shrugged. "You know how it is."

Ryan did know how it was. Once an operator, always an operator. Tracking down terrorists, cartel sicarios, serial killers, and sex traffickers was a righteous passion that every man at Trident shared, including Ryan and Mango. While Ryan loved diving both commercially and recreationally, he liked the thrill of the chase and he felt at home riding in the Explorer with Scott, strapped up and locked in on a suspect.

Scott drove them through the suburbs of Miami. It was hard to tell where one town ended and another began, because there was hardly any difference in the buildings or the street names. Lining the streets were strip malls and office buildings. Jammed in between those were narrow apartment buildings. The Trident operator pulled the car into a grocery store parking lot and put the transmission into park.

"See that bodega across the street with the cell phone sign in the window?" Scott asked.

"Yeah," Ryan said, looking across four lanes of traffic at a two-story building. Sandwiched between a Cuban restaurant and a hair salon on the first floor was the bodega in question. Above them were law offices and a massage parlor.

"That's where Barry's surveillance footage came from. There's nothing special inside. I've been in there and bought a six-pack and a burner phone. Speaking of which ..." Scott rummaged in a bag, plucked out a phone, and handed it to

Ryan, along with a pair of Bluetooth earbuds. "I programmed everyone's number into there."

"Thanks." Ryan scrolled through the numbers and checked their location on the map application. "Where's Pops at now?"

Scott consulted his phone and showed the screen to Ryan. "He's making his drop at the horse track. He'll go to the post office and then the strip club."

"Who does he meet with at each place?"

Scott pulled up pictures of two people. The bookie was a Latino-looking male with dark hair, bronze skin, and brown eyes. He had acne scars and looked rough from running the streets. The strip club owner could have been Emily's twin: tall and slender, with thick blonde hair and a winning smile.

"What do you think?" Scott asked after Ryan and Emily had looked at both pictures.

"We need to know who he's passing the cards to before we move, but my guess is that it's the club owner. I don't think the bookie has access to the track's accounts."

"I agree," Scott said.

"When do you think Pops will be back to get more cards?" Ryan asked.

"If he sticks to his schedule, he'll be back tomorrow," Scott replied.

"I wonder how we can track the cards?" Ryan mused.

"What are the chances that Pops records the numbers for each card?" Emily asked.

Neither man had an answer for her. Scott shrugged, and Ryan asked her what she was thinking.

"What if we get a batch of cards and swapped them out? We could put a tracker in with them, and Barry could track the numbers."

"That might work," Scott said. "Where do we get one hundred prepaid cards?"

"We just have to buy them," Emily said. "We know they're blue, so we get lookalikes."

Ryan nodded. He liked the idea. Not only would they know where Pops handed the cards off and to whom, but they would also have access to the money. They could let the bad guys finance their counter-operation.

Emily opened her door and climbed out. "I'll be back in a minute."

She crossed the street at the light and walked into the bodega. A few minutes later, she reappeared with a plastic grocery sack. The two men in the Explorer watched her walk west along the street.

"Where's she going?" Scott asked.

"She doesn't want to retrace her steps in case someone is watching her. Drive down the street, and we'll pick her up."

Scott put the Explorer in gear and pulled into traffic. Ryan saw his girlfriend turn south at the next cross street and told Scott to continue west and make the turn at the next light. When he did, they found themselves in a residential street lined with small apartment buildings. Scott hit the accelerator and exceeded the speed limit.

Ryan suspected Scott had the same queasy feeling that he had about letting a beautiful blonde walk through the rough neighborhood. They caught up to her, and she hopped into the SUV before it came to a complete stop. She handed Ryan a cold Mountain Dew from her bag and gave Scott a Red Bull that matched the empty can in the center console.

Scott navigated them back to the main thoroughfare and headed east.

"Where are we staying?" Emily asked.

"It's an old local place on U.S. 1," Scott said. "Wait, you're from here, aren't you?"

"North. Hollywood."

Ryan hadn't bothered to ask her how she felt about

coming home. She hadn't lived on the East Coast in over a decade, and she'd told Ryan that there were good reasons for her move. Chief among them was her ex-boyfriend, who was still a sheriff's deputy for Broward County. Hopefully, they didn't run into that asshole or Ryan would probably deck him. She hadn't told him everything, but Ryan had heard enough to know that her ex had physically and verbally abused her, and Ryan wouldn't stand for that shit. Cop or not, he might just kick her ex in the nuts, but that was a worry for another time. They had an errand man to track down.

Scott made several stops at bodegas, convenience, and grocery stores, but they only came up with half the cards they needed.

Turning to Scott, Ryan asked, "Where are Jinks and Rick?"

"They're following Pops."

"Emily, send them a picture of the prepaid. Tell them to buy fifty more cards and meet us at the hotel."

WHEN THEY ARRIVED at the hotel, the group gathered in one room and Ryan told them their plan. Barry smiled and said he had just the thing they needed. He rummaged around in his computer case and pulled out a small clear package. He held it up in triumph for everyone else to see.

"That's a great idea, Barry," Carmen said.

"What is it?" Mango asked.

"This is a tracker," Barry said. "It looks just like the chip on a credit card, but we'll put it in the blister pack. If we replaced a chip on a card, they would catch it, because the card wouldn't load."

"What makes you think they won't find it?" Scott asked.

"We don't know if they will or not, but hopefully they

have someone opening the cards who isn't paying attention. Anyway, we insert this into the cardboard of the blister pack and, *voilà*, we track them to their destination."

"Can that pinpoint the target or just give us a general building?" Scott asked.

"Once you're close, it will give you the exact position inside the building or wherever else the cards go."

"I like it," Mango said.

"By watching the numbers on the cards you bought, we can see what account they're using to load them and track them through the network," Carmen said.

"Exactly," Ryan agreed. "Then we can round up the accomplices. By taking out the network, we might force The Armorer to come out of hiding."

"It's as good a plan as any," Scott agreed. "But I was looking forward to roughing up a few bad guys."

"Don't lie," Carmen said coyly. "You just want to do a stakeout in a strip club."

Scott grinned and shrugged. "The job comes with some perks."

Ryan glanced at Emily, who just shook her head. He had no plans to go into the club. He had all the woman he needed.

He changed the subject by saying, "We need a game plan for the swap tomorrow."

"The first thing we need to do is separate Pops from the cards," Jinks said.

"This is how I think we should do it," Ryan said, then outlined his plan.

CHAPTER FORTY-TWO

They knew the route that Pops normally drove because of the GPS tracker on his car, and they knew where he made stops besides those related to his business. It was at one of those places that Ryan wanted to exchange the cards. From the intel that Scott, Jinks, and Rick had collected, they knew Pops liked to stop at a Cuban restaurant for *café con leche* and he always left his batch of prepaids in the car.

As Ryan, Scott, and Emily sat in the Explorer in a nearby shopping center parking lot, they watched Pops wheel his antique Cadillac into the lot, get out, and slap down the door lock. He swung the giant door closed and headed into the café. Scott had also observed that the old man had a penchant for younger women and often chatted them up if he saw one he fancied. Scott had never seen him leave with a woman, but Pops certainly thought he still had a few moves left in the tank.

No sooner had their target swung his door shut than a car pulled in beside him and Jennifer and Carmen climbed out, dressed to make any man glance their way. And Pops did more than glance. The old black man put his hand over his heart and let out a long breath as the scantily clad women walked past him. Carman tossed her hair over her shoulder with a shake of her head and glanced back at him. She blew him a kiss, and he staggered backward, faking being blown away.

"Think that will keep him occupied?" Scott asked.

"That should keep *any* red-blooded male occupied," Ryan said.

"I hope *you're* not occupied, sailor," Emily said from the back seat.

They continued to watch as Rick and Jinks pulled in beside the Cadillac. Rick slid out of their Chevy Tahoe and went to work opening the Cadillac's locked passenger door. Ryan had given him the job because Rick had grown up with a pickpocket for a father who had done time for robbing a jewelry store. Before joining the Army, Rick had boosted cars to help pay for college until the cops had busted him with a hot Porsche. If his ROTC instructor at the University of New Orleans hadn't helped him out of the jam with the owner and the cops, Rick might have gone to jail. As it was, the owner hadn't pressed charges, instead he'd mentored Rick as he worked his way through school.

Within a matter of seconds, Rick had the window pulled away from the door seal, allowing him to slide a carefully bent wire coat hanger around the lock knob and pull up, popping the lock. He quickly transferred the replacement cards into Pops's old paper bag and took Pops's cards with him. The entire process took less than two minutes, and Jinks drove away as soon as Rick was back in the Tahoe.

Ryan sent a quick text to let Carmen know the deed was done, and the women disengaged from Pops and walked out of the café. He set his phone down, and a moment later, it dinged with a texted photo of an envelope. The addressee was Hotshots, Inc. Ryan showed the photo to Scott and Emily.

The puzzle pieces were falling into place.

The operators spread out through the city to cover the stops they knew Pops would make. Scott headed for the strip club while Ryan worked on finding more information about Victor Quintero and his defection to the United States. The only thing of note was a small article in the *Miami Herald* that said Quintero was cooperating with the U.S. government.

"Do you suppose our case will poke holes in the story Quintero is telling the Feds?" Ryan wondered aloud.

"If he's got their protection, we might have to turn everything we have over to them," Scott said.

"Yeah, and that would be a shame, because they probably won't do anything to him," Ryan said.

"Should you talk to Landis about it and see what Homeland has on him?" Scott asked.

"Not yet," Ryan stated. He wasn't ready to hand over what he had because it was all circumstantial, and he knew for a fact that if Homeland or the FBI were working with Quintero, they would tell him to back off. "Let's see where this card thing goes first."

Pops's first stop was the horse track, and Jinks reported that he'd carried a paper sack into the casino.

Ryan called Rick, who had gotten into his own chase car, and asked him if he knew what was in the sack. Rick said he hadn't seen another bag in the Cadillac and, according to the GPS, their bag of cards hadn't left the car.

They didn't need to wait much longer for the cards to move. Pops drove to a pink concrete block building and climbed the back stairs to what Scott told Ryan was an office. Above the building's main entrance was a neon sign that read *The Pink Flamingo Cabaret,* and beside it was a neon bird of the same name. The club sat on the Little River across the street from a gas station.

Ryan craned his neck around to take in the sites around

them as they sat at a red light beside the club. He told Scott to circle the block. On the corner opposite them was an abandoned twelve-story building with its windows broken out and the demolished walls around the bottom two stories revealed its skeletal interior. On the west side of the strip club was a run-down apartment building with overflowing dumpsters.

"The cards are moving," Ryan said, watching the GPS tracker.

"What do you want to do?" Scott asked.

"Pull into the gas station and back into a spot where we can see the club's parking lot."

Scott parked, and Emily went into the gas station. She came back with drinks for the three of them.

"It seems a little ridiculous sitting across the street at a gas station," Scott said. "Why don't we go over there and avail ourselves of the amenities?"

"How many bouncers are in there?" Ryan asked.

"On a busy night, I counted six."

"Strapped?"

"Uh, yeah," Scott scoffed.

"So, how many times have you been in there?" Ryan asked.

"A couple," Scott said. Then quickly added, "I was trying to get the lay of the land."

"Do you mean 'get the *lay* of the land' or 'get *laid*,' because we both know there's no sex in the Champagne Room," Ryan said with a grin.

"Don't give me an assignment if you don't want a thorough firsthand report."

Ryan continued to smile as he shook his head. "I'm sure your hand was the only thing you took home after spending time in there."

"Here's my hand." Scott held it up with his index, middle, and ring fingers extended. "Read between the lines."

"I hope you didn't talk to the girls like that," Emily said.

Both men laughed, but their good-natured ribbing stopped when Ryan's phone rang. He tapped the speaker and asked, "What's going on, Barry?"

"They're loading the cards and using an account from a local bank. And get this. The name on the account is Hotshots, Inc. It receives *a lot* of cash deposits."

"All in one-dollar bills?" Scott asked.

"There's probably some. You know it's superstitious for a stripper to leave the club with one-dollar bills, right?" Barry said.

"Why am I not surprised you know that?" Ryan said.

"I may have invested in a strip club before," the hacker said.

Ryan laughed. "Putting ones in a G-string is not 'investing.' Tell me about the account."

"They routinely deposit at least one hundred grand a night," Barry replied. "In one-dollar bills, that's …. about two-hundred-and-twenty pounds, give or take. They'd need an armored truck to carry that."

Scott whistled. "I was in that place. There's no way they're pulling in a hundred G's a night in cash."

"There are a lot of credit card receipts as well," Barry said. "Millennials are using apps like Venmo to pay phone-to-phone."

"Great. So, we might never know where the money is coming from," Scott lamented.

"It's true that there are a lot of individual transactions connected to the club," Barry said. "Most of the workers are independent contractors who get paid either via cash or electronic transactions, but this is getting into the weeds. For now, I'm focusing on the money from the club, not the workers. If it's as you say, and the club can't show correct receipts for the big deposits, then something is definitely fishy."

"Glad we cleared that up," Scott huffed. Turning to Ryan, he said, "What now?"

"Barry, can you take the money off the cards as fast as they're putting it on?"

"Sure. I'll just move it into an escrow account that I use."

"Great. Do it, and we'll see what happens when they try to use them."

"Okay. I'll start now," Barry said.

"Thanks," Ryan said and hung up.

Scott leaned his head back against the headrest and blew out a sigh. "How long before they notice the money is missing?"

"Who knows," Ryan said.

"I wonder how many times we could switch cards before they'd notice?" Scott asked. "We could scam a ton of cash that way."

Ryan shrugged. He had thought about the same thing. He could have Barry dip straight into the account and bypass the cards all together. That would *definitely* get someone's attention. They needed to know where the money was coming from. Some of it was proceeds from the club as a legitimate business, but stealing it all would scare the hell out of everyone up and down the power structure.

As they watched, a black Lincoln Town Car pulled into the parking lot, and the club owner got out of the passenger seat. She wore a dark blue business suit with a skirt similar to the one she'd been wearing in the picture Scott had shown Emily and Ryan. Her heels were around three inches high, and she carried a briefcase in one hand. Behind her was a tall, beefy man.

"Who's the guy?" Emily asked.

"That's her EP—executive protection," Ryan said, noting the way the man constantly scanned his surroundings and kept his principle close at hand. He was packing in a shoulder holster beneath his suit jacket.

"She has to know her club is being used to launder money and who she's laundering it for," Emily said. "I think we should talk to her. We need to push this along. I'm ready to look for another boat and get back on the water."

Ryan turned to look at her, knowing full well his mouth was open in surprise.

She smiled coquettishly. "I like Jenn and Mango's cat. We should get something like that."

Scott flicked his wrist and made a sound like a cracking whip.

"Don't be jealous, Scott," Emily said.

"What's this chick's name?" Ryan asked, referring to the club owner. Turning around to face the street, he gave a glance into each mirror to check their flanks.

"Candice Vaughn," Scott said.

Ryan chuckled. "That sounds like a stripper name."

"I've seen her in the club. The girls said she used to work on stage and suddenly came into some money and bought the place."

"Maybe Uncle Quintero financed a new business venture to help launder his cash?" Ryan suggested.

"Could be," Scott replied. "She has a nice apartment near Haulover Inlet, too."

"Do you have a tracker on her car?" Emily asked.

"No, but I can put one on it," Scott volunteered.

"What do you know about her EP?" Ryan asked.

"Just that he's always around."

"Put the tracker on," Ryan said.

Scott ran across the street and planted the tracker under the rear of her vehicle while Ryan moved to the Explorer's driver's seat. They pulled away as soon as Scott was back in the SUV.

Two blocks later, Emily said, "Vaughn's GPS says she's moving."

Ryan swung into a shopping center and parked until they could figure out which direction Vaughn was heading. Vaughn's black Town Car passed them and continued north. Ryan fell in behind it while Scott called the others to tell them they were in pursuit of the club owner and gave them her license plate and vehicle description.

Vaughn's driver turned left and headed west.

Ryan turned their Explorer around and followed discreetly, but he couldn't help wondering if this was just another wild goose chase.

CHAPTER FORTY-THREE

Twenty-five minutes later, Ryan, Emily, and Scott watched as the black Lincoln Town Car they'd been following pulled into a parking structure beside Marlins Park, the stadium where the Miami Marlins played. Ryan pulled into the parking lot of a shuttered gas station across the street.

"Get in there, Scott," Ryan ordered.

Scott glanced down at the tablet they'd been using to follow the tracking device on Vaughn's car, then got out and ran across the street. There were two massive parking garages that looked like many of the shopping plazas and apartment buildings around the greater Miami area. Palm trees lined the street, obscuring the view of the retail spaces on the garages' ground floors.

Emily climbed over the center console into the front seat. She gripped Ryan's hand, and he returned the squeeze without taking his eyes off the parking structure. Neither of them lost their focus on the job as they held hands. Candice Vaughn had connections to Hotshots, Inc. and was the sudden recipient of an infusion of cash that had allowed her to purchase the strip club, and someone was loading the prepaid cards in her office. She was a key piece in The Armorer's money laundering operations. They couldn't afford to lose her now, and this was the perfect place to get lost in a crowd.

"There's a silver Range Rover coming out of the west garage," Emily said.

Ryan saw it pull up to the stop light and make a right turn without slowing. "Shit, that was Vaughn's EP in the driver's seat." He grabbed his phone and dialed Scott. When the former SEAL answered, Ryan asked, "Have you found the Town Car?"

"Yeah, I've got eyes on it."

"Is there anyone inside?"

"No, there's no one inside."

"Get back here, *now*," Ryan ordered. "They left in a different vehicle."

Ryan hung up without hearing Scott's acknowledgment and dialed Jinks and Rick Hayes on a conference call. When both men were on the line, he told them that Vaughn had changed vehicles and gave them a description before telling them the Range Rover had turned east on Northwest Seventh Street and they were in pursuit.

"He's turning right," Emily said, pointing at the silver SUV.

Scott ran out of the garage, and Ryan gunned the Explorer through the red light, slowed at the curb just long enough to let Scott hop in the back seat, and took off again. He made the same turn the Range Rover had into a residential neighborhood. They rolled through two blocks before making two more turns and heading south on to Northwest Twelfth Avenue.

"Who's with me?" Ryan asked into the phone.

"This is Jinks. I'm on your six and see you and the Rover. Fall back and I'll take over."

"Got it," Ryan said, slowing to make a turn off the main road and watching his mirror as Jinks sped past in his Jeep Wrangler.

"Where are you, Rick?" Ryan asked.

"I'm on I-95, passing downtown Miami. Where do you want me?"

"I don't know yet," Ryan said.

"I'll keep heading south."

Jinks said, "I'm going to pass them. Ryan, you take over again."

"Give me one minute. We're stuck at a red light."

"Tell me when," Jinks said through the Explorer's radio speakers.

Ryan stopped at the red light and threw the transmission into park. He glanced at Emily. "Chinese fire drill?"

She grinned, and they threw open their doors and ran around the vehicle. Ryan hopped into the passenger seat, and Emily got into the driver's side. They picked up the Range Rover after two blocks. Ryan told Rick to take I-95 until it turned into U.S. 1.

When Vaughn turned onto U.S. 1, Rick fell in behind her until she turned into a parking lot for a small park overlooking Biscayne Bay. Rick kept going, reporting Vaughn's location over the cell phone.

Emily coasted the Explorer to a stop in another lot for the same park. Through the trees, they could see Vaughn and her EP climb from the Range Rover and head toward a group of boys playing soccer. Ryan and Emily got out of their SUV and followed, hand in hand, across the green grass.

The EP stopped and let his principle walk ahead. Ryan and Emily walked past him, watching Vaughn take a seat on a park bench beside a man with a newspaper.

"Scott, do you see this?" Ryan asked into his Bluetooth earpiece.

"I see them, but I don't know who the guy is."

"That's Victor Quintero," Ryan said.

"*Holy* shit."

"You got the camera?" Ryan asked.

"Yeah. I've got a few shots already. I'm on the far side of the soccer game."

Ryan saw his partner squatting in the grass, photographing the boy's game and their two principles on the bench. "Get a couple of good ones and let's get out of here before the EP or Quintero's security spot us. He has to have people somewhere."

"Roger that," Scott said.

As they retreated to the Explorer, Rick Hayes walked past eating an Icee from a cup. He didn't acknowledge them as they passed, turning toward the bench where Quintero and Vaughn were sitting. A moment later, Rick said into the phone, "I've got eyes on two guys I think are Quintero's EP. They look and smell like Feds."

"Jinks, you and Rick stay with Quintero. Let's find out where he lives," Ryan said.

"You got it, boss. I have to say this is better than deploying to Mauritania, where Greg had a team scheduled to go."

"Are you putting your name in the hat for Caribbean operations, too?" Ryan asked.

"Beats Africa," Jinks replied, and Scott concurred from the back seat of the Explorer.

"Just follow Quintero," Ryan said, and ended the call. He drove south along Bayshore Drive, passing glittering marinas full of giant luxury yachts on the east side of the road and million-dollar homes and towering condo buildings on the west side. He turned onto Pan American Drive on Dinner Key and circled around the front of Miami City Hall, which sat on the edge of the water, overlooking the bay and Dinner

Key Marina. He stopped in a City Hall parking lot beside Regatta Park, a lush green space that occupied the rest of Dinner Key.

"Did you know that Miami City Hall used to be the main terminal for Pan Am's flying boats?" Emily asked.

"That's cool," Scott said.

The phone rang, and Ryan pressed the button on the steering wheel to answer Rick's call. "Vaughn is leaving, and Quintero is on the move."

"Stick with Quintero," Ryan said.

"He's heading south."

A few minutes later, Jinks called and reported, "Quintero's SUV just pulled into the Grove at Grand Bay."

Emily pointed across the street. "That's those twin towers over there. They call them the Twisted Towers."

The two towers looked like someone had rotated each floor just a little more than the one below it, giving the structure the visual effect of twisting around its axis.

Ryan realized Emily knew or spent more time in South Florida than she'd told him. It was one of the boating capitals of the world, so she probably came here on business. He dialed Barry's number and asked if the hacker could get into Candice Vaughn's cell phone. Barry scoffed and complained about it being child's play, then asked what Ryan wanted to know because he was already inside her Android operating system.

"Give me the number for Quintero. It should be one of her last calls."

Barry read off three numbers with no caller ID while Ryan typed them into a note-taking app. Before Ryan could hang up, Barry said, "I know who hacked my system."

"Who?" Ryan asked.

"It was a group based in Ukraine. Rumor has it they're part of the Russian Federal Security Service."

"Are they tracking you now?"

"No. I'm running off a server farm in Argentina and using a VOIP that masks my identity, plus—"

Ryan cut off the hacker. "Can you move all the money out of every account associated with The Armorer?"

"Sure. Yes. Hell, *yes*, I can do that. It'll take me some time to set up some shell corps and I'll have to bounce it around a bit, but yeah."

"Good. Call me when you're ready to press the button. When I tell you, I want every account balance zeroed out. If you have access to prepaid card numbers, ding those, too."

"Okay. I'll let you know as soon as I have everything set up."

Ryan ended the call, and Emily asked what he was doing.

"If Quintero is The Armorer—and I suspect that he is—then he has protection as long as he's here in the States and working for the U.S. government. Normally, I wouldn't care about some defecting undersecretary and I hope they squeeze him for every ounce of intelligence he has to give, but this guy has killed a lot of people to get where he is. If we zero his account balances, I think we can flush him out. I think he'll run toward someplace he has money stashed, and that will give us an opportunity to put an end to all of this."

"And what about the money you take?" Emily asked.

Ryan shrugged as he gazed out the window at the luxury towers where Quintero lived. "We could use a new sailboat. I'm sure Scott and the rest of the crew would like to get paid for riding all over the Caribbean, and we'll figure out how to give the rest of it back to Venezuela. If we can't get it there, we can fund some other charities."

"I don't like it," Emily said.

"It's this or Quintero sits up in that apartment, fat, dumb, and happy," Ryan said. "I can't stand the thought of that."

"Me, neither," Scott chimed in.

"So, what's the plan?" Emily asked. "How will we know if he's running, and to where?"

"The one thing he's proven to care about is the money," Ryan explained. "Once it's gone, he'll have no assets here. If I were him, I'd have a boat or plane on standby. I doubt he'll drive because there's nowhere for him to go. This state is one giant peninsula with limited roads in or out."

"He could drive to the West Coast or to the Keys and get on a boat there," Emily objected.

"True, but from here, it's a straight shot to the Bahamas, where we know he has accounts. It would be an easy run. We stake out the bank and put a sniper round in his brain as he walks in the front door."

"Taking the money will spook him," Emily said, "but if there's anything we've learned about Quintero, it's that he has plenty of resources. What are you going to do to make him run?"

"I'll call him and tell him I know everything," Ryan said. "Then Barry will zero his accounts. He'll check them and see that the only one left is the one in the Bahamas. We'll cut off all his lines of communication to the bank and force him to go there."

"What about the FBI?" Scott asked. "If they're babysitting him like Rick said, then they'll be pretty pissed about what you're doing."

"Once he rabbits, I don't think they'll care," Ryan said.

"I think they'll be seriously pissed if you take him out. Maybe you should talk to Landis," Scott suggested.

"I've had that conversation before," Ryan replied. "He'll say that Quintero enjoys the good graces of the DEA or whatever alphabet agency he's working with, and we're not to interfere with their ongoing operations."

"I know you think this is best," Emily said, "but there may

be more at stake than we know. I think you should discuss it with Jinks—or Greg, at least."

Ryan drummed his fingers on the steering wheel and glanced in the rearview mirror at Scott, who shrugged. He wanted to see Quintero pay for what he had done to Oscar, to Oscar's team, for killing Rincone and Kirshen, and for fleecing the Venezuelan people. Ryan needed to do something, and he was afraid that if he spoke to Landis, he would be told to back off and no one would bring Quintero to justice. The defector would probably spend the rest of his days living on his ill-gotten gains and receiving subsidized housing courtesy of the American taxpayer.

Ryan wondered if it would interest Maduro to know the whereabouts of his turncoat Undersecretary to the Minister of Defense. It wouldn't be hard to send in Latinos to spy on Quintero's activities; they seemed to be everywhere. Castro had done it many times, and there was probably a contingent of covert agents from every country operating in and around Miami. Ryan and his Trident team were just a drop in the bucket.

"I can see the wheels spinning," Emily said.

"What if we did nothing but make a phone call?" Ryan asked.

"What do you mean?" she asked.

Scott leaned forward to hear better.

"Colonel Estevez is training troops in Colombia. What if I called him and let it slip where Quintero is living, and he sent someone to take care of the problem?"

CHAPTER FORTY-FOUR

One Month Later
Tampa, Florida

Whiskey Joe's Bar and Grill had become Ryan's de facto hangout. The waitresses knew him by name and, whenever he sat down at the bar, they automatically placed a glass of water in front of him followed by a margarita on the rocks with salt on the rim. Shortly after, a plate of grouper tacos would arrive, and after eating, Ryan would spend the afternoon soaking up the sun on the little beach beside the bar.

In the mornings, he'd run the Courtney Campbell Causeway Trail from Emily's apartment on Rocky Point to the causeway boat ramp and back, a distance of six miles. Some days, he'd swim there and back.

When sitting at the bar or in an Adirondack chair on the restaurant's private beach, he spent his time staring at a laptop. He divided his time between surfing the Internet for a new sailboat and checking the news, expecting to see something about the death of Victor Quintero.

He took a drink of his margarita, the ice pressing against his upper lip. Not long after calling Colonel Estevez in Colombia, Ryan and Scott had driven to a duplex in a tree-lined suburb less than a mile from Quintero's home in the Twisted Towers. After entering through the back door, a lawn service truck had pulled up in the front and disgorged a zero-turn mower from an enclosed trailer. A crew of three men ran string trimmers and the mower while a fourth walked to the duplex's front door.

The man wore green pants and a green shirt with the sleeves rolled up. An embroidered name tag read Henry. Ryan let him in and shook hands with the smaller, balding man. Henry sat at the table and read through the entire folder Ryan and his team had put together on Quintero. When he finished, Henry said, "This is excellent work. May I ask how you found him?"

"It was a long and complicated process," Ryan said.

Henry nodded. "I didn't believe Colonel Estevez when he called me, but he assured me you'd have proof." He tapped the closed folder.

"What will you do now?" Scott asked.

"What difference does it make?" Henry said. "You called me for help, and I will do what is necessary."

"Do you need anything else?" Ryan asked.

"No. You have been more than helpful."

Ryan recounted that conversation often in his mind and wondered when Estevez's men would act, assuming they would move immediately on Quintero.

He took another drink and went back to looking at catamarans online. Picking out a new boat was harder than he'd thought. His tastes had to match Emily's, even though she had told him that whatever he picked out would be fine. He had learned otherwise. Whatever boat he found had to receive her stamp of approval.

"Hey, Ryan. The paper came in," Cheri, the bartender, said. "Do you want to see it?"

"Yeah." He held out his hand, and she put the *Tampa Bay Times* in it.

He flipped through the pages quickly and spotted a story from Miami. The headline grabbed his attention:

FORMER VENEZUELAN DEFENSE UNDERSECRETARY SLAIN IN EARLY MORNING HOURS.

According to eyewitness reports, men on motorcycles had pulled alongside the Chevy Tahoe Quintero was riding in and fired point-blank into it, killing both Quintero and the driver. The police said they were pursuing several leads and believed the killing was retribution for Quintero's defection.

Ryan folded the paper and laid it on the bar beside the computer. Cheri brought him a fresh margarita and took the paper. After she walked away, he sent a text to Barry Thatcher and told him to move the money. While they'd decided not to drain all of Quintero's accounts, they would take enough to pay the team and for Ryan to buy a new boat and recoup the cost of giving Oscar López a proper burial on St. Thomas.

Barry immediately returned his text, telling him he had moved the money as soon as he had heard the news of Quintero's murder. The text also contained the account number and SWIFT codes for Colonel Estevez's new bank account, funded by Victor Quintero. Ryan forwarded the text to Estevez, then took apart the cell phone, removing the battery and the SIM card.

After finishing his drink, Ryan paid his tab and left the restaurant, depositing the phone in the trash on his way out. At another trash can along the causeway, he tossed the SIM card and kept walking to Emily's apartment.

Surprisingly, she was home. She had been working almost non-stop since their arrival in Tampa two days after meeting with Henry.

"Hi," he said, taking in the wine glass in her hand and the two cardboard boxes on the kitchen table.

"I have something to tell you," she said.

Ryan fetched a beer from the fridge and leaned against the counter. After a long swig, he looked at her expectantly.

She smiled. "I quit."

"Quit what?" he asked.

"My job. Well, I didn't fully quit. I just changed jobs. I'm now an independent contractor, like you. The Ward and Young Board of Directors didn't want to lose me completely and asked me to take the contracting job."

It wasn't a complete surprise to him. She didn't need to work now and neither did he, but Greg was already ringing his bell about jobs around the Caribbean, everything from working with Trident to inspecting oil rigs. Even Travis Wisnewski had called and asked him to come back and dive with the crew on the salvage vessel *Peggy Lynn*.

"That's awesome, babe," he said. "Now we can go look at that catamaran I found today."

"Here in Tampa?"

"No, it's in Annapolis, Maryland."

She smiled coyly. "You couldn't find one closer?"

He sat beside her on the sofa and opened his laptop. The boat he showed her was a Fountaine Pajot Saba 50, a beautiful catamaran with an interior that rivaled some luxury hotels, and there was more closet space in the master stateroom of the Saba than in all of his old boat combined. The boat had four staterooms—one of which Ryan planned to turn into a workshop—a compressor for filling diving tanks, and plenty of space to entertain, along with a spacious galley.

"I like it," Emily said after scrolling through the pictures. "When do we leave?"

"Whenever you want, now that we have no obligations other than to each other."

She grinned mischievously. "I'm an *obligation* now?"

Ryan rolled his eyes and heaved himself off the couch. He glanced around at the apartment's interior. It had come furnished, and what Emily owned would fit into a small storage unit. Most of it was clothes and knick-knacks. Pausing by the table, he saw a framed photograph in one of the boxes. Jennifer Hulsey had snapped it right before Emily and Ryan had taken off for the Florida Keys on his old Sabre 36 *Sweet T*. They had spent several wonderful days sailing and diving together on that trip.

"Where did you get this?" he asked.

"Jennifer gave it to me on the way to Puerto Rico. She wanted us to have something because all of our other things burned up on *Windseeker*."

"That was an enjoyable time."

"Other than those hitmen trying to kill us."

He flipped out the frame's stand and set the photo on the counter. "So, not everything was perfect."

"Have you called about the boat?"

"Yeah. I talked to the broker. They're doing a survey for us."

She came over to where he was looking out the window at the water. Slipping her arms around his waist, she asked, "Are you getting antsy, being cooped up in here?"

"A little," he said.

"Greg called. He said you weren't answering his calls."

"I threw my phone away after sending a message to Colonel Estevez," Ryan said. "His men took out Quintero yesterday morning."

"I saw the news article this morning."

"Our hands are clean, but did we do the right thing?"

Emily kissed his shoulder. "Quintero would have gotten his comeuppance one way or another. Estevez and his men just hastened it along."

He turned and kissed her. "You're right, baby. Anyway, I'm excited about getting another boat, and I'm excited to see where it takes us."

"Let's go tomorrow," she said.

"What about the apartment?" he asked.

"Okay, the day after. We can clean it out tomorrow, and I'll sort through what I want to take and what I want to keep in storage."

Ryan picked her up, carried her to the bedroom, and closed the door with his foot. Tomorrow, they had work to do, but tonight he wanted to nestle in her arms and make love. The world was starting to make a little more sense, and it thrilled him to have her by his side for the next stage of their lives.

EPILOGUE

Wrightsville Beach Marina
Wrightsville Beach, North Carolina

The Fountaine Pajot Saba 50 was too wide to fit into a slip, and she extended into the Intracoastal Waterway behind a one-hundred-and-fifty-foot mega yacht and a seventy-five-foot sportfisher, all tied to a finger pier. The catamaran had a new name, *Huntress*, christened in honor of Emily.

Ryan had sailed it down from Annapolis with the help of an employee of the yacht broker from whom they had purchased her. Ryan had gotten a first-hand lesson in sailing a catamaran, his only other experience being aboard the Hulsey's Lagoon 52.

The couple had driven from Tampa to Annapolis, then Emily had driven the Jeep to Wrightsville Beach by herself and made arrangements with Ryan's old friend and mentor, Henry O'Shannassy, owner and manager of Wrightsville

Beach Marina, to dock *Huntress* there while they spent time with Ryan's family. Henry had welcomed her with open arms and told her many stories of when a young Ryan Weller had worked for him during his high school years.

When Ryan had arrived on the boat, Emily and Henry had both been there to help dock the big cat, and when they'd finished tying her off, Henry came aboard and gave Ryan a bear hug. "Welcome home, me lad," he'd said in his heavy Irish brogue.

After spending their first night together on *Huntress*, Ryan and Emily had walked to his parents' home, just up the street. It had been a warm Sunday morning, and Ryan's parents usually spent the early hours on their back deck, sipping coffee and reading the newspaper.

Ryan had knocked on the door and waited for someone to answer, his hand sweaty in Emily's palm and his heart thundering in his chest. He hadn't been home in over two years, and he had never brought home a woman for his parents to meet.

Kathleen and David had made more fuss over Emily than they did their prodigal son, but as Kathleen had promised Ryan during one of their last talks, she had fixed a giant pot roast with potatoes, carrots, and onions. She'd also invited Ryan's siblings and their children to dinner.

That had been a week ago, and Ryan and Emily had been busy prepping *Huntress* for the sail south and customizing her to their specifications. Having lost everything in the fire aboard *Windseeker*, they spent a lot of time shopping for replacement parts, gear, clothes, and equipment. Ryan built himself a go-bag, found novel places to stash his new firearms, and assembled a full complement of scuba gear.

He had one more stop to make before he returned to the boat for the night and the party he and Emily were throwing aboard for his family and friends. As he walked into the jewelry store, the owner greeted him like an old friend and pulled the engagement ring from the glass case.

"It is sized just as you asked, Mister Weller."

Ryan held the sparkling band of white gold and diamonds up to the light. Emily had pointed out a similar one at a store on Antigua, and Ryan had searched the shops in Wilmington until he'd found the perfect match. Now, it was sized just for her finger. He handed it back to the jeweler, who slipped it into a blue velvet box and carried it to the register. Ryan swiped his debit card through the machine and put the box in his pocket.

Their guests were just starting to arrive as he parked the Jeep and walked with his parents to the boat. Emily gave him a questioning look about why he was late getting back, but he just grinned, and she couldn't help but smile back. The rest of the guests arrived within the hour, and Ryan and Emily served them wine, beer, and sodas for the kids before the caterers from the nearby restaurant arrived with the fish and steak tacos.

After dinner, Ryan stood and clinked his glass to get everyone's attention. As the crowd quieted down, he had Emily stand beside him. "I wanted to say thanks to everyone for coming out today. I'll make this quick, but I have something I wanted to share with you all." He glanced at Emily for a second, trying to steel his nerves. "They say the two happiest days in a boat owner's life are the day he buys her and the day he sells her. I have to say, I've never experienced that. I've been lucky enough to have had three exceptional boats in my life, and I've been lucky to have shared them all with the same woman.

"Emily, you are the best thing to ever happen to me. You know my strengths and my weaknesses. You know how to calm my fears and smooth troubled waters. We've been through a lot together, and I thought I had lost you until fate brought you back into my life. I am so lucky to have you, and I want to spend the rest of my life with you." He dropped to one knee and removed the blue box from his pocket. "Emily Hunt," he said, opening the box and showing her the ring. "Will you marry me?"

Tears ran down Emily's cheeks, and she nodded her head while covering her mouth with her hands. Then she threw her arms around his neck and cried, "Yes. Yes! I'll marry you!"

Ryan took the ring from the box and slipped it onto her finger, then stood and kissed her. The family clapped their hands and shouted encouragement. Ryan's brother, Mark, shouted, "Don't do it!" Ryan gave him the finger, and their mother admonished them both.

The newly engaged couple sat at the table on the aft deck, holding hands and sipping beers. All was right with the world, and for the first time in a long time, Ryan Weller believed he had found true happiness.

ABOUT THE AUTHOR

Evan Graver is the author of the Ryan Weller Thriller Series. Before becoming a write, he worked in construction, as a security guard, a motorcycle and car technician, a property manager, and in the scuba industry. He served in the U.S. Navy as an aviation electronics technician until they medically retired him following a motorcycle accident which left him paralyzed. He found other avenues of adventure: riding ATVs, downhill skiing, skydiving, and bungee jumping. His passions are scuba diving and writing. He lives in Hollywood, Florida, with his wife and son.

WHATS NEXT :

If you liked *Dark Path* or any of Evan's other books, please leave him a review on Amazon.

If you would like to receive a *free* Ryan Weller Thriller Short Story, please visit www.evangraver.com and sign up for Evan's newsletter. You can learn more about Evan, his writing, and his characters.

Made in the USA
Monee, IL
03 May 2021